DAWN OF THE SHADOW

DAWN OF THE SHADOW

LEGACY OF THE SHADOW'S BLOOD™ BOOK 4

E.G. BATEMAN

MICHAEL ANDERLE

THE DAWN OF THE SHADOW TEAM

Thanks to our Beta Readers:

John Ashmore, Kelly O'Donnell, Larry Omans, Rachel Beckford

Thanks to our JIT Team:

Micky Cocker
Paul Westman
John Ashmore
Larry Omans

Editor
SkyHunter Editing Team

Carolyn peeked out from the tree line and took her boyfriend's hand. "See? No one's here. It's okay. Come on."

With a giggle, she tugged insistently and pulled him into the small circular clearing and toward the stone altar in the center.

She wasn't supposed to bring outsiders to her coven's place of ritual but she was fairly certain he was allowed to go wherever he wanted.

He looked around nervously and held back. "You didn't tell anyone we were coming here, did you? I don't want to be turned into a groundhog by a coven of angry witches."

A smile crossed her face as she stood in front of him, took his other hand, and hauled him closer to the altar. "Of course not. My parents would hit the roof if they found out I was dating a Kindred. They'd prefer I found a nice, boring boy from a witching family. Anyway, why do you care? Are you ashamed of me?" She pouted.

When she released his hands, he put an arm around her neck and drew her closer to kiss the top of her head. "Silly. I thought this might be blasphemous or against the rules or something." He relented and walked beside her for a few steps before he stopped again. His face twisted into a grimace and he shuddered and rubbed his cheeks. "I feel like I walked through a spider's web."

"That's the wards. My witch magic has given you access to the circle."

His grin was a little teasing. "Well, thank you, ma'am."

She looked at him and raised an eyebrow. "I'd have thought you would be more familiar with our practices. You're supposed to be leaders of all the supernatural communities, including us witches."

They reached the center of the circle and strolled past the tall unlit torches affixed to posts driven into the ground. He smiled at her. "We try to not get too involved. We're here to protect you, not control you."

Carolyn stood with her back to the altar, leaned her elbows on the smooth stone, and shook her blonde hair. She gazed at him with a playful expression. "You could control me if you like." She raised her eyebrows and bit her lower lip suggestively.

After a glance at their surroundings, he moved close, slid his arms around her, and lifted her to sit on the altar. He stood on a stone step beside the edifice and stroked her hair.

She looked into his eyes, then down and toyed with a button on his shirt. "I'll be sad when you have to leave. I assume that'll be soon?"

"We've interviewed everyone we needed to. I'm convinced the shifters know something—particularly the guy who runs the bar and maybe a couple of other people—but the higher-ups won't give us permission to investigate further."

"Investigate further?" She frowned. "You mean extract their memories? That seems barbaric."

"Do I look like a barbarian to you?" He swept her hair behind her ear. "The rogue we're after is a kidnapper and murderer. Besides, I've come up with a plan. I think I'll be able to stay a little longer."

Carolyn beamed at him. "Really?"

Ignoring the question, he slid his hands down her sides as he kissed her neck and whispered in her ear, "Give me a buzz again like last time. That was so hot."

The young witch flinched. "It made me hot too. It burned my hands, remember? I don't think our magic is meant to mix like that."

He took her hands and kissed the palms. "I fixed it, didn't I?" He grinned "Besides, it's exciting to do things we're not supposed to do."

Without waiting for a response, he took her hands and placed them on his forehead but she pulled back.

When he frowned, she shrugged.

"I need an earthly substance to conduct the magic." She unstoppered the vial of oil she wore around her neck and put a drop in her palm before she resealed it and rubbed her hands together.

Again, he took her hands but this time, lowered his face to them and inhaled deeply. "Mmm…my lavender girl." He moved her hands to his forehead.

She didn't resist this time and instead, whispered the incantation.

His breath caught as the magical energy flowed from her into him. Her palms grew hot and she started to pull her hands away but he caught hold of them and covered them with his own. "I'll use the magic to protect your hands. Let's see if we can get it to flow through us in circles."

"Would that bind us? I could be your new blood match." She frowned slightly when he stiffened.

"That's already a complicated situation." He kissed her. "But I have big plans for you, beautiful."

Carolyn considered his idea of drawing the energy in circles. It might work, and if they reused the same energy, it wouldn't exhaust her. She was also curious about sorcerer air magic and wondered if it would feel as good for her as her earth magic did for him. Persuaded, she began the incantation again.

Her eyes widened when the white energy in his unhealing scar began to turn red and she looked into his face. He looked enraptured with his eyes closed and muttered words she couldn't hear. She had no pain in her hands this time so she assumed his spell was working.

After about a minute, it occurred to her that he seemed to be receiving far more from this than she was. In fact, she began to feel a little dizzy. She swayed and he moved a hand to her back to hold her close to him. The burning heat returned to her hand and she tried to pull it away from him, but both seemed to have melted to his skin. His face was feverish. As she stared at him in pain and consternation, he began to change. It was as though a glamor began to fade. She gaped when she realized that was exactly what was happening.

The young woman's expression froze in shock when she was suddenly able to see the madness in his eyes. They were filled with swirling red energy and magical scars traced all over his face. He wasn't the kind and playful Kindred who had seduced her for the past couple of weeks. Panic mounted when she reached the unequivocal conclusion that he was insane.

"Babe? I can't… Let me…" Everything blurred and went dark.

Warren held the young witch and muttered his spell to keep the magical energy flowing. He breathed deeply while the power streamed into him until it finally stuttered to a halt and settled to burn in his core like molten lava. He withdrew his arms and she slumped forward.

"Are you still with us, Caroline? Carolyn? Whatever your name is?" He tapped her face and shook her. She looked drawn and empty. He laid her along the length of the altar and checked her carotid with no result. "That's a no, then." The legacy stepped back and looked absently at his surroundings as he paced in thought. There was no room for error. He had to be sure he'd thought of everything.

He giggled, then frowned. The magic made him giddy and he shook his head to clear it. It was time to execute the next part of his plan. He stared at his hand, muttered a few words, and grinned when it grew long, pointed claws. His expression almost gleeful, he stepped closer to the girl's body and proceeded to slash and gouge it methodically. When he had finished, her face and body were raked with bloody wounds. His hand returned to normal and he wiped it on his jeans.

The smell of blood hung heavy in the air, sweet and metallic. He knew he must be drenched in it. Warren snatched the lavender vial around her throat and tugged it free. He stepped away from the altar and gazed at his handiwork. Blood ran in rivulets down the sides of the edifice. Satisfied that he'd accomplished his purpose, he translocated to the edge of the clearing.

Lights glimmered through the trees to catch his attention and he paused in shock. He hadn't realized the circle had been so close to a house.

The legacy cloaked himself and approached cautiously. He must still be within the wards of the coven to have come so close. He moved onto the deck and stepped silently to a window.

Inside, a young, attractive woman sat at a large wooden kitchen table. Her dark hair was plaited and hung over her shoulder. A look of concentration narrowed her eyes. Behind her, an old man stood and busied himself at the countertop.

She brought her face close to a delicate-looking flower in a pot and sniffed. Her eyes narrowed. "Hmm… No fragrance."

"Problem, Heidi?" The old man remained at the kitchen counter with his back to her.

She leaned back and looked at the items around her. "I swept the room, blessed my athame, and lit the candle." She looked at the herbs. "I'm sure I put all the necessary herbs in the oil before I uttered the spell. I know I did." Heidi folded her arms and stared at the flower like it was all the blossom's fault. "And I said the right words."

"I know you did. I heard." The old man turned, carrying two cups. "Here's your hot chocolate."

"Thanks, Grandpa. But what did I do wrong?" It had been clear from the tone of his voice that he knew exactly where she'd gone wrong.

"Where were your fingers when you spoke the words?" He creaked and groaned into his chair.

She looked at her hands and frowned as she focused on him.

"Were they in the pot and touching the dirt the plant grew from?"

Heidi's shoulders dropped. "Well, shit."

"You mind your language, young lady."

"I'm nineteen—" She stopped speaking, rolled her eyes, and turned her attention to the flower. After a sigh of irritation, she plunged three fingers into the dirt and spoke the words again. The blossom opened fully and puffed its perfume into the air. "There, I did it." She gave him a satisfied grin.

"Did that little flower give up a season's worth of fragrance simply to make this room smell nice?"

The young woman picked a small vial up and slumped. She'd clearly intended to use it to collect the fragrance.

Her grandpa stood, groaned again, and lifted his cup. "I'll take this to bed. Goodnight, sweetheart." He stepped to the back door, locked it, and paused as he glanced toward the window.

She looked at her grandfather. "Is something wrong?"

Warren froze and his heart rate accelerated. The old man seemed to look directly into his eyes, even though he was cloaked.

"Something…" He squinted as if to focus for a moment before he shook his head and turned to walk down the hall.

The legacy sighed with relief. Of course the old man hadn't seen him. They were only witches.

Heidi blew on her beverage and took a sip. She yawned and stood to gather the herbs and oils and the still-empty glass vial. Carefully, she put it all into the apothecary cabinet on the other side of the room. The watcher didn't like that she'd turned her back to the window. He glanced down and noticed a bottle close to his foot, kicked it, and watched as she spun. He couldn't believe he'd done that.

I'm still high on the witch's magic.

The sound drew her gaze to the kitchen window. She stepped across warily and looked out into the darkness. Finally, she shrugged and seemed to think nothing of the sound. She returned to the cabinet.

Warren turned to the circle and muttered a spell to light the torches. He continued to watch her.

She had returned to the flower and now lifted the pot and sniffed it. As she placed it onto the window sill, the flicker outside caught her eye.

"Is that flames?" She looked in the direction in which her grandfather had disappeared but seemed to think better of disturbing the old man. With a shrug, she strode to the kitchen door, unlocked it, and stepped onto the deck. She put her hand into her pocket, retrieved a little bag of sand, and scattered it around. "Reveal the hidden."

Nothing happened. The legacy was relieved that he'd translocated to the tree line a moment before. He glanced toward the circle. The torches were visible through the small copse that surrounded the altar. Carolyn had told him that it wasn't unusual for a coven member to leave an offering for the goddess as part of a private request, but people were expected to clean up after themselves. They had a rule about leaving the space as they had found it. He almost chuckled out loud. *I sure didn't do that. My bad.*

He watched as the woman, unable to see him, looked around

and finally stepped onto the grass. A warm breeze brought an unpleasant sharp smell to his nose and he wondered if she could smell it too.

She walked to the tree line and he could see that she grasped her athame tightly. The small blade wouldn't have been much use as a regular weapon but as a ritual blade, it could hold considerable power and probably did given how confidently she moved. As she drew a little closer, she frowned and narrowed her eyes.

The legacy could tell from the way she tilted her head that she saw something on the altar but couldn't discern what it was.

Heidi stopped beside the torches.

From Warren's place at the edge of the woods, he could see the light reflect on shiny blonde hair. She would have seen it too.

"Who is that? Carolyn, is that you?"

She took another step and muttered an incantation. The torches brightened, the flames surged like flamethrowers into the night, and she saw the woman on the altar clearly. She raised her hands to her mouth and screamed when she saw that her friend's face and body were rent by deep claw marks and her clothes soaked in blood.

Warren wondered why she hadn't run away. Was she fascinated? Or rooted to the ground, unable to make her feet move. In the next moment, he heard her grandfather run to her, his breathing labored.

The old man put his arm around her and turned her face away from the horror. He started to take her back to the house but stopped and looked into the trees where the watcher stood cloaked. He prepared to do battle, but the old man shook his head and guided his granddaughter into the house.

The legacy knew he should be long gone, but the young woman had interested him. He was curious to see her face after she had seen her friend and coven sister's mangled corpse. Ignoring the voice of caution, he crept to the window again.

Heidi looked pale and sickened. "Was it an animal? Was she

attacked by a bear or something?" Her grandfather muttered soft words and handed the young woman her beverage. She drank it and immediately began to look drowsy. Her face seemed placid and detached from the awful sight she had witnessed.

Warren watched her grandfather as he picked the telephone up. "It's Louis. We need help."

The young woman wept and gulped, so Louis spoke more quietly. The legacy missed most of the conversation but he had no need to hear anything beyond the word "shifter." His work was done and well done too. He gazed around him with a feeling of smug self-congratulation but when he looked into the window again, the old man stared almost directly at him as though he could discern his presence in some way. It unsettled him and he almost swore.

Louis stepped back and spread his arms wide, his palms upturned and face raised. Warren recognized that it was time to leave. Before the man could utter a word, he grinned and with the witch magic coursing through his veins, he translocated several miles away and whistled as he continued to walk.

CHAPTER TWO

The corners of Lexi's mouth twitched into a tiny smile as she lifted her tank top up and slowly revealed toned abs.

Scott stared, then closed his eyes. "Will you stop doing that? You're distracting me."

Her katana flashed and delivered a light tap to the side of his head. "Then don't let it distract you. Don't focus on anything. Concentrate on broadening your gaze. Take in my face, my eyes, my stance, my grip on the weapon—everything."

"I'm trying to." He brought his blade up to meet hers as she attempted to chastise him with another slap. Clearly pleased to have seen it coming, he grinned.

They parried a few times as he went through his practiced actions. The young woman watched his face and the mask of concentration as he recalled the order of the rehearsed movements. She would attack from the left and the right and turn, and he would stab at her back while she would spin and defend.

Not this time.

The girl attacked from the left then the right. She turned, Scott stabbed, but she didn't whirl to meet his blade. It slid into her back. He screamed, recoiled, and dropped the blade with a loud clatter as she faded away.

"Wow, that was loud." She wiggled a finger in her ear as he spun to stare at her where she now leaned against the wall a few feet away.

"Why would you do that?" Scott stepped toward her, caught her arm, and spun her to scowl at her back. She allowed him to see she hadn't been stabbed.

Lexi shrugged. "You were starting to get complacent."

He put his hand over his heart and dragged in a deep breath. "And how did you do it? You couldn't project an image of yourself at all yesterday and now, you do it perfectly."

"I merely approached it from a different perspective. When you translocate, you can leave the shadow image of yourself behind. I realized that it was easier to make you believe I was still there." She grinned as she sheathed her blade. Honestly, she couldn't resist it. She appeared behind him as he stood and stared at her image and whispered, "Boo!"

The young man jerked his head around. "Jesus! Stop doing that."

She snorted. "I could do this all day." Of course, she wasn't entirely certain she could do it all day. She wasn't sure how she managed it at all, only that she'd done it a few times when she was alone and now tried to discover the limits of her new abilities.

Scott narrowed his eyes. "Are you saying you used magic on me to make me hallucinate that you were still there? That was risky. I'm not sure how I feel about that."

"It worked fine." She deliberately sounded flippant to annoy him.

"Your magic doesn't always work the way you expect it to. What if you lobotomized me in the process?" He glanced at her unhealing scar filled with black energy and sighed. "If we were still bound, I'd have known what you were doing."

After a second or two, she shrugged.

The mage stepped closer. "Listen, I want to try something. Hold your hands out, palms up."

Lexi rolled her eyes. He constantly did this, trying new things in an attempt to make their connection work again. She held her hands out.

He faced her, grasped her wrists, and indicated that she should do the same. As he muttered a few words, white streams of energy came from his fingers and bound their arms together.

His speech became more forced and she looked into his face. Sweat had broken out on his forehead and his teeth were clenched in a grimace. His cheeks were turning red.

Unfortunately, she couldn't feel anything. "Whatever you're doing, it isn't working." She pulled away and the streams broke and disappeared.

Scott looked crestfallen. "I thought I had it that time. I won't give up and you shouldn't either. I won't accept that our bond is broken."

"What's the point in disappointing ourselves repeatedly?"

The young man turned away. "You don't look very disappointed."

Lexi opened her mouth to reply but a tone sounded. She snatched her towel up and walked to a large, free-standing, transparent screen. She tapped it and Dick's face appeared and filled the giant screen when he stared into his cell phone. He looked at her and leaned forward. He was so close that all she could see was his eyes and nose and she took a step back involuntarily.

"Woah!"

The vampire narrowed his eyes "Where are you?"

She wiped her face with the towel. "We're training. What's up?"

"You're in that funny little room, aren't you? Well, out you come. We have a visitor."

The mage stepped forward to join her. "Who is it?"

But Dick had already disconnected and no reply was forthcoming.

Lexi stared at the screen. "Vague much?"

They returned their weapons to a rack on the wall and she looked around her dojo. Both she and Scott had copied aspects of their dimensional pocket designs from Bryan. She had a wall of screens connected to a cabinet full of backup drives. This was how she chose to represent and protect her memories.

He gazed at the comms screen. "This place is beginning to look like the Bat-cave."

She grinned. "Come on then, Alfred."

"Wait, I'm Alfred?"

They appeared in the kitchen of the Las Vegas condo and hurried to Dick's residence next door.

Briskly, she knocked as she opened the door. "It's only us."

They walked in to where both Dolores and Dick waited for them.

Her face brightened at the sight of the older woman. "Do you have a job for us?"

Dolores shook her head. "I thought I'd look in and see how you're doing."

She narrowed her eyes. "I don't get it. You usually have more work than we can handle. Is this related to the Fae Elders investigating you?"

The visitor shrugged. "That's all gone quiet and there seems to be no further investigation. The Elders called me in on another issue, however. They asked me if I was present when Caleb died. I wasn't and that's what I told them. It seems his headless body was found in the grounds of Emmersley. They suspect he was murdered by a wendigo, which was subsequently killed by the residents of the facility. Except they can't determine what happened to his head." She slid her gaze to Limpet, the demon disguised as a cat. He was curled with Marcel in the dog's basket and merely glanced at her before he snuggled again with supreme indifference.

Lexi smirked. "So you didn't tell them the cat got his tongue."

And everything around the tongue.

Dolores stared at the creature. "I'm surprised you trust him near Marcel."

Limpet returned her gaze and managed to look highly offended. He nudged the dog awake and flounced to the other side of the room with him following. They settled under the dining table and snuggled again, and both began to snore within seconds.

Lexi turned to the little fae woman again. "So why is there no work?"

Their visitor patted her arm. "Why don't you simply appreciate the break? The wards are in place again and haven't been tampered with. Enjoy the quiet."

Scott narrowed his eyes. "It's interesting that the problem with the wards ended when Caleb died. Does that mean he was behind it? I wonder why." He frowned. "For the stolen casino money?"

"Pfft!" Dick fluffed a throw pillow. "That was chump change for someone like Caleb. He had hundreds of millions, probably billions of dollars." He stopped what he was doing and looked away for a moment. "I wonder what happens to all that money now he's gone."

Dolores shrugged. "I guess we'll never know what he was up to. Well, never mind. I expect you'll want to get out to the pool."

Lexi shook her head. "No, I'm bored. I want to work."

The fae sighed. "How's your training coming along?"

She folded her arms. "What do you mean?"

"Aren't you learning how to use your new abilities?"

"So that's it." The young woman narrowed her eyes. "You've benched me."

"I'm merely giving you time to adjust to it all."

"I'm showing her what I can," Scott interjected, "but honestly, it needs someone who understands how dark sorcery works. And since they all died out hundreds of years ago, we're doing our best but little more."

Dolores thought for a moment. "Why don't you talk to someone who was around then?"

"You mean like a ghost?" He shrugged.

Dick put a finger in the air. "Or a vampire."

The fae frowned in thought. "Or someone else. But for now, I do have a job. I intended to pass it on to someone else but if you feel up to it—"

"Yes," the three of them said immediately.

"In fact, I believe it's an old acquaintance of yours. A member of the supernatural community in Peoria, Illinois."

Lexi frowned. "Mike?"

Scott looked at her. "Who's Mike?"

Dolores shook her head. "No. Louis."

The young mage turned his head to look at her. "Who's Louis?"

"What happened?" the girl demanded

"All I've been told so far is that a witch from his coven has been murdered. The indications are that the killing was perpetrated by a shifter."

She checked the time. "I'll be ready in five."

"Not yet. It sounds like Kindred has made a thorough examination of the scene, and the coven is casting to try to speak to the girl's spirit tonight. I'll meet you at the diner tomorrow morning." Dolores walked to the door but turned to face Scott. "You'll have to do something about those two." She pointed at Lexi and Dick. "I've already heard whisperings about a day-walking vampire. I don't want to hear rumors about a dark sorcerer as well."

"I'll get right on it." He saluted.

The fae fixed him with a stern look, then left.

Lexi turned to her teammates. "Well, that's okay. I don't have to change my plans with Ali. We're meeting at six."

The vampire checked his watch. "I'm heading to Albin's so I could drop you off."

She grinned. "We could all meet for drinks."

He frowned. "Do you mind if we don't? You make Albin uncomfortable."

"Excuse me?" She glared with pretend offense.

Dick gestured toward her. "You...undress him with your eyes."

The girl rolled said eyes. "Everyone undresses him with their eyes."

"No, they don't. Most women blush and look away demurely."

"Bullshit. He's an incubus. It's not my fault."

The vampire patted Scott's shoulder. "Well, it makes poor Scott uncomfortable."

"Don't bring me into this." The mage selected an apple from a bowl, crunched into the fruit, and backed away.

She raised an eyebrow. "Thank you. A ride would be great."

Lexi glanced across the bar at Scott and Bryan who were ordering the drinks. She continued her conversation with Alicia. "How's Bryan doing?"

Her sister raked her hand through her hair and sighed. "He's not coping well. He's behaving very strangely."

"In what way?" With a small frown, she looked toward the bar again.

"The part of him that worked so efficiently for Kindred—the strong, focused part—was destroyed by Caleb. The man who's left...honestly, I don't think he has the stomach for it."

"Are you sure? He came with me into that tower to save you. I could see he was terrified but he still did it."

"I suppose that's a good sign." Ali shrugged. "We were on a job in a cemetery last week to dispatch a couple of zombies some new voodoo practitioners had inadvertently created. I went in and did the messy part as usual and… I don't know, he looked at me like he didn't know me. In fact, when we got home, he said, 'What are you?' And slept on the couch."

"Perhaps this part of him needs to be trained." Lexi eyed the strange pink concoction Bryan carried to the table. "What in the hell are you drinking?"

"It's for you." He put the glass in front of her.

She turned it, removed the fruit-laden parasol, and sniffed it warily. "What is it? Pepto Bismol?"

"I remembered you like pink." He looked proud of himself.

Scott's features writhed in facial gymnastics to avoid laughing.

"I like pink?"

"I remember you had a whole collection of Hello Kitty—"

Lexi's eyes widened. "Stop talking."

Alicia smirked.

Bryan looked confused. "But you used to like—"

"But now I like sharp, pointy things." She felt bad when he frowned and lowered his head. They'd just been talking about how he struggled to cope and she had blundered in and made it worse. She took a sip. "Wow! This is nice." She coughed. "And strong. Okay, you're forgiven."

He turned to Scott. "See, I told you she'd like it." He retrieved a pink plastic stirrer from his pocket. "Here. They said you don't need a stirrer with this drink but I stole it for you anyway."

She took it and looked at the molded pink flamingo on the end. "So now I'm an accessory after the fact." She took another sip of the cocktail and saw a look pass between Alicia and Bryan. "What?"

Scott made the helicopter signal with his finger. The music

around them reduced instantly so they could hear each other easily and not be overheard.

Her sister leaned forward. "We've had a ton of questions about what happened to Caleb. They're not happy with the answers. Someone's coming to perform an extraction tomorrow."

Lexi scowled. She believed the magical procedure of invading the privacy of someone's mind and extracting their thoughts was even worse than taking their memories away magically, a process called counseling. "I don't know how you can still work for them. They shouldn't be allowed to do that. And they shouldn't keep doing it to us."

"I don't want someone going through my head," Alicia continued, "but more importantly, I don't think I could stop them. I'm worried they'll learn about you. They'd know we're in contact and that you're a dark sorcerer. I think it might put you in danger."

She bristled. "I can look after myself."

Her sister looked doubtful. "With the whole of Kindred looking for you? I won't risk that. Bryan will counsel me tonight."

Lexi narrowed her eyes. "But he'll only remove the information about my new ability, right?"

Alicia sighed and focused on her drink.

Bryan leaned forward and put a hand over hers. "I might not have to remove anything forever. I've discussed it with Scott. He suggested we back you up to the cloud."

His wife frowned. "I don't understand."

"Well, in this case, back you up to me. My magic supplies your dimensional pocket, so I should be able to send your memories of Lexi to my dimensional pocket."

The woman smiled. "That's genius."

Lexi squeezed her hand. "I hope you can do it. It's not fair to have to lose each other again."

Bryan sipped his drink. "If I leave any trace of you where they can find it, they'll counsel her anyway. There's no official record of the two of you meeting. I don't think Caleb even reported it because whatever he was doing was completely off the books."

The thought of losing her sister again made her feel like she'd been punched in the stomach. "As far as you know. What if they do know we're in touch and they expect to find some memory of me in there. If that is the case, they'll know you tampered with her."

He shook his head. "They know Caleb kidnapped us. It's more likely that they'll think any memory gaps were Caleb's doing. I think we'll be okay. And I think they're more concerned with covering his suspicious activity up."

Bryan knocked his drink back. "We have to cut this short, then. We have considerable work to do and not much time to do it in."

Alicia raised her eyebrows. "We have to do it now? Urgh! I think I have a headache coming on."

Lexi stood and embraced her sister. "I'll see you on the other side. When you remember me again."

"I'll make sure she remembers you. And your penchant for Hello Kitty." Bryan grinned.

After the couple had left, the two friends walked along the Strip. As usual, it bustled with people enjoying all Las Vegas had to offer. As they crossed the street near the Paris hotel, the mage stood rock-still. She took a few steps and turned when she realized he was no longer beside her.

"What are you—" Her gaze followed his.

An incredible light show took place inside the Arc de Triomphe. Bright purple, green, and blue lights wavered and clashed together with flurries of sparks. Her first thought was the same as everyone else who had gathered to watch—that it was another Vegas light show. "It's very pretty."

He caught her arm and yanked her closer. As they approached, the hairs stood up on the back of her neck. "Oh. Is that what I think it is?"

He nodded. "The Paris and Planet Hollywood each have their wards up and they're clashing." He turned to her and did a double-take. "Your eyes are black."

"I can feel it. I get a heavy charge from this."

"But that means it's opening a portal to—"

A giant tentacle uncurled from the middle of the light and slapped onto the ground a few feet from onlookers, who screamed and jumped away as it swished and writhed. Lexi raised an eyebrow. "A demon realm."

She glanced at the spectators in time to see the famous Vegas magician step out and she dragged Scott back. "It's not our problem. Kindred's on the scene."

The magician walked toward the display, held his arms up, and muttered a few words. The tentacle thrashed wildly, curled in on itself, and vanished with a pop.

The lights dissipated and the crowd went wild, clapping and whooping. He bowed and offered discount tickets for his show.

The two teammates walked away. After only a few steps, Lexi flicked a hasty look over her shoulder and her gaze settled on a man who looked directly at her with his eyes narrowed. "Someone's watching us."

CHAPTER THREE

Scott stopped immediately and spun but Lexi punched his arm. "Don't look!"

He continued to stare. "Where?"

She glanced back. "Oh! He's gone." She searched the crowd for a few more seconds before they continued to walk.

The young mage knew better than to doubt that she was correct. "Who do you think it was?"

"A mage maybe?"

After a moment's thought, he nodded. "It could be."

Lexi thought for a few seconds. "But how would he be able to translocate? You can't."

"I can go into my dimensional pocket. Maybe that's what he did. Or he was merely a guy who walked away."

They were under the Eiffel Tower when she stopped again. "You know what I don't understand? Paris and Planet Hollywood are owned by the same company. Why don't they simply share a ward?"

He shrugged. "It has something to do with different unions."

They turned off the Strip and began to traverse the few blocks to the condo.

Scott glanced at her a few times before he finally spoke. "Are you okay?"

"Yes… No. What if something happens? If she can't get her memories back and she doesn't remember me."

"Then you'll introduce yourself to her all over again." He grinned. "You could even have another big fight and pound each other's faces again."

She blew a sharp breath out. "No thanks. When she had all the legacy juice, it was like being hit by a truck." She didn't want to think about it. Instead, she glanced over her shoulder. "The Council will have to stop the casinos from using individual wards."

"You're not wrong. We almost died twice stopping Caleb from letting Azatoth through, and portals now open here by accident. What if those monsters with all the eyes we fought in Palm Springs start to emerge here? Or worse." He shuddered.

Lexi smirked. "They'll probably make a few bucks on the Strip posing for selfies."

They continued for a few steps before she spoke again. "I've enjoyed having somewhere to stay for more than a couple of nights, but I'm beginning to wonder if we shouldn't think about leaving town. These problems with the wards will draw more Kindred attention if they haven't already."

"We're leaving tomorrow. Maybe Kindred will be able to talk the casinos into dropping their wards since the city's have been stable for a while. It could all be settled by the time we return."

She sighed inwardly. "Maybe."

"Who are Mike and Louis?"

The girl raised an eyebrow. She'd expected this question. "You remember I told you about when I met Dick for the first time?"

"I remember. You said you were beating the snot out of a witch who had cursed a girl over a boy." Scott shook his head.

"The other girl was Louis' granddaughter, Heidi."

He nodded somberly. "The girl who died."

Lexi frowned. "I didn't say she died."

"You said it was a death sentence. I assumed."

She shook her head at the memory of what she'd had to do to save Heidi and shuddered. "It was a death sentence. But in the end, it wasn't hers. We managed to save her."

"And Mike?"

"A shifter bar owner. I worked on the door for him for a while. He seemed like a good guy but as it turned out, not so much. He told Kindred where to find me."

"Oh, and they sent Dick. I suppose it worked out okay, though."

"I suppose." She still felt the sting of being betrayed by the man and hoped she wouldn't see him this time.

Her companion remained silent for a few more steps. Finally, he looked at her. "Do you think we'll ever get our bond back?"

"I don't know." She glanced at the unhealing scar hidden by her sleeve and knew it would be filled with black energy instead of the white energy she had gained through her blood match with Scott. "The fact is, we don't even know if it's safe to mix white energy with dark. What if we tried to force it and we melted or blew ourselves up or something?"

He grinned. "Well, we'd know for sure."

The next morning, Lexi stepped out onto the deck and looked at Scott. "I can't believe you're sunbathing with your beanie on your head." She chuckled as she tapped her hand on the back of his chair. "Have you seen any sign of Dick?"

He repositioned his headgear and grinned as if proud of his weirdness. He gestured to the coffee he'd poured for her. "He's in the pool. Don't forget we have work to do. Dick's vampire nature is hidden and we should see to yours next. I'll get my stuff together and we can do it before we leave."

She gazed at the calm surface of the seemingly empty pool.

With a frown, she wandered to the edge and watched as Dick's muscular, tanned frame glided silently from one side to the other at the bottom of the pool. He turned onto his back and waved at her before he rocketed to the surface with a grin.

Ignoring his smugness, she raised an eyebrow. "People will think you're a fish."

He placed his hands at the back of his neck and floated while he wiggled his toes on the surface. "Why thank you, Lexi. Yes, I am considered quite a catch."

She rolled her eyes. "I'll go see Scott and get ready to leave. We're waiting to hear from Dolores."

The vampire clambered out of the pool and she smirked at his tiny Versace swimming briefs.

He threw an arm over her shoulder. "You know what they say. If you have it, flaunt it."

She pushed him away. "Eww! You're wet."

Unperturbed, he retrieved his towel. "It wouldn't kill you to get pool time. I'm sure a swimsuit could be found that would flatter those thighs."

Lexi rounded on him and poked his chest. "There's nothing wrong with my thighs. Why are you always picking on my thighs?"

Scott joined them. "Dolores will meet us at the diner in about an hour."

Dick grinned. "Ah, Scott. Great timing. I have a question for you. Have you ever been close to death?"

The mage raised an eyebrow. "You're kidding, right? Usually twice a week."

"And what flashed before you in those terrifying moments?"

The young woman knew instantly where he was going with it and groaned. "Not this again."

"My life, you mean? I guess—"

"Not always. You know what flashed before me in my dying

moments the last time I went to Illinois? Lexi's thighs as they crushed my vertebrae. That's the vision I almost took to my grave."

She held her hands up in surrender. "My bad. But seriously, stop picking on my thighs or I'll do it again and this time, I'll throw you in the dumpster behind a snow crab buffet."

Dick's face screwed up in disgust. "You are pure evil."

"What can I say? I'm a dark sorcerer." Lexi smirked as she headed into the condo.

Scott followed her inside. "Speaking of which, take a seat. This should only take a minute."

The girl sat on a barstool at the counter while he held a hand over her head and muttered a few words.

He frowned. "Hmm… It's not working." He sighed. "We should have done this yesterday."

Lexi looked at the clock. "Well, we don't have the time now." She slid off the seat and headed upstairs to gather her belongings.

She stood in front of the dresser, took a few items she needed from a drawer, and was about to close it when a glint caught her eye. After a moment's thought, she lifted out a little bracelet with a pentacle dangling from it. She took the chain downstairs to Scott. "Could you try it on this?"

"That's the one you wore before we were matched." He looked away and she could see he felt awkward talking about it. "Pass it to me. I'll give it a try." He held it with his eyes closed. "I can still feel that it's been spelled before. I can't do anything with the charm but since the chain has been spelled by a mage, I can enhance that."

After holding it in his hand for a few minutes, he secured the clasp around her wrist. He gave her a thumbs-up. "You're all good. But you know the pendant I gave you would have worked."

Lexi kicked herself mentally for not thinking of it. "I love that pendant. I worry I'll lose it."

He stooped to pick up his low-tops, but she could see he was smiling.

A rat-tat-tat sounded at the door. "Can we come in?" Dick and Albin were halfway down the hall before she could say anything.

The mage looked up from tying his laces and smiled. "Hey, Albin, how are you?"

"Good, thanks." He narrowed his eyes at Lexi. "I see you're in disguise too. I don't sense anything—no legacy and no sorcery. Like Dick, you smell weird and human."

Scott nodded. "Good. It's working then. What will you do while Dick's away?"

"I'll look after Marcel."

She raised an eyebrow. "The management's okay with that?"

"I'm paying a fortune for that suite so they'd better be okay with it."

Lexi began to slip various sharp objects into her vest and leather pants. "When will you go back to your apartment?"

Albin shrugged. "When I feel fully assured that the city wards will remain in place. Maybe another year." He chuckled.

She couldn't even begin to imagine how strange it was for the incubus. The poor man had to hide within the safety of the wards because his looks could drive people insane with lust.

Dick coughed and she realized she was staring at Albin again. She frowned and looked away. "The wards barely contain it as it is."

"Sorry." The incubus shrugged.

"It's not your fault. It must honestly suck. Would an ugly spell help?"

The vampire's eyes bulged. "Don't you dare make my boyfriend ugly."

Albin merely laughed.

Limpet yawned and sat where he'd lounged on Scott's duffel bag. He looked from Lexi to Marcel to Albin, slid off the bag, and sat at the incubus' feet.

She scowled at him. "You're choosing Marcel over me?"

He threw his arms around the puppy's neck and Marcel licked his face.

Scott looked at Albin. "Do you mind looking after the demon?"

The man gave him a little wave. "Dude. I'm a demon too."

"Oh, right. I forget that."

"It's no problem. He'll be company for Marcel. What does he eat?"

The two young people looked at each other. She knew they both recalled how Caleb had met his end.

The incubus grinned. "Kidding." He turned to the vampire. "Bring me something pretty."

Dick narrowed his eyes. "Pretty?"

"Well, something in a pretty bottle." The man wiggled his eyebrows.

"That's more like it. Mission accepted." They kissed and Dick crouched to Marcel's level. "Come here, boy."

The puppy remained where he was and wagged his stumpy tail.

Albin frowned. "Maybe I should try to teach him some commands."

"I wouldn't bother. I think he's untrainable." Dick turned to Marcel. "Come here, sit, lie down, roll over."

The animal tilted his head and simply stared at him.

Dick looked at Albin. "See? Nada."

Limpet straightened and looked sternly at Marcel, who returned the stare. The puppy finally stood, walked to Dick and sat, lay down, and rolled over before he sat with his tongue lolling out.

The vampire looked from Marcel to Limpet and back again. "Did anyone else see that?"

Lexi and Scott shared a look and both said, "Nope."

He patted the dog's head. "You be a good boy and do what

Albin tells you." He looked at Limpet. "Don't eat anyone unless they try to hurt Marcel or Albin."

Albin widened his eyes. "Careful. What if he understands you?"

Dick stood and lifted his traveling trunk. "I'm one hundred percent certain he understands me."

They reached the diner in Boulder City and found Bill at his usual table near the door. He inclined his head at Lexi and she nodded in return.

Dolores sat nearby at a table for four, with coffees and a Bloody Mary already waiting for them. "You didn't bring the kids?"

Dick sat. "Albin's babysitting."

She raised an eyebrow at him. "You know, he's a lovely young man. You could do worse."

His jaw dropped. "What are you? My mother?"

The fae smiled before she looked closely at him and Lexi. She nodded to Scott. "Good work. A couple of regular humans if ever I saw them." She passed the sugar to the young woman. "Now that I think about it, it's a wonder Caleb didn't sense the dark magic in you."

Dick stirred his drink with the celery stick and removed it from the glass. "That room stank of demon. There's no way he could have sensed her."

Lexi thought about that. "It's good that he didn't. He wouldn't have turned his back on me. In fact, he'd probably have killed me the moment I was frozen by his trap."

They finished their drinks and Dolores led them to the diner's front door. When she opened it, they gazed at a huge parking lot and cloudy skies.

"Oh, that was sneaky." The girl stepped through the fae door into Peoria, Illinois.

Scott followed and turned to gaze at a storefront. "Oh! We're at Target. I love this place. Do we need anything?"

Lexi looked around and turned to see Dick come through with their boss. She returned to the little fae woman's side. "This is where we met."

Dolores patted her arm. "I suppose you could say that."

She narrowed her eyes. "Well, I would say that because it's true. I ran straight past you when I was being chased by Kindred and you rescued me. My hero."

The woman smiled. "I'll see you soon. Call if you need me."

Dick frowned. "Aren't you forgetting something?"

"Oh, goodness." She took the tiny car from her pocket and put it on the ground.

Lexi scanned the parking lot. "No one's looking."

The fae leaned down and tapped the tiny car. They all stood back and watched as the vehicle expanded quickly to its real size.

Dick slid behind the wheel and Scott sat in the back. Lexi stood in silence and waited until Dolores had disappeared, along with her fae door. She climbed into the passenger seat and they headed over the river toward Louis' home outside of town.

The streets became more familiar as she gazed out of the window. She'd only stayed in Peoria for a couple of weeks, sleeping in the cellar of the bar she worked at, but she remembered the town as a pleasant place.

When they passed Mike's bar, she glanced up and saw Louis standing outside. "Wait—stop. I saw Louis."

They parked but when she climbed out, there was no sign of the old man.

"He must have gone inside." Lexi was annoyed. She'd far rather have slipped in and out of town without seeing Mike and his business again. She leaned against the car and folded her arms.

Scott started to walk toward the bar but stopped to look at her. "What's wrong?"

With a sigh of reluctance, she unfolded her arms. "This belongs to Mike."

"Oh?" He sounded quite curious.

Lexi checked the time. The bar would have only just opened. They entered and Lexi wondered if Mike might sense something different about her with his shifter nose. As she headed to the office with Scott and Dick following, the phone rang within.

"Mike's Bar," her old boss said.

She pushed the door a little but didn't enter. He would know people were there.

"No, I haven't seen her since—" The man turned to face her. He frowned in confusion, glanced at her companions, and turned to the phone again. "Yes, she's here, Louis. Which I'm sure you already knew."

Lexi was conflicted. It was good to see Mike in a way. He'd been kind to her—right up until the moment he betrayed her to Kindred.

The man continued the conversation. "I've just opened the bar… Well, if it's urgent, sure. I'll get one of the guys to watch it."

She didn't bother with a greeting. "Where's Louis?"

"He's waiting for us at the house."

Confused, she narrowed her eyes. "He can't be. I saw him outside. That's why we… You know what? Never mind."

His gaze drifted over the others. "Are you going to introduce me?"

"This is Scott and Dick, my colleagues." She turned to them. "This is Mike."

Dick tutted, obviously annoyed at how she had introduced him. She'd wondered if they might have met when Mike squealed on her. The vampire leaned forward and proffered his hand. "Pleased to meet you. Dick Erwin—that's Erwin, German for honored friend."

The shifter nodded and shook his hand but froze almost instantly.

"Sorry." Dick withdrew his quickly. "Cold hands, warm heart."

Mike frowned in suspicion and the two young people both stared at their teammate, who usually observed the formalities when meeting other supes. She assumed with his vampire nature hidden, he felt it was safe to act like a human.

The bar owner turned to Lexi. "It's been a while. How have you been?"

She blew out an irritated breath. "It's a long story."

He picked his wallet up. "You can tell me in the car. I hope you have one because mine's in the shop."

The friends climbed into the car and waited while he dispensed instructions to his barman. As he slid into the back, he muttered, "Thanks for not driving off without me."

Lexi smirked from the passenger seat but didn't turn to look at him. "No problem." She recalled the last time they had seen each other. He had insisted on going to Chicago on a job with her but she had ditched him. The smirk slid from her face as she recalled why she hadn't wanted to see him again. She wondered if she could forgive him, but it was a lot to forgive.

CHAPTER FOUR

After a half-hour of questions from Mike and one-syllable answers from Lexi, they turned off the road toward the single-level house Louis had shared with his granddaughter Heidi when she had last been there.

The shifter unclipped his seatbelt. "So, from what I've been barely able to glean, you seem to have had a busy year. Except that most of it was top secret."

"We have to be careful. There's no telling who it might get back to." She unbuckled, waited for him to leave the car, and hoped the barb had hit home.

Dick leaned closer to her. "Thank you for that awkward, fractious journey."

"You're welcome." She stepped out, looked at the house, and saw Louis on the deck. Unable to resist, she raised her voice. "You sure get around."

He smiled in response but pulled her into a hug when she approached.

She introduced him to Scott and Dick.

The old man raised an eyebrow when he heard the vampire's name. "Erwin…that's interesting."

"It's German for honored friend."

Lexi made a mental eye-roll. She'd heard that line at least a hundred times since he discovered she had chosen the name for him. At least seventy of those had been while he stared at himself in the mirror. She turned to Louis. "No Heidi?"

"I sent her to the market to pick a few things up. I wanted to speak to you alone. Come on in." He led the way and gestured to the big wooden kitchen table.

She sat and focused on him. "Tell me, what's the problem? How can we help?"

"A dear friend and member of our coven was murdered two nights ago."

Mike froze with a hand on the back of a chair. "Murdered? Who? Why is this the first I've heard about it?"

"It was Carolyn. Her body was left on the altar out back. Heidi found her and she's very upset."

The shifter sat heavily.

Lexi looked at him. He was visibly shocked. "Did you know her?"

"Everyone knows everyone in the supe community here. I know her father and her brother well. They come into the bar. They must be... I can't imagine." Mike exhaled sharply. "What happened?"

"She was mauled," a woman said.

They turned to where Heidi stood in the doorway and stared coldly at the shifter.

He turned to Louis. "Do you think it was a shifter?"

The elderly man nodded. "It looks that way."

Scott frowned as he considered what he'd heard. "Don't you have ways to communicate? After?"

Their host sighed. "We held the ritual over the body last night. It should have brought her spirit forth, but nothing appeared. Her family is distraught. We all are."

The mage straightened. "Can I see where it happened?"

Louis turned to his granddaughter. "Sweetheart, can you take the young man to the circle?"

Heidi paused, then nodded.

Lexi put a hand on her arm as she passed. "It's good to see you."

The young woman froze and studied her for a moment. "Something's different about you."

Mike stood. "Should I go too?"

"No." She didn't turn as she headed to the door.

He turned to Louis. "I swear if it's one of my community, I'll find out."

"I know you will, son. That's one of the reasons I asked you here. These are difficult times." Louis turned to Lexi. "There's a darkness the like of which hasn't been seen for hundreds of years. And there's a war coming."

Goosebumps prickled on her arms.

A darkness that hasn't been seen for hundreds of years. Is that me?

She shook the ominous feeling off. "Don't tell me—the war of the blood."

His eyes narrowed. He had certainly heard that term before. It looked like he intended to say something but·in the end, he remained silent. She let it go.

Mike shook his head. "Jeez. We had that Kindred guy around for days. Now, they'll be back again."

Her head jerked toward him. "Kindred has been here for a while?"

"He asked questions about you and he threatened to extract what he wanted, but I don't think he got the go-ahead from his bosses. When I first saw you, I thought that's why you were here."

"At least he bothered to ask permission. They've simply pulled information directly out of my head in the past." Dick frowned and turned to Louis. "I'd like to help. I'll see if I can find a trail."

The shifter watched him leave, waited for a few moments, and turned to Lexi. "Is he—What is he?"

Unable to resist, she smirked. "According to him, quite a catch."

"It's all true," the vampire called from the yard and much too far away for a human to have heard.

Lexi looked Mike sternly in the eyes. "Kindred is not to know about him."

He shrugged, "Okay." He seemed perplexed by her tone.

She rubbed her temple. "I thought that when I resolved everything with my unit, I could stop looking over my shoulder for Kindred." She stood, walked onto the porch, and gazed into the trees.

Louis stepped through the door and she turned to him. "Did you and Mike have a falling out? The atmosphere seems a little frosty."

A heavy sigh escaped before she could stop it. "When I went to do that job in Chicago, he called Kindred and told them where I was."

The old man looked at her "Why on earth do you think it was him?"

"He and you were the only…" She swiveled her whole body toward him. "It was you?"

"It was. When I tried to eavesdrop on your progress, I had a visitor from the ancestor realms who gave me a vision of the friend you call Dick and told me he was looking for you and that he must find you. So I thought I'd help."

Lexi stared at him with a slack jaw. "You didn't consider simply passing his number on?"

"I had my instructions." Louis shrugged.

She narrowed her eyes. "What do you mean by the ancestor realms? Do you practice voodoo?"

"I don't source my magic from there but I do visit with my grandmother on occasion."

"And she told you I was supposed to meet Dick. What was so important about us meeting?"

"When you receive such instructions from the other side, you do what you're told. And it might not be him who is important. Perhaps you've met other people you wouldn't have met otherwise."

She thought of Dolores, Scott, and Alicia.

With a heavy sigh, she scrunched her eyes as though in pain.

Louis looked concerned. "Are you all right?"

"I will have to apologize to Mike. I've been a real asshole."

Within a half-hour, Scott, Heidi, and Dick returned.

Lexi looked at the mage. "Did you see anything?"

Dick frowned and shook his head. "A ton of blood."

"Was it a shifter?" she pressed.

He looked puzzled. "There's a strong smell of shifter in the vicinity—ridiculously strong for two days after the murder. But I couldn't tell which direction he went in. Frankly, it's quite puzzling."

Mike put a hand on Louis's arm. "I can't sense anyone familiar but I might if I were a little closer. Although I have to say I don't think it's any shifters from hereabouts. Maybe one from out of town or a were. I don't know anyone capable of that."

The old man shook his head. "I don't think you want Kindred to find your scent at the scene."

He raised his eyebrows and nodded his agreement.

Lexi looked behind the men and noticed that the other young woman had left the room. "Where's Heidi?"

Louis nodded toward the hallway. "She went to her room. You know where it is."

She approached and knocked on the door. "Can I come in?"

Shuffling sounds ensued and Heidi responded. "Yes."

Quietly, she entered and sat on the end of the bed. She looked around the girl's room. It reminded her of the one she had grown up in. The posters here were of Brandon Urie and The Weeknd. Her books were herbalist and magic books. "Do you think Mike had something to do with this?"

"Maybe." The young woman looked at her and tilted her head. "You've changed."

"You can tell that, huh? I'll have to cut Scott's pay. He was supposed to hide it."

Heidi's gaze moved to the pentacle dangling from the chain around her wrist. "My pentacle knows."

Lexi touched the charm the girl had given her to help her hide from Kindred. "This kept me safe for quite a while, thank you." She put her hand on top of hers. "We'll find out who did this."

The young witch looked away. "Do you ever think about Stacey?"

She thought briefly about Stacy, the witch who had hexed Heidi. To reverse it, she had beheaded her. "I was Kindred, remember. I have many deaths to feel bad about but Stacey isn't one of them. The pure malevolence that came from that girl still makes me shudder. I've met demons nicer than her."

A short while later, the four visitors drove away from the house in silence. Finally, Lexi turned to look at Mike in the back of the car. "Should we drop you at the bar?"

"If it's not a problem."

They drove the relatively short distance and parked. She dragged in a breath and mumbled, "I'm sorry I didn't come back before. I'll explain tomorrow."

He climbed out of the vehicle and headed across the street to the bar.

Dick eased onto the road.

Scott leaned forward and put his hand on his shoulder. "Something's wrong. Can you pull over?"

They stopped a little farther up the street from the bar.

The vampire squinted into the rear-view mirror. "What are we looking for?"

"I don't know." The young mage gazed out of the back window. "I feel...icky."

"Icky?" Dick repeated.

The doors to the bar opened and Mike was led out by two men.

Lexi sighed. "Kindred."

Scott spelled the car hastily and the unit drove past without noticing them.

She looked at Dick and spun her finger around. "Let's see what's going on."

He stared at her.

Impatient, she shooed him with a curt gesture. "Move."

His mouth formed a silent "O." "Right. I thought you were doing the no one can hear us thing. Maybe you should use a different action—" He stopped speaking when she leveled a warning gaze at him and turned the car to move closer to the bar. They entered and found the main area empty so they headed to the office. A man sat there surrounded by the contents of drawers and cupboards strewn around. The room looked like it had been ransacked. She recognized him as one of the bar staff.

He looked at her and frowned. "I remember you." He looked at the desk.

Lexi nodded. "Liam, isn't it? What happened to Mike?"

"Kindred took him."

"We saw that part. What happened before that?"

"Kindred came and searched the bar. They found a pendant, said it belonged to a dead witch and that he'd—"

Dick folded his arms and leaned against the doorframe. "Do you believe it?"

"No. But they had evidence." Liam seemed conflicted.

Lexi narrowed her eyes. "So suddenly, you trust Kindred. No one ever trusts them."

"But he's a mage." He pointed at Scott. "Is this some kind of trick?"

She made a mental eye-roll. "Where did they find the pendant?"

"In the cellar."

After a moment's thought, she gestured for Scott to follow her. They hurried down the stairs to the cellar. It hadn't changed since she'd been there and she remembered it as being not a bad place to hide out.

He whirled his hand around, then did it again with no result. "This is the cleanest cellar I've ever seen. Not a speck of dust. Does that strike you as unusual?"

"I slept down here for a couple of weeks. Trust me, it's unusual."

Scott shuddered. "I'd say he's been set up."

She stared at him "What's wrong with you?"

"I don't know. I merely feel—"

"Icky?"

He shrugged. "Who would do this? And why?"

A loud thump sounded above and the two of them returned to the office to find Liam sprawled on the floor.

Lexi looked at Dick, who shook his hand with a scowl on his face. "Would you like to share with the class?" she asked.

"His face went kind of glassy and he picked the telephone up. I asked if he'd like me to step out and give him privacy. He said, 'I have to call Kindred to tell them Lexi's here.' I think I'd have had a fight on my hands if he'd realized what I am. I was able to surprise him before he could shift."

Scott crouched and held a hand over the man's head. He closed his eyes. "Yes. It's there. Only that command, I think." After a few minutes, he nodded. "I've removed the compulsion and his memory of us." He picked a bunch of keys up. "Do these belong to this guy or Mike?"

She studied them. "I have no idea."

The young mage looked around the desk. He leaned across and picked up the trackball mouse, tipped it up, and dropped the ball into his hand. "Let's get out of here."

Lexi exhaled slowly. "I think it's time to call Dolores."

Dick retrieved his cell phone and pushed a button as they walked to the door of the bar. "Hi, Dolores?"

She pushed the door open and froze.

"Yes?" The fae stood in her living room on the other side of the door.

He disconnected the call. "Marvelous. I hope you have some bourbon in here."

They stepped through and closed the door. Lexi could see through the blinds on the opposite wall that the back of the magical apartment opened onto Lake Norman.

"I was coming to get you." Dolores glanced at Scott. "A friend has been in touch to let me know that Warren has been seen around here."

He nodded grimly. "That explains the icky feeling. He always has magical feelers out for me but I'm not usually this close to them."

***

Lexi turned to Dolores where they sat outside the fishing shack. "You had no intention of giving this job to someone else, did you?"

"If you hadn't been up to doing it, I most certainly would have."

She sighed. "When was Warren seen?"

"Today. But my friend's been asking around and he's been there for a few days."

"He didn't arrive to investigate the murder? I'd guess he's the one Mike mentioned. This is about Scott, isn't it? He's following an old trail of mine and looking for someone who can lead him to us." She lowered her head into her hands.

Her cell phone rang a moment later. "It's Bryan." She accepted the call. "Bryan? Hi."

His voice seemed hesitant. "Lexi…I need to talk to you. It's about Alicia."

"Is she okay? What happened? Did she lose her memories?"

"I have them and they're fine. She's with Kindred now. It's not that but I'm worried about her."

Lexi rolled her eyes to Dolores. "She's worried about you too, but I think it's something you'll both have to work through together or with a…uh, professional."

"Oh… Well—"

"Listen, Bryan, I'm in the middle of something. I'll catch up with you both when I finish this job." She disconnected.

The fae woman smiled. "Well, you wanted a family."

She sagged. "Sure, but not a career change."

While she had her cell phone out, she called Louis.

"Hello, Lexi."

Startled, she narrowed her eyes. "How did you know it was me?"

"Caller display."

"Oh right, of course." She looked at Dolores, who smirked with amusement. "Listen, Mike's been arrested. It sounds like they found Carolyn's pendant at the bar but I think it was planted."

"I see. What are you thinking?"

Lexi honestly had no clue and opened her mouth to say as much when Dick appeared at the door. "Scott wants to take a look at the body."

She cleared her throat. "Would it be okay to see Carolyn's body?"

"You'll have to go now. She's being cremated at midnight."

"We'll be there ASAP. Can you text me the address?"

A few minutes later, she entered the apartment. "We need to go now."

C H A P T E R   F I V E

The three of them sat in the car outside the funeral home.

Lexi looked at her enchanted chain, then at Scott. "Could you alter the spell on this? I want to appear to be a legacy."

He touched the chain as it hung on her wrist and muttered an incantation. "Keep your jacket on. Anyone sensing you should believe you're a legacy but I'm worried your scar will say something else."

They knocked on the door and waited with no response.

She reached out tentatively and pushed the door. It swung open so they stepped inside. The entrance hall was lit by lamps on side tables. The floorboards creaked as they walked across the room and she glanced at various chairs and side tables scattered against the walls. The smell was musty and the only sound came from a tall grandfather clock that ticked loudly in the corner.

A gaunt, overdressed man gazed sternly at them from a framed painting on the wall. His eyes seemed to follow her as she walked and the three companions all paused to stare at it.

Finally, Dick muttered. "Well, this isn't at all creepy."

"You should try working here," someone said from directly behind them.

The vampire screamed and darted past Lexi and into a side room at vamp speed, which gave the scream a Doppler effect.

A stiletto blade materialized in Lexi's hand at her side. She looked at the man's gaunt, familiar face. Confused, she looked at the painting, then at him again. He was possibly the thinnest man she'd ever seen, his scrawny frame exaggerated by his height which could only have been a couple of inches less than seven-feet.

She almost reached out to touch him. "Are you—"

"Related? Yes. That's my great-grandfather. How may I assist you? It's rather late for visitors."

"We've come to pay our respects." Lexi felt an odd vibe from him. He wasn't human but she couldn't work out what he was.

"As I said, it's rather late."

"We've come to see Carolyn. I understand she's leaving you soon."

"Ah. Yes. Well, this is highly irregular."

"My name's Alecia Rand. We're from Kindred."

"I see. I'm Julian. Please, follow me." He turned to walk down the hallway.

Dick stepped beside her. He leaned closer and muttered, "You wanted to ask him if he's a ghost."

Lexi swiveled her head to look at him. "Of course not. Don't be ridiculous."

That was exactly what I was about to ask him.

The vampire turned to Scott. "Your heart didn't race."

"I knew he was there." The mage looked at the blade in Lexi's hand. "That was interesting."

She stared at the weapon. Unable to make it disappear in the same manner it had appeared in her hand, she slipped it into her dimensional pocket.

They stepped into the hallway, where Julian held a door open at the other end and looked pointedly at his watch. They took the hint and walked faster. No one wanted to upset the creepy proprietor.

In silence, they followed him down a staircase and through a door into a brightly lit room with a casket on a gurney in the center.

The mortician opened a door in the cabinet and slid a covered body out. He drew the sheet away from the face.

Lexi stopped while Scott stepped closer to the dead girl. She knew he hated seeing things he couldn't unsee but he was good at his job. His lips moved with no sound as though his softly whispered incantations might wake the dead.

He turned to Julian. "Do you have any artificial tears?"

The man grimaced. "I'm afraid they wouldn't be of any use. They aren't there."

Dick took a couple of steps closer. "What's not there?"

The young mage sighed. "Her eyes. I wanted to try the reflective surface spell." He leaned over the body. Lexi assumed he was checking the eye sockets and stepped farther away.

After a moment, he turned to Julian. "Do you think it was a shifter?"

"Your Kindred colleagues think it was. I've never had two visits from you before."

"We want to be sure. What do you think?"

The man paused and studied him. She had seen the look before. He was weighing up whether or not he wanted to share his true thoughts with Kindred. Finally, he seemed to reach a conclusion. "I think the same as you. Her eyes were plucked out, not clawed out. The scratches across her eye area seem to be a clumsy attempt to hide it."

"You didn't say any of this to...our colleagues?"

"No. The young man was quite unpleasant and not interested in my opinion. He seemed unusually keen that I sign off on the cause of death."

Scott nodded and turned to the body to examine the claw marks. He picked her hand up gently and looked at the nails.

The mortician stepped beside him. "There are no defensive wounds and nothing under the fingernails."

"And no polish. I was looking for another shiny surface." He turned her hand over, then checked the other, his eyes narrowed. "What did you make of this?" He pointed at silver burn marks.

"The burns? I thought they were old."

The young mage brought the hand closer to the man's face. "They were magically healed as they were burning, which accounts for these circular ridges." His cell phone appeared in his hand and he took a couple of photographs of the burns. "I think we're done here. You can cover her. Thank you."

Julian covered Carolyn's body, slid the drawer back, and closed the door.

While his back was turned, Scott raised his hand and twisted his fingers in the air. The man froze.

He touched the mortician's head, "You've had no visitors this evening." He muttered a few words and turned to Lexi. "Let's go. He won't remember we were here."

Her jaw hung open. "You counseled him? Why?"

"His suspicions are enough to get him killed. The girl wasn't killed by a shifter. She was killed by sorcery."

They returned to the car and Dick looked at her. "Where to now?"

She turned to Scott. "Well?"

"We need to speak to her family."

"I'll call Louis." She took her cell phone out.

"It's quicker if I simply go there." He vanished without warning.

The vampire started the car. "Will you simply disappear too?"

"There's no sense in both of us translocating. I could use the time to think." She closed her eyes.

He tutted loudly. "You mean nap."

Her cell phone rang and she answered and listened to Scott. "Yes? Sure, I'll do that for you."

She rang Louis. "Hi. Scott's at the edge of your property. It seems he translocated into your wards and almost knocked himself out. Could you let him in? Thanks."

With a low chuckle, she turned to her companion. "He impressed me tonight."

Dick nodded. "His work with the body was focused and professional. I'll be honest, when I first met him, I thought he'd be a liability."

Lexi smirked. "I'm about one hundred percent certain that's not what went through your mind when you first met him."

Unoffended, he laughed. "He's growing up. You need to be careful. If the two of you are no longer bonded, he might go off and bond with someone else. Some young thing will likely come along and sweep him off his feet."

She cocked an eyebrow. "Good for him if he wants that kind of drama in his life. Seeing it from the outside is all the motivation I need to stay well clear."

"Alicia and Bryan?"

After a moment's hesitation, she nodded. "I think the part of Bryan that loves her the most might be the part that she loves the least." She exhaled in frustration. "I can't begin to imagine how to navigate that."

"But look at me and Albin. We're an interspecies couple and it's going fabulously."

"I thought you and Edward might—"

"Edward is wonderful but he would always put his pack first. My ego simply wouldn't stand for it." He thought for a few moments. "Hmm... I should invite him over."

Lexi's eyebrows almost reached her hairline. "I'm moving out. I refuse to listen to a full-on sex orgy through those thin walls."

"Don't be silly. You wouldn't have to listen. Edward likes the ladies too."

"Maybe I should translocate to Louis's house. I think I'd prefer to pound myself against the wards at the speed of light than listen to this."

"Ha! That was so easy. You're such a prude."

Her face flushed. "I'm not a prude. I merely don't have the time for that."

"Oh. Well, maybe Scott would be interested."

She pointed a finger at him. "You leave him alone."

The vampire slid his gaze to her, then back to the road. "Okay, but only because your black eyes are scaring me."

Startled, she leaned back in her seat and closed her eyes.

Relax. Relax and make the creepy black eyes go away. And try not to kill Dick.

Her mind entered her dimensional pocket. She stepped close to her martial arts test dummy and decided it would be more enjoyable to beat it up if it had the vampire's face. She threw magic at it absently.

His horrified face appeared before her. "What the fuck? Where did the car go?"

"Shit." She pulled them both back into the car.

His hands wobbled on the steering wheel as he straightened. "What was that?"

"I went into my dimensional pocket to meditate and somehow pulled you in there too." Lexi's face was aflame.

I need to understand how this magic works.

A little shaken, he kept his gaze on the road. "Fine, let's go with that. Perhaps you could meditate sitting right there. Or nap. I'll drive and we won't die."

Honestly, she felt ashamed. She had always been quick to anger but having all this magic was a liability.

It was so much easier using Scott's magic, so much...lighter.

She closed her eyes.

"We're here."

Lexi scowled. "Damn. I did it again."

Dick turned the engine off. "Fell asleep when you were trying to meditate? I'm the same. I've never been able to do it."

Scott exited the house. "The coven is starting to gather out back. Carolyn's brother and mother have arrived."

As they entered the house, Lexi could hear Louis speaking. "I'm not asking you to do it for me or them or even you. Hear them out for Carolyn."

A woman's shrill voice penetrated the walls. "How dare you use her name as a bargaining tool."

Lexi entered the room. "I'm sorry for your loss—"

The woman interrupted her. "I know you. You were here before. You're the one Louis sent to Chicago to save Heidi."

She wondered briefly if that might earn her a reprieve. "You need to know that a shifter didn't kill your daughter."

"Why should we believe anything a Kindred says?"

Her brow furrowed in confusion before she remembered the mage's handiwork. "Scott, remove all enchantments from me. Oh, except the one that hides me from Kindred."

He did as she asked.

Carolyn's brother jerked in his chair. "What are you, a demon?"

Louis looked unsurprised. "She's a dark sorcerer."

"What?" Carolyn's mother snatched a pouch from her purse. Scott flicked a finger and it disappeared.

She spun to face Louis. "What is this?"

The young mage answered. "Sorry. It's in your purse. No one needs this to escalate. What we have to discuss is too important."

The old man sat. "Karen, my home is not a battlefield. We are here to discuss vitally important issues."

The woman grasped her pentacle pendant. "Dark sorcerers died off for a reason."

Louis raised an eyebrow. "Really? Would you like to tell us that reason?"

"I... I..." She knew nothing, it seemed, and her lips drew into a tight, thin line.

He addressed her and her son. "Dark sorcerers aren't what you think they are."

"They're... We're not?" Lexi gaped at him in astonishment.

He delivered a line she'd already heard from her friends. "Do you feel evil?"

"No." She thought about what she'd recently done to Dick. "Well, I sometimes think I have my moments."

"We'll get to this," Louis interrupted before she could elaborate. "First, we need to discuss Carolyn. Scott?"

The young mage took a deep breath. "Lexi's right. Your daughter wasn't killed by a shifter." He looked sadly at the girl's mother. "I think she was killed by a Kindred legacy called Warren."

Dick swiveled to stare at him. "The psycho did it?"

He nodded. "I think he's still in town."

"Waiting for us to show up?" The vampire raised an eyebrow.

"Perhaps." He shook his head in a non-committal way. "It's more likely that he thought he'd get the chance to arrange an extraction on your old friend, Mike."

Lexi frowned. "We need to find him before they perform that."

Karen snarled. "Why should we care about that?"

Dick raised an eyebrow. "Because he's innocent?"

"There's more," Scott continued. "I think Warren took Carolyn's magical essence."

Heidi took Karen's arm as she swayed and helped her into a chair. "That's why she didn't come to us in the ritual."

Louis looked interested. "Why do you think that?"

"I grew up with him. As you know, everything has some form of magical energy inside it. He used to try to leech the energy out of everything, especially animals. I recognized the...signs. As a child, that energy used to dissipate and he couldn't do anything with it. As a matched legacy? I honestly don't know."

The old man frowned. "Her essence might be recoverable. We need to get to this Warren."

A pair of headlights flashed through the window and Heidi looked out. "The funeral home car is here."

Karen stood. "We can't have the ritual now."

Lexi considered what she'd said. "Kindred will expect you to cremate the body tonight. Warren will think all the evidence is gone."

Louis nodded. "We can hold a different ritual. Scott, can you tell me more about what he did to the creatures?"

She turned to the mage. "Can you stay and help them? I need to find Mike."

He took the trackball from his pocket and dropped it into her hand.

Surprised, she looked at him and raised an eyebrow. "You trust me to do this?"

"It's a locator spell. You'll be fine. Take Dick with you."

The vampire stood and smoothed an eyebrow. "I'll be your muscle."

The two of them stepped out and headed to the car. She waited for him to start the engine, retrieved Mike's computer trackball, and held it close to her face.

The dark sorcerer stared at the object. "Okay, shiny gray ball. Lead me to Mike."

Dick groaned. "Good grief, Lexi. You completely lack finesse."

CHAPTER SIX

Alicia stared into the mirror, a little dazed, and shook her head. "Wow, I zoned out there."

Bryan picked his shoes up from the floor. "No shit." He headed to the bedroom door.

She looked at him through the mirror. "What?"

"Nothing." He walked out of the room and left her wondering what was wrong with him this time.

She pinched the bridge of her nose and rubbed her temples. He would give her a migraine when they had to go out on a job. She had to hope the painkillers kicked in fast or it would be a nightmare to deal with his shitty mood. Scowling, she took the bottle, dropped a couple of pills into her hand, and swallowed them with water. It was time to get to work. She yanked her linen vest over her head, secreted blades here and there, and clipped a shuriken to the magnet before she zipped her boots and headed into the kitchen. She watched Bryan from behind as he put a cup into the cupboard. "Are you ready?"

"I'm good to go." He smiled but it didn't reach his eyes. She turned and headed down the stairs to the front door. As she moved, she drew on his magic to top up her unhealing scar.

He muttered from behind her as they reached the door. "Leave some for me."

They stepped out onto their New Orleans street in the French Quarter and she turned on him. "What's your problem?"

"I talked to you for ten minutes and you didn't even listen. Do you know how offensive that is?"

"If you only noticed after ten minutes that I wasn't listening, you weren't talking to me, you were talking at me. And you think I'm offensive." Alicia sighed. "I'm sorry, okay? I have a headache coming on and it's annoying."

"I could tell you were annoyed. I thought it was me."

She stepped close to him. "Never." She kissed him. "Did you pick a sack up?"

Bryan held a hessian sack up with magical symbols drawn on it. "And a net in case."

"Right, then. Let's catch some pixies." They began to walk down the street.

He sighed. "We need to talk about the counselor's visit."

"I'm very sure that's where my headache came from. Can we talk after we get this job out of the way?" She looped her arm around his as they walked.

He groaned. "Fine, but it's important." He held the sack up. "I can't believe we have to do this. I feel like such a dick."

"Why?"

"Pixies are so...cute." He shrugged.

"You're kidding, right? They're vermin. And they eat sprites." She shuddered.

"But they look like little Disney characters—cute, annoying, and psychotic Disney characters."

"Don't worry, it should be over quickly. At least it'll be easy to find them when we bring their favorite food source. Where are we meeting the sprite? Varda, is it?" She checked her watch.

"Her name's Valda." Bryan shook his head. "She said we should call when we're in the area. She doesn't want to hang around there alone before we arrive."

Alicia raised an eyebrow. "Understandable."

They walked through the French Quarter and finally arrived at the dark alley where the pixies had last been seen. Bryan held a stone up that glowed blue. "They're still in the area." He took his cell phone out and dialed. "Hi, Valda. We're here."

A fae door appeared at the entrance to the narrow street and a beautiful young sprite floated through. "I hope you have your running shoes on because I don't want pixie bites. I have a date later."

Alicia smiled at the tiny being. She felt a little high when the air filled with ozone at the sprite's arrival. It made her dizzy but even better, the unsanitary smell of their surroundings faded.

Everyone nodded to confirm they were ready and they moved forward into the area.

A natural glow emanated from Valda in her true form, so Bryan cast a spell that kept him and Alicia in the shadows. Within seconds, they began to detect small movements in the trash scattered around. Rustling sounds and metallic and glass pings followed as glasses and cans were rolled aside.

A tiny face peeked from inside a paper cup on the ground. Bryan was right. Their features were similar to troll dolls—perfectly sweet and innocent until you saw their teeth. With no other warning, the pixies emerged from even the most unlikely places and surged toward Valda from every direction. She elevated sharply and Bryan cast a freezing spell. For a few moments, the only sounds were the tiny thuds of frozen pixies falling one after the other. While they lay paralyzed by his spell Alicia tiptoed around with the net, scooped them up, and dropped them into the sack.

She held one up by the foot and turned her nose up in disgust. "These things stink."

"I know. They're revolting." Valda had returned and now

watched proceedings from a safe distance. Once they were all in the sack, the woman grasped it tightly at the neck. "There. Job done."

The sprite moved closer. "That was faster and less inconvenient than I expected. What will you do with them?"

"Flush them," Alicia answered.

Bryan narrowed his eyes at her. "She means we'll send them back to fae."

Valda smiled sweetly. "I could take them for you since I'm going that way."

As though he'd anticipated the offer, he shook his head firmly and quickly. "Sorry, Valda. I know there are restaurants that pay for pixies by the pound."

"Oh, you know about that." She shrugged.

He removed his freeze spell and Alicia turned to lead them away from the alley.

A loud screech issued from somewhere behind them.

The legacy turned to where a pixie had attached itself to the end of Valda's nose by its pointed little teeth. While she stared at the sprite, another of the tiny beasts landed on her hand and bit hard on her knuckle. She dropped the sack and all the others tumbled out and woke from their magical slumber. They scrambled to their feet and lunged toward Valda again.

Alicia roared her indignation. "I don't think so." She punched the wall and the pixie that still had its teeth in her knuckle burst in a little explosion of gore.

Bryan whirled his arm and froze them again. Valda slapped the pixie on her nose and it came loose and fell.

The little sprite flew directly to Bryan. "Is it bad? Can you fix it?"

"Let me see. I'll do what I can."

The woman was barely aware of the conversation between him and the sprite. She moved through the alley, stamped on the pixies, and thrust their ruined bodies into the sack. When she finished, she kicked the garbage out of the way to see if any more were hiding there. Finding none, she returned to the entrance.

Bryan was examining the bite and shook his head. "You might have to glamor this for a couple of days." He turned to Alicia as she approached. "Jesus, what have you done?"

She looked down at herself and realized she was covered in spatters of pixie blood.

Her sigh was one of exasperation. "Well, this will never come out."

Valda stared at her and the sprite's mouth was a perfect "O." She called her fae door and vanished without another word.

Alicia frowned. "What's up with her?"

"You look like something from a horror movie. Let's get home. I'll cast a glamor on you to hide the blood so you don't frighten people."

They hurried home and entered the apartment, and he directed her immediately into the bathroom. "You have a shower and I'll make coffee."

When she emerged a short while later, she sat beside him on the couch. "I hate pixies."

"Yeah, I'm starting to see that. You know squashing pixies isn't exactly allowed, right?"

She showed him the bite on her knuckle. "One of those little fuckers bit me." She put her head on his shoulder. "I truly hate pixies."

"Let's watch some TV." He sounded troubled.

Alicia wasn't in the mood for whatever his latest problem was. "No. I still have a headache. I'm going to bed."

She slid into bed and put her cell phone on charge beside her, then scrolled through the recent calls. It seemed she had received a missed call from someone stored in her cell as *L*. "Who's L?" She shrugged and slid onto her back.

CHAPTER SEVEN

In one moment, Lexi had been in the car with Dick outside Louis's house and in the next, she stood in a small square cell and stared at the door.

"Where the hell did you come from?"

She jumped and spun to see Mike seated on the bed. "I... Well, that wasn't supposed to happen. I came to see if you needed help." She looked at her surroundings. "I'm thinking you do."

The shifter rubbed his face. "They're saying I killed Carolyn but I swear I didn't." As he spoke, the cuffs rattled around his wrists. He wore K-cuffs, which worked in a similar way to the bracelets at Emmersley. They stopped him from shifting or contacting his pack through their mind link. Not only that, but she knew they would also drain the strength from his body. She could only imagine how vulnerable he must feel.

Lexi waited for him to look at her. "It's okay. We know it wasn't you. Where are we?"

He looked around the cell. "It's a police sub-station. They don't use it twenty-four-seven. The front desk and offices were all dark and locked up when we got here."

"Well, I can get these off." She moved toward the cuffs but

stopped when she heard a door open and footsteps coming toward the cell. "Shit." She didn't want to leave him but couldn't think what else to do and tried to translocate. When her attempt failed, she looked around the cell and panicked.

Mike whispered, "Aren't you going to disappear?"

"I'm kind of new at this," Lexi whispered in return. She stood to the side of the door as the little observation hatch slid across and keys rattled.

Grimly, she closed her eyes and reached into the well of power she was still becoming acquainted with.

Frustrated, she muttered, "Come on. They mustn't see me. I need to disappear." She stared at the door in horror as it opened.

A man entered and she recognized Warren instantly. He looked at Mike without so much as a glance in her direction. A little confused, she looked down and could still see her body. Mike's gaze flicked to catch her eye and she knew he could also see her.

Her intention had been that the newcomer wouldn't see her and she guessed that she had somehow manipulated Warren's mind the same way she had done with Scott while they were training. She hadn't done it intentionally this time and wasn't even certain she could replicate it. A little startled by the realization, she stood frozen to the spot.

As she stared at the crazed legacy, she saw now with the help of magic what Scott had been talking about before. Slashes across his cheeks and down both arms were unhealing scars. He also had two welts which were mostly healed on his forehead.

Warren sneered. "Mike, isn't it? Let's talk about what you did to Carolyn."

The shifter looked at him in disgust. "Let's talk about you planting evidence at my bar. I didn't touch her."

His captor stepped closer and put a hand on his head. "But what if you did?" She felt the air change briefly. It was heavy with magic but as quickly as he had done it, he stepped back.

She returned her gaze to Warren. His scars were filled with a swirling red energy. She'd never seen anything like it and wondered briefly if she should snap his neck while she was there. It seemed a pity to miss the opportunity, but Kindred would blame Mike.

Lexi looked at the shifter. His eyes glazed over and after a few moments, his face contorted in horror. "No. That wasn't what... What did I do? Oh, God, what did I do?"

"Now, we'll have considerable time together to work on what you know about that bitch Lexi." The legacy stepped out of the cell and locked the door.

She rushed to the shifter.

He pushed her away. "Get away from me. You don't know what I've done. I'm dangerous."

Ignoring his protests, she grasped the sides of his face and made him look at her. "You're not. You didn't do it. He did something to you. Whatever you think you remember, you're wrong." She bitterly regretted not killing the legacy when she had the chance.

Mike was weeping and stared at his hands. She couldn't make him listen and scowled when she heard voices in the hallway.

Warren's whiny voice came closer. "I didn't do anything. I was merely checking on him."

Lexi looked at the shifter. "I won't leave you here." She put a hand on his shoulder and pulled him into her dimensional pocket. "I don't know why I didn't think of this before instead of panicking."

He sat on the floor and jerked his hands away from his face. "Where are we?"

The girl looked around the room and shrugged. "It's difficult to explain."

An expression of revulsion crossed his face and he stared at his hands again. "You need to lock me up. Put me in a cage."

She thought of Bryan locked in a prison he had created for five years and shuddered. "You'll be fine." She focused on Louis' deck and told herself firmly that she should be able to do this. After a deep breath, she put a hand on his shoulder and willed herself to be there.

"Yes!" Thankfully, she had indeed appeared at the house. Scott and Dick stood a few feet away. She turned quickly and scowled when she realized Mike wasn't with her. "Damn."

The young mage jumped at her sudden appearance. "I need to apologize for all the times I did that to you."

Dick raised an eyebrow. "Some traveling companion you are. You left me behind. Where did you go?"

"Well, I thought the ball would lead us to where Mike was and it dropped me next to him in a jail cell. Look, I have a problem. He's in my dimensional pocket. I tried to pull him out but it didn't work."

Scott grasped Dick's arm and they translocated into her dimensional pocket.

The vampire gazed around curiously. "Finally, I get to see your funny little room. It's not so little but would it kill you to decorate?"

The mage looked at Mike with his eyes narrowed. "He's not here."

Lexi looked from Scott to the shifter and back again. "He's right there."

Dick stepped closer to the man and poked his arm. "He's kind of here but something's not quite right. He has no heartbeat for one thing."

"You've brought his consciousness," Scott continued. His body is probably still in the cell. It's similar to when we're in a dimensional pocket and also in the outside world."

She narrowed her eyes. "Similar but not the same?"

The mage shook his head. "No. When we exist in both, our consciousness is in both."

Mike finally looked up. "Is that bad?"

Lexi facepalmed. "They could be performing the extraction. Warren was there and he did something to him. It was weird magic. Now, Mike thinks he killed Carolyn."

"I did. I remember doing it. I shifted and I ripped her to pieces." He returned to looking at his hands.

Dick looked at the distressed shifter, who was seated on the floor. "Surely they won't perform an extraction if all they have is an empty shell."

Scott leaned closer, put his hand palm out, and held it over him. "You're right about that magic. I can't sense how he did it."

She remembered her shock at seeing the legacy. "Warren's face and arms… He has unhealing scars all over him."

He sneered. "Oh, you saw that."

Mike looked from one to the other. "I didn't see that."

"He must have been hiding it behind a glamor." The mage shrugged.

"And he had two welts on his head like burns. But I don't understand why the energy in his scars was red."

Scott's eyes snapped to her. "Red?" He looked away, deep in thought. "We need Louis."

He vanished and reappeared moments later with the old man and his granddaughter.

Heidi gazed around the room while Louis looked unfazed. He walked directly to Mike.

The girl walked nervously to him. She still seemed half convinced that he had killed her friend and was a few feet from him when she stopped, her face ugly with disgust. "I can smell Carolyn all over him."

Her grandfather was more objective. "Tell me."

Lexi explained what she had seen.

Heidi stepped closer. "I sense it's her magic."

"I don't feel so good." Mike swayed.

Scott held onto him. "They're trying to pull him back." He

turned to Louis. "Is there anything we can do to get the memories out of him?"

The old man frowned. "Can't you do that counseling thing you people do?"

He threw his hands up. "I tried but I can't shift it."

Louis sighed. "This has been done with a mixture of sorcery and witch magic. It might be that's what it'll take to remove it. I'll need to work through you, Scott. Do you trust me?"

The young man nodded and glanced at Lexi. "We need to know what they're doing in the cell."

"What if I find myself completely visible and standing in front of Warren?"

Scott stepped close to her and put his hands on the sides of her head. "Close your eyes."

She did as he asked.

"Where do you feel your body is?"

With a slight frown, she focused on the light breeze around her. "I'm on the deck outside Louis's house."

"In here, all you are is consciousness. Return your consciousness to Mike. You won't be seen."

When he removed his hands, she focused on going to the cell and shifted her mind.

A stinging blow caught her cheek immediately. "Son of a bitch."

Her voice didn't sound right. It didn't sound right at all.

Warren sounded smug. "There, you see. He's fine and just in time for the counselor to see what secrets he's hiding."

Lexi looked at a pair of jeans and a plaid shirt. The sleeves were rolled up to reveal hairy arms cuffed in front of her.

She was in Mike's body. "Oh, shit."

The legacy laughed. "That doesn't even cover the trouble you're in, murderer."

Aghast, she stared at Warren from Mike's eyes. Eric, the grandfather of Colorado, stood behind him. She turned to another man beside her who she assumed was the counselor. What would they do when they found out she was inside the shifter? She decided that shouldn't happen.

Instinctively, she closed her eyes to think about what she needed to do. She would have to time it perfectly.

"This won't hurt. I'll merely look at your memories from the night in question. If you're innocent, you'll be able to go home." The man had a soothing voice. It reminded her of the counselors who had visited her family throughout her life. She wondered briefly if it was part of the training.

He rested his hand on Mike's head.

It was easier than she had expected. He had already initiated a magical link between their minds. She let him believe he was taking thoughts from the prisoner's head while she allowed her mind to travel through the link and search his thoughts. He wasn't happy to be there and had been writing a letter in his study. She watched as he wrote his name and address at the top of a sheet of expensive paper. His phone rang. Eric was on the line, asking him to come. He did this as a favor for Eric but didn't like the white-eyed Grandfather. He was afraid of him and the psycho kid. She couldn't blame him for that.

A few minutes later, Warren shifted his weight from the wall he'd been leaning against. "Well?"

It brought Lexi back to what she was trying to do. She decided to try a little more direct manipulation.

She sent a thought to the counselor. *I'm afraid you have the wrong man.*

He sighed. "I'm afraid you have the wrong man."

The legacy stepped forward. "That's not possible."

Extractions don't lie. I have all his movements from the night of the murder. It wasn't him.

"Extractions don't lie. I have all his movements from the night of the murder. It wasn't him."

Warren looked livid. "But—"

Eric stepped in front of the younger man. "Thank you, counselor. I'm sorry to have wasted your time."

The man removed his hand from Mike's head. "No trouble, Eric. I'm happy to help. I'll write my report and submit it to head office."

Warren stormed out of the cell and Lexi fought to keep a smug grin on the inside.

"That won't be necessary. This was a bust and you're off the clock. Let's simply say you owe me one less favor."

"As you wish." The counselor gathered his belongings.

Lexi asked. "Can I leave now?" She almost giggled at the deep voice. Then the idea of Mike giggling almost made her do it again.

I need to get a grip.

Eric stared at her. "There's still the issue of the girl's pendant found in your cellar."

She looked into his face. "That was obviously planted by that lunatic. I hope you'll investigate that with a little more diligence."

Her error was immediately made apparent. The man took a step and backhanded Mike's cheek. It was the same one Warren had punched and she felt the blow as though it were her face. The shifter wouldn't be happy if she caused him to be beaten to a pulp.

The man stepped back, turned, and left, and the way he did it was chilling. He seemed completely without emotion. He and Warren were a match made in hell.

"That wasn't the brightest choice."

It took her a moment to realize the counselor was speaking.

He circled to face Mike, then glanced at the door before he turned to face him. "I don't know who you are, but I think we might need to talk." He took a business card out and dropped it into the shifter's shirt pocket. "Just in case you don't remember my name from the letter you saw me write. You were quite clumsy and you didn't see anything I didn't want you to." The man turned and left the cell.

Lexi felt the heat of embarrassment mingle with the sting from the blows. She heard the counselor's voice in the hallway outside. "He can go."

A police officer walked in and released the cuffs. She rubbed the painful wrists and attempted to stand before she became light-headed and settled Mike's body heavily onto the bed again.

The officer stared at her. "I got other things to do, man. You can stay here all night if you want."

She tried again. The problem was the size of Mike's body. It was like trying to drive a tank—huge and unwieldy. It was all so...big. She lurched out of the cell and stumbled down the hall-way. The cop looked at the prisoner as though he suspected he was on drugs.

"Inner ear infection," she muttered.

The guy chuckled. "Jeez. You are having a shitty day."

"You have no idea." She rolled Mike's eyes.

The cop led the shifter's body to a side door that opened onto a parking lot. "The gate will open for you."

She turned quickly. "Have you got—" The door slammed in her face.

Somewhat nervous about what she might find, she felt in the shifter's pockets. Gum and a cell phone were, thankfully, all she could find. She guessed she didn't need to collect anything so walked out onto the asphalt lot.

The gate opened automatically and she stepped through onto the street and it closed behind her. She took a few drunken-looking steps and stopped to study her surroundings. Someone was watching but she couldn't put her finger on which sense told her that and how she could know exactly who it was. She desperately wanted to vacate Mike's body and see what was going on in her dimensional pocket, but if she was right and Warren had her under surveillance, she couldn't leave his body vulnerable.

CHAPTER EIGHT

L exi stood on the street and tried to get her bearings in an area of the town she didn't recognize. Uncomfortable in Mike's body and suspecting that Warren watched her from somewhere, she lumbered along until she reached an alley.

This might be a safe place to get Mike into his own body.

She stepped into the shadowed space and readied herself to shift her consciousness.

Suddenly, the vision in Mike's eyes blurred and she began to lose her balance. She flattened her palm against the wall and tried to steady herself. The body felt suddenly weary. Her thoughts became foggy and difficult to process, and the shifter's knees threatened to buckle. She knew what a psychic attack felt like and so kept to the shadowed side of the alley and glanced out beyond the wall. A man walked casually along the street in her direction. It was Warren.

As she stumbled farther along the narrow road, she tried to shake off the debilitating dizziness and took refuge behind a dumpster. The body she inhabited wasn't capable of fighting the legacy while under this psychic attack. She began to panic. Then, from deep within Mike's chest, came an explosion of pain and anger. Her vision flickered and pressure built throughout the body, tugging her in every direction. She opened her mouth to curse but it came out as a whine.

"*What the fuck?*"

"*Who is that?*" The voice was so loud that she tried to turn, thinking that someone stood beside her, but her feet somehow tangled and she stumbled. She realized with shock that there were four feet beneath her, and she now stared down a long furry snout.

"*I've shifted?*" She yelped.

The voice spoke again. "*I said, who is this?*"

The voice wasn't close. It was inside her head.

This must be Mike's pack. How the hell can I explain that I'm a friend of his who's trying to protect his body.

The chatter was instant and distracting. She struggled to separate the many voices but her hackles rose and she was acutely aware that Warren now stood at the beginning of the alley where she'd entered it moments before.

"*You've inadvertently taken possession of Mike's body which has now shifted because it's under threat.*"

She realized she only had to think the words. "*Well, that helps. Yes.*"

"*I won't pretend to understand how that happened. Take in your surroundings a little better so we know where you are.*"

Lexi glanced left and right and tried to notice the details. She poked her head out to look at the alley in the direction of Warren's silhouette and toward the street at the other side, closer to her. "*I need to get Mike out of my pocket and back into his body.*"

A new voice spoke. "*How is Mike in your pocket? That makes no sense.*"

"*Shut up, Kevin.*"

"*Sorry, Alpha.*"

That surprised Lexi. She'd always assumed Mike had been the alpha.

The wolves guffawed at her thought.

She felt the alpha's brief amusement.

"You're a wolf now. Pay attention to your other senses."

Her first instinct was to inhale. The smells spoke to her in a way she couldn't believe was possible. That single breath told her there were a dozen animals in the vicinity. She could smell the sweat from Warren, the businesses nearby, and a stationer. How could she know that? When she sniffed again, she realized it was the paper and the ink. She could smell Mike's scent glands—*gross!* —and the witch-magic on her stalker.

The crazy legacy took a step into the shadows. "It smells like dog in here. You haven't shifted, have you? In a public place? You know that's in breach of the Kindred Code. I'm perfectly within my rights to kill you right here."

The alpha's voice continued. *"I need you to do something for me. Sit."*

Lexi's borrowed wolf butt hit the dirt. *"Hey!"*

"That's good. You have the compulsion to follow commands. You'll have to make a run for it. But you have four feet so it'll feel difficult and unnatural, so I will command you to run. The command should take over the physiology of the body you're in."

She nodded her understanding even though the alpha couldn't see her. As she readied herself for the command, a bright flash bounced off the dumpster beside her with a crash and threw sparks onto Mike's fur.

"Run."

The body didn't allow her a second's thought. She bolted out of the alley and zigzagged to avoid two more blasts before she sprinted around the corner, across the street, and into another alley.

She stopped, panting. *"He's here. He's caught up with me."* She spun but no one was there. Before she could relax, she felt him behind her again and whirled several more times.

The dry voice in her mind sighed. *"You're chasing your tail."*

Lexi made a mental eye roll. It wasn't only the tail, she realized. There were all kinds of stuff back there she wasn't used to.

She glanced over her shoulder. *"Jesus Christ! I have balls."*

Her mind filled with raucous laughter.

"I can smell you and whatever's chasing you. You should be able to scent us now. I'm at a junkyard a couple of streets away."

Another small explosion caught the edge of Mike's ear and she yelped. Spurred into action, she raced away in the direction of the junkyard and sprinted the rest of the way. She bounded through the open gates and skidded to a halt inside.

She could smell the other wolves there but couldn't see them immediately.

Moments later, Warren appeared, already holding his long blade. "Who's been a naughty boy, then?"

Lexi growled and bared the body's teeth. At this point, she wasn't sure who the wolf belonged to and it felt all her. Other growls joined hers and snarling wolves stepped out around her and Warren.

The legacy looked at them and grinned. "I don't think you want to get in the way of Kindred in the pursuit of a criminal." He threw what was supposed to be another energy ball at her but it sputtered and died. He'd run out of Lucy's magic. She realized she hadn't sensed the young mage at all and wondered where she was.

Warren must be drawing on the magic through his unhealing scar from some distance. That could kill Lucy, not that he'd care.

"You're Kindred?" several voices asked in her mind.

Lexi wondered if these wolves could read her whole mind. *"This is worse than an extraction. I'm not Kindred anymore but the guy following me is. And he's crazy."*

She sniffed with Mike's sensitive nose and scented the earthy tones of witch magic. The smell came from Warren and she realized that he must have been mostly cloaking it. Now that his mage magic was depleted, there was no way to hide it. He had indeed taken the witch's energy.

As she considered this, she kept her gaze on the legacy and wondered why he hadn't attacked them with the earth magic. Instead, he gazed at the wolves with an arrogant expression before he simply turned and ran.

The need to pursue rippled through her and she decided it seemed a waste to allow him to live while she had all these teeth. No sooner had she thought it, however, than the might of the Alpha's mind was brought to bear on her.

"Down."

The wolf hit the dirt.

She pictured Carolyn's body to show them what he'd done to the young witch but the alpha continued to pour his will upon her. Finally, she surrendered. With the threat gone, everything blurred and she was in Mike's human body again.

One by one, the wolves shifted and she was surrounded by a group of men and women.

A large man with a scarred face approached her. "We don't need to be in the middle of a war between Kindred and witches."

Lexi wondered how tall this guy must be if he seemed large compared to Mike. "You're already in the middle of it. I know that if I could smell the witch magic in him, you could too. He killed Carolyn." She recognized the stubbornness in the man's face and gave up.

The alpha smirked. "It feels odd introducing myself to a face I've known half my life. I'm Terry."

"Lexi." She sighed and gave him a curt nod.

"I need to make sure Mike's okay." She contemplated translocating her mind to where the others were but so many unexpected things had happened this evening, it seemed safer to simply call them. She took the shifter's cell phone out. "Fingerprint identification, thank God." She opened the device and called her number, then put it on speakerphone. She listened to it ring with a frown and nervousness kicked in when it reached its seventh beep.

"Hello?" It was Scott.

"Hi, it's me." When she heard the deep voice coming from Mike's mouth, she rolled her eyes. "Lexi."

She heard the shifter in the background. "Wait, is that me?"

A young man stepped forward and stared from his packmate's face before him to the cell phone. "Mike?"

Lexi recognized his voice from the wolfpack chatter. It was Kevin.

"Kev?" Mike sounded baffled.

Kevin's eyes bulged as he stared from Mike's face to the cell and back. "This is so fucked up."

Ignoring the man, she sighed with relief. "Scott, I thought you wouldn't answer. What took you so long?"

Scott sounded uncomfortable. "I went out and brought your corporeal body into your dimensional pocket. I didn't want to simply leave you standing there with no one at the helm. Then I had to take your cell phone out of your pocket. I was trying to be respectful."

Kevin grinned. "While she's been looking at Mike's balls."

"What?" Mike's voice was a squeak.

Lexi ignored him. "What's the situation?"

"Louis and I managed to reverse the spell together," the mage replied. "I've never seen anything like it."

She considered vacating Mike's body but didn't know if Warren had stayed in the area. Instead, she chose to remain in it until she had it safely with her team. "I'll call a cab and come to Louis's place."

The alpha stepped forward. "No need. One of the guys will take you."

The huge man had a few more questions for her which she answered patiently. She checked the time. "If you don't mind, I need to get Mike's body to his consciousness. While we're talking, Warren could be powering up again."

"Kev, take him…her, or whatever, to wherever he needs to go. Make sure Mike's okay and confirm with me."

Lexi followed the young shifter out of the yard to a car.

Kev pulled out onto the road. "Where did you say Mike's mind is again?"

"His consciousness is in another dimension that can be accessed in corporeal or non-corporeal form."

"And that's where your body is?" He seemed blown away by it all.

"That's right." As she spoke, she became aware that the car had suddenly slowed. "Is there a problem?"

She stared at Kevin as his head slumped against the wheel and the engine cut out. "Shit." As she looked to see where the danger was coming from, she reached toward where her dimensional pocket should be. Of course, it wasn't there. Her vision blurred and a moment later, she was overcome.

Lexi was woken by excruciating pain. She couldn't move but could see she was still inside the shifter's body, now seated on the ground. It took a moment to register that a knife was buried up to the hilt in Mike's thigh and she looked at Warren, who stood in front of her with a smirk on his face.

The crazed legacy's expression brightened. "You're awake. That's great."

Mike's cell phone rang. It lay in the grass a foot away, but she couldn't move her arm to reach it. The body she inhabited was bound by a spell. Warren took two steps and stamped on the device. When he removed his foot, they both looked at it in confusion. It continued to ring and the screen wasn't even cracked.

She fixed a disdainful look on her captor. "Not had your oatmeal this morning?"

He delivered a blow to the side of Mike's face and kicked the cell away. Lexi heard a *plop* as it landed in the water.

I need to be more careful with Mike's body.

Briefly, she wondered if she could shift again. She tried but didn't seem able to grasp whatever had made her shift the last time. Given that she sat with a knife in her leg, it wasn't like she wasn't motivated. Warren's spell must be blocking it.

Her next idea was to try to override the paralysis spell but nothing happened. The man was talking but she made no effort to listen and instead, focused her thoughts on trying to find the solution. She'd been able to use her abilities on the counselor while inside Mike's body but it didn't work on Warren. Why?

He flicked the knife handle with a finger. Mike's voice howled and she felt nausea-inducing pain.

"Listen, we'll have to move this along. I've never performed an extraction before. I'm not even sure I can. Counselors go through years of training and I simply don't have that kind of time to get what I need from you. I have some extra juju that might help, or it might fry your brain." Warren crouched. He took a vial out and tipped a little oil onto his palm, rubbed his hands together, and placed them on either side of Mike's head. "Let's get to it then."

CHAPTER NINE

Lexi closed her eyes, relinquished the body, and took her consciousness to her body in the dimensional pocket.

She sat bolt upright and turned to Scott, who was bent over Mike on the floor, muttering spells.

"Warren has Mike's body."

"No shit!" Mike sprawled on the floor and clutched his leg. "What the fuck did he do?"

"He stabbed you in the leg. Now, he's trying to perform an extraction."

The mage's face dropped in horror. "He's what? A legacy can't do something like that. Even with borrowed magic. This is bad. He could obliterate Mike's mind."

"But Mike's mind is here."

"He's still connected to that body." He pointed to the shifter, who continued to groan in pain.

"What can we do? I tried to cast a spell on him but it didn't work."

Scott frowned in thought. "That's probably because your body is here. I think you'd need a mind-to-mind connection with him."

Mike screamed and clawed at his head.

79

Lexi looked at the shifter. "Like that!" She lay down quickly.

The young mage turned to her with a confused expression. "What are you—"

In a split-second, she was in Mike's body again.

Warren held a hand on the shifter's head. "Where are you, you fucker? No one meditates this damn deep." His scars glowed red as he stared into his captive's eyes. "Good. Hold still."

As Mike's eyes closed, she allowed her mind to travel along the stream of tangled red and white energy that emanated from the legacy. She didn't have a clue what she was doing now and acted on pure instinct.

In her mind's eye, she stood and reached out to the red mist. "Carolyn."

It jerked in response.

"Carolyn, come to me." She touched it with her mind and that was all it took. The witch's energy surged, half-pulled and half-pushed through the mind link into Lexi's consciousness.

Warren fell back and looked drained. "What's happening?"

She didn't hang around to answer. Instead, she pushed to a seated position again in the dimensional pocket and screamed. Her unhealing scar seared with pain as it flashed red.

Scott was at her side immediately. "What did he do to you?"

"She's here. I have Carolyn's energy inside me. She's not happy."

He raced to his backpack and yanked things out of it. A moment later, he crouched next to her and put a handful of crystals and Dolores' power bank into her hands.

Her teeth gritted, she focused on the collection and tried to force the energy from her. "She won't go."

The mage disappeared and returned with Louis. The elderly man shrugged him off. "What the—"

"Can you help her?"

Lexi lay motionless, half-aware of those around her and half-lost in the red maelstrom of power that coursed through her body. It was agony but the feeling of power was incredible. She felt like she could do anything.

Louis took a handkerchief from his pocket and rubbed his hands with it. He placed a hand on her head and one under her chin. Suddenly, he was inside the whirling, crashing magical energy. "Carolyn."

"Louis? Where am I? I'm frightened."

"It's okay, baby. I'm here to take you home. There's nothing to be scared of. Follow me."

The old man groaned.

Lexi opened her eyes to see sweat on his face and his face twisted in a grimace.

He breathed deeply. "You have to let it go, girl."

She thought he was talking to Carolyn but in a moment, she recognized the truth she'd been keeping from herself. Stunned, she reached out to Scott, caught his hand, and drew on his magic. He sobbed as the mental pathways between them opened more fully than they ever had. She looked at him. "Help me let her go."

Her eyes struggled to focus on the red magic in her unhealing scar. It flooded out of her and into Louis, washed away by the white.

For a few moments, she closed her eyes, felt the presence of her mage, then opened them.

"I need to get back to the house." Louis looked as exhausted as she felt.

Scott stood and grasped the old man's shoulder and they vanished.

The mage returned moments later and was silent for a moment. He looked at her arm and raised his eyebrows in surprise.

Lexi looked down to see what had startled him. The magical energy in her scar was like a river of silver. "That's pretty."

He looked at her. "Are you able to carry on? We need to get to the body. Mike can re-inhabit it and we'll finish Warren."

Before she could respond, a retching sound drew their attention. Mike was still on the floor, holding his leg, but he now vomited water.

She was horrified. "We were near the river."

Scott tried to tug her closer to the shifter but she pulled back. His eyes were closed and his legs jerked. "We can't put him back in that condition. He won't make it." She took Scott's hand. "Hold your breath."

"No—" His protest cut off.

A moment later, Lexi was in Mike's body again. It thrashed wildly under the water. His lungs were burning and she instantly lost the ability to reason. Her hand flexed and tried to take hold of something. Vaguely, she recalled that something important had been in her hand but she'd lost it. Now, it was only water.

She began to lose consciousness when she felt a strong arm around Mike's chest. Barely aware of her surroundings, she felt herself drifting away. The thud of being dropped onto the ground brought her mind momentarily to awareness and a warmth spread through the breastbone of her borrowed body. As though through a fog, she heard Scott's voice.

"Lexi, can you hear me? Get back into your body if you can." He sounded desperate.

In fact, he felt desperate. The rawness of his fear pulsed through their link.

She merely wanted to sleep.

The surge of water from lungs to throat to lips brought her to full consciousness. She coughed up more water than she imagined possible and continued until she was sure it was gone. Finally, she looked into her mage's relieved face, sat quickly, and pulled him close to hug him tightly.

His pained voice broke through her momentary panic. "Lexi, you'll break my ribs. Also, you need a shave."

Lexi remembered she was still in Mike's body. She tried to

apologize but her throat stung. The words emerged as a groan and she tried to stand.

"Wait, you're bleeding." He put a hand over the shifter's leg and muttered a few words. "I've closed it. His shifter healing should stop any infection now."

The mage pulled his cell phone out and called Dick. "I don't know where Warren is. We're getting our corporeal selves the hell out of here and back to Louis's house."

She put Mike's arm around his shoulder and he translocated.

In an instant, she stood outside Louis's kitchen. Still leaning on Scott, she walked in and groaned at the aches in the damaged body as she dropped into the chair next to Dick, who was drinking an ominous clear liquid from a mason jar. She wiped Mike's hands down his chest. It didn't help that he had no breasts. She was certain it contributed significantly to the lack of balance.

The vampire slid the mason jar across the table. "It's like a tonic, trust me. You two are soaked. What the hell happened?"

Louis turned to Heidi. "Sweetheart, get some blankets, please."

Lexi looked at Mike's wet clothes and shivered. "I assume he didn't get the answers he wanted from Mike and dumped him in the river."

Dick rolled his eyes. "So you came back and grabbed Scott. Couldn't you think of someone else who could help underwater? Someone who doesn't need to breathe?"

She was speechless.

Mike's borrowed gaze focused on him. "Right. I need to get him in here because this body needs to pee and I'm not going there."

He raised an eyebrow. "Surely once you've seen a man's—"

When she gave him the kill-stare, he simply shrugged. "Weirdly, it's more intimidating when you do it with your face."

Lexi closed her eyes and opened them. She now lay on the couch in her dojo while Mike paced up and down.

It was great to feel her body again. "That was some *Freaky Friday* shit I don't ever want to do again. Let's get you home."

He walked toward her. "Wait, I want to know why you were looking at—"

She took hold of his shoulder and they appeared in the kitchen.

"My balls," the shifter croaked and looked at the others. "Never mind."

"I didn't intentionally look at them. I happened to glimpse them when I was looking at your tail."

"You shifted?" Scott and Dick asked in unison.

Mike looked down. "I'm soaking. And I think you peed myself."

Lexi suddenly remembered Kevin. "Mike, you should contact your alpha. Kevin was in the car with me when Warren attacked."

He nodded.

Louis patted the shifter on the shoulder. "I'm glad you're okay. We'll head out for Carolyn's ritual now."

Dick lowered the mason jar and screwed the top on. "We'll make ourselves scarce."

"You're very welcome to join us." Carolyn's mother spoke from the doorway.

Lexi, Scott, Dick, and Mike followed them to the circle. They stood a little beyond the gathering as the witches began their chant. The altar blurred and Carolyn's body rose from the stone. Louis stepped closer to the body and whispered words over it. As he spoke, tendrils of red mist left his mouth, curled around it, and settled into it before it rose and took the young woman's shape.

"I'm sorry, Mom."

"It wasn't your fault, honey." Karen stepped forward.

"My lavender girl," said Warren's disembodied voice.

Karen raised a hand to the spirit. "It's okay, Carolyn. We know what happened. You don't have to go through that again."

Louis put a hand on the woman's arm. "We'll need to witness it for evidence."

The woman looked directly at Lexi. "This won't be handled through Kindred justice."

She nodded her agreement. Carolyn's mother wanted Warren dead and she was happy to oblige.

The spirit drifted to the edge of the circle where Lexi stood. "Thank you." She looked at Scott. "He hates you. He wants to do the same to you as he did to me."

Carolyn drifted to the altar. "I have to go. Grandma's calling."

Karen sobbed. "Well, your grandma can wait. She'll have all of eternity with my baby girl."

Lexi felt keenly that they had seen enough. She looked at her companions, who all had wet eyes. In silence, they left the circle and drove to Mike's bar.

They entered and walked directly to the office.

The shifter pulled a drawer open and retrieved a bottle of bourbon and a glass.

"Oooh!" Dick's face brightened. He was still holding the mason jar.

The other man looked at it. "Is that Louis's moonshine? That stuff will rot you from the inside out." He gazed at the hopeful faces around him. "I guess we all need one of these." He pointed to a glass-fronted cabinet behind Scott. "Would you mind?"

The mage turned and took out three more glasses.

Mike knocked his drink back. "What next? Do you think he'll come for me again?"

Lexi considered the question. "Warren probably thinks he scrambled your brains before he dropped you into the water. I'm sure he thinks you're dead."

Dick picked a glass up. "Where do you think he is now?"

Scott answered before she could. "If I know Warren—and I'm sorry to say I do—he'll put as much distance as possible between himself and Mike's assumed death."

The shifter leaned down to a sports bag and pulled out some sweats. "I need to get changed and make a call."

"I'll give you some privacy." She wandered out of the office and walked into the quiet bar where she sat at a table and put her feet up.

"Penny for them?" Dick sat next to her.

"Mike was here for me when I needed someplace to lie low. I'm ashamed by how poorly I've repaid him. I'm what brought Warren here. No one deserves that."

"Don't take it all on yourself. He's after Scott, not you."

"But Scott was never here and I was. When will that lunatic stop?"

"Never. We know that now." Scott joined them and put refilled glasses on the table. "I'll have to deal with him."

"We," Lexi corrected him. She picked her drink up. "There isn't much more we can do here. Let's get to the hotel. I'd like to see Louis and Heidi before we leave in the morning."

They turned as someone entered the bar. It was the alpha Terry with a couple of the pack, including Kevin.

Mike emerged from the office. He'd changed into the sweatpants but still had the same damp shirt on.

Terry's eyes narrowed. "Mike? Is that you?"

"It's me. Come and meet Lexi."

They walked to the table.

Quickly, she stood. "It's good to meet you again."

The alpha gave her a wry smile. "You look different. Have you changed your hair?"

"She's lost her balls." Kevin guffawed.

Lexi frowned and raised an eyebrow. "Would you like to test that?"

The man shuffled awkwardly. "It was a joke."

After a moment to prolong his discomfort, she grinned. "It's good to see you're okay." She turned to Scott. "Can you make sure he is okay?"

The young shifter regarded Scott with suspicion and stepped back.

Dick spoke to Terry. "Warren could have done something to him while he was unconscious. It's best to know."

The alpha nodded and Scott extended a hand to Kevin. After a few seconds, he shook his head and smiled at the nervous young man. "Nothing. You're fine."

She finished her drink. "Right, let's get out of here before anything else happens." She took a couple of steps toward Mike, leaned closer, and pulled the counselor's business card from his shirt pocket. It was unharmed by its dip in the water.

He narrowed his eyes. "What's that?"

"It's evidence that I'm not as smart as I think I am," she replied with a lopsided grin.

Mike looked at the mage. "You saved me twice today."

Scott shook his head and raked his hair back. "It's my fault you were in danger in the first place."

His cell phone beeped and he looked at it. "Dolores will meet us at the parking lot tomorrow. She wants to know a time."

Lexi turned to Mike. "What are your plans?"

Terry answered for him. "We'll stay here, drink all night, and sleep where we fall."

"I recommend the basement. It's surprisingly cozy." She smiled and her ex-boss chuckled, which made her feel that maybe they were okay now.

CHAPTER TEN

"Honey, I'm home." Warren whistled as he climbed the stairs.

Lucy gathered the papers spread across her bed, shuffled them frantically, and stuffed them into the folder before she pushed it under her pillow. She knew she should have hidden them when she felt her magic being drawn repeatedly as he translocated back to her. Now, she tried not to let the feeling of dread escape, knowing he could feel her emotions through the bond. "You've been gone for days. I was worried."

The legacy appeared in the doorway of her room. He was grotesque to look at after he insisted that they conduct the bonding ritual repeatedly. For some reason, he was convinced that he gained more power with each unhealing scar and that he could compensate for her not being as powerful a match as Scott would have been.

A little shiver raced through her when she realized she'd been staring too long. She frowned at the welts on his forehead. "Your face is injured. Do you want me to fix it?"

He strode to her bed, lay on his side, and rested on his elbow next to her weak, fragile body.

His brief smile was playful, but he stared at her and raised his eyebrows. "You don't fool me. You were watching." He tapped his temple. "From inside here."

"I had a night...a dream. I don't know what was real and what was the dream." She felt she was walking on eggshells, something she always did with him.

He shoved his arm in front of her face. "But you see the red welts on my head. I don't hide anything from you. You know it was real. That red power was like riding an unbroken stallion." He tapped the tip of her nose with his finger. "Silly."

"I suppose." She noticed that while most Kindreds referred to the white light in the scar as energy or magic, he called it power.

"What happened to you? I was surrounded by wolves and your pathetic magic gave up on me."

Lucy looked away. "I fainted. I couldn't draw enough magic from the air to replace what you were taking." She looked at him after a moment. "Did your witch's magic let you down too?"

Warren glanced up, clearly noticing the barb, but ignored it. "I don't seem to be able to use it without our power to carry it."

He shifted onto his back. "It felt amazing, though. My head's still buzzing. I could feel it curl around my bones like smoke. Do you want some next time?"

"No thanks." *Next time? Dear God.*

He rolled toward her and onto his elbow, dangerously close to the hidden folder, and put a hand on her face. "Are you sure? Do you want me to show you how I did it?" His hand was warm and began to heat noticeably. He would burn her face and she was virtually defenseless because he had drawn so much of her magic that it had left her physically weak.

She tried to turn away. "It might mess my magic up. Then there'd be none."

With a disapproving sigh, he removed his hand. "So. What have you been doing while I've been away?"

"I've tried to get my strength back."

"Get it back? Where did it go?" It was like he dared her to complain.

You know where it went, you psychotic bastard. "I've felt a little under the weather."

"You're lucky we live in Eric's big house with people to look after us and cook our food. We'd starve if we had to rely on you."

You could try doing something yourself. She wanted to say it but it wasn't worth the slap she knew would follow.

Warren traced a finger across her collarbone, over her shoulder, and down her arm.

Lucy trembled.

"You're so full of nerves that you fascinate me. You remind me of the pets I had growing up—like a delicate little mouse, so brittle I could simply snap you in my hand." He clicked his fingers and she jumped.

A flood of excitement surged through the bond they shared. He liked it when she was frightened.

She resisted the urge to shudder again but she swallowed loudly.

Warren laughed and sat. "Since you haven't asked, I'll tell you. I've had a shit couple of days."

He would continue whether she asked or not so she remained silent.

"I should have had access to that shifter's memories. Something went wrong with my spell. It should have worked."

"Mixing magic can be unpredictable." She shrugged.

"Thank you for the lesson, Lucy."

"I didn't mean—"

"I did it right. I know I did." He thought briefly about the pretty witch girl in the kitchen who had spoken those same words. "The memories were implanted. He was crying like a baby when I left him. But somehow, after a two-minute relaxing meditation session, he was fine."

"Perhaps he carried a witch charm."

"No. I'd have sensed it. And even more so since I was juiced up with the witch's power."

Lucy flinched. He'd murdered a woman without a second thought. She was nothing more than a source of energy and a way to get into the shifter's mind.

He turned to her again and moved toward her on the bed. "Can you fix the burns on my head? They hurt."

"Of course." She sat, placed her hands over the welts, and closed her eyes, more because she didn't want to see his face than for any other reason.

Not looking proved to be a mistake as she didn't see his arms move until he'd clapped his hands over hers. He began to mutter under his breath. Her eyes jerked open when she realized what he was doing. She was in the same position as the witch had been, but instead of looking into the face of the terrified victim through his eyes, she now looked at his cruel face.

"Ah, Warren. You're home." Eric stood in the doorway. "Have I come at a bad time?"

Lucy shifted her gaze from the young legacy to Eric and back. Her Kindred partner paused but finally sighed and released her hands. He turned to the door with his glamor in place to hide the horrific scars on his face. "No. It's fine. What do you need?"

Relieved, she scuttled away from him and across to the other side of the bed. Neither man even looked at her.

"I've received a message. They want to see me tomorrow. It looks like I'll get the position on the Kindred Council. I'd like you to come along. I've recommended you for a position at head office."

"An office job? Me?" Warren laughed. "I'm still working on the murder investigation." He turned to her and winked as though they were co-conspirators. "We can't let that savage get away with it."

She knew he was thinking of the witch he'd watched in the

kitchen. It wasn't easy to forget that when she'd seen the girl through his eyes and felt his hunger.

"I'm impressed by your dedication but you're not supposed to work jobs in Illinois. It's not in our jurisdiction. It was convenient that you were on vacation there when it all took place, but I think the investigation's a bust for now. A shifter has the taste for blood. He'll strike again and Kindred will catch him next time." Eric glanced at his cell phone. "And no. It's not an office job. I've recommended you for a position in the Overseers' office."

Warren's eyes widened. "The Overseers? But that would give me jurisdiction over the whole country."

Eric nodded. "Yes."

"So I could continue working the case."

The older man raised an eyebrow. "You go where they send you."

Lucy sighed. She was conflicted. If he continued to translocate alone, it could kill her. But she had made her mind up. All this had to stop. She couldn't talk to Eric. He frightened her as much as Warren did—and maybe more because he was both perfectly sane and utterly ruthless. While she feared the effect Warren's traveling had on her health, the two of them being away would be perfect.

Eric glanced at her when she sighed loudly. "Don't worry, Lucy. You'll come with us."

She felt the legacy's irritation so strongly that she was fairly certain he wouldn't have felt hers. It came as no surprise. She knew he didn't want her around and only wanted her magic.

Conscious of the older man's attention, she managed a half-smile. "Great."

He frowned. "You look tired. Get some rest or you won't be strong enough to take us. I'll send dinner up." He looked at Warren. "Let's chat about the job."

As they headed to the door, Lucy spoke quickly. "I'll try some energy-building spells."

Warren glanced dismissively at her. "Yeah, you do that."

Without another glance, he closed the door behind him.

It had been a deliberate ploy. He would now expect to sense her using magic, which was what she wanted.

Lucy waited for at least a minute before she drew the manilla folder out from under her pillow. She glanced nervously at the door. It was stolen property several times over.

The heading was already imprinted in her mind. *Property of Kindred Document Library, New York, New York.*

She had stolen it from Warren's room. He had stolen it from Eric's office, and she was fairly certain that the older man wasn't supposed to have it either.

The label at the top read, *Alexa Braxton (Texas Unit) - Legacy. Status: Missing.* She flicked through the sheets.

Father: Unknown

Mother: Elizabeth (Surname unknown) Legacy - (Unit unknown.)

Sibling: REDACTED

Unit Leader: John Braxton

Unit Siblings: REDACTED

Margaret Braxton - Mage,

Isaac Braxton - Legacy,

Robert Braxton - Mage

With a frown, she returned her attention to the incomplete lines and wondered why the names of a blood sibling and unit sibling would be redacted. She glanced at the mother. *Why no surname?* She read on.

Alexa scores low in legacy abilities and no affinity for any super-nature stands out. However, she compensates with highly developed skills through a solid training regimen.

She scores very high on moral code, justice, ethics, and loyalty. Counseling sessions weighing heavily toward these traits are recommended.

The young witch turned the sheet sideways to read the notes

scribbled in the margin in Warren's handwriting. Everywhere Lexi's name appeared, he'd written *Bitch*.

Quickly, she flicked through more sheets and skimmed reports from her last few operations with her Kindred unit.

On the last page was a report by Eric naming the fae woman Dolores as possibly harboring Lexi and Scott, and a report on the cafe where they had almost caught her in New York and an unknown subject had shot Warren through the neck with a bolt.

It's a shame they didn't kill him.

Finally, she glanced at the hand-drawn sketches by the legacy. One was of Lexi's severed head.

The frail young woman climbed off her bed and held onto the nightstand when she wobbled from weakness. She picked her jewelry box up, unzipped her cosmetics bag to retrieve her compact mirror, and opened it with a frown. It was broken and only a single shard of mirror remained. When Warren had seen it, he said she should throw it out. She had told him it had been her mother's. While the compact had been her mother's, the shard of glass was from one of the mirrors in the coffee shop in New York where they had caught up to Lexi and he had unfortunately not died from a projectile through the neck.

It had been her job, after the attack on her, to identify the shooter from evidence in the bathroom. With the projectile missing and most of the glass obliterated by Warren's energy ball, it had been simple to obscure Maggie and Isaac from all but one shard. She took an earring from the jewelry box and held it to draw the magical energy she had imbued it with. After a moment, she already felt better. She gazed into the shard and whispered her spell.

Lucy had never shown Warren this spell. He'd spy on her all the time if he knew it—her and everyone else. She watched through the shard of glass as the vision of Isaac and Maggie in the bathroom vanished. The picture became a swirling gray mist and she focused on it while she continued to murmur. This was the problem. The spell only worked if the people she sought were in the vicinity of a mirror.

She was aware that the clock was ticking. Warren would be up to torment her before he turned in for the night. She had begun to consider giving up when the mist swirled and revealed Maggie and Isaac entering a room—a bedroom from what she could tell.

"Help me. Can you hear me? I need help." She whispered close to the mirror so she wouldn't be heard by Eric and Warren, but the couple couldn't hear her.

Maggie put her arms around Isaac. "Exactly how tired are you?"

The young mage rolled her eyes. She could hear them perfectly well.

He smiled and kissed her nose. "I'm not tired at all."

"That's not what you said downstairs."

"I lied." He tugged at her t-shirt.

A giggle came from somewhere in the room and they stepped apart.

Maggie grinned. "Come out, you rascal."

A little boy appeared as though from thin air. Lucy was shocked at how young but proficient he seemed.

The woman in the mirror raised an eyebrow. "Bobby, what have I told you about spying on people?"

"Not to get caught." He gave her a dazzling smile.

"Not to do it, munchkin." She mussed the boy's hair.

"How come the lady can do it but I can't?" He pointed at the mirror.

They turned to face Lucy in surprise. She sighed with relief and mouthed, "Help me."

Isaac stepped in front of Bobby. "Isn't that Lucy? The psycho's mage?"

She nodded frantically.

Maggie sat at the dresser, closer to the mirror. "You can hear us? We can't hear you."

Lucy's gaze flicked to the door and back to the mirror.

Isaac stepped beside Maggie and put a hand on her shoulder. "She's trying to be quiet. Can we do anything this end?"

The other woman muttered some words while she continued to whisper.

Suddenly, their faces indicated that her voice was audible. "I need help."

His eyes narrowed. "Where's Warren?"

She turned the mirror in a full circle around the room and back to her. "He's downstairs but he'll be here soon. I can't take it anymore. He'll kill me."

They studied her with a dubious expression. "You've looked better. Not much, though. Why now?"

"I think he's planning to simply use me up until he can get Scott back. I'm not strong enough. I can't regain the energy he wants. He's been translocating all over the country without me."

Maggie's jaw dropped. "Without you? No wonder you're such a mess."

"Can you contact Dolores? She got Scott out, didn't she? Can she get me out? I'll keep this shard of mirror with me all the time. She can use it to find me."

"How do we know this isn't a trick so Warren can capture Scott?"

Lucy burst into tears. She heard someone on the stairs and looked desperately into the compact. "Please, tomorrow, midday. They're going to New York. I think I can swing it so I'll be alone."

She watched as Maggie picked a snow globe up and threw it at the mirror. Her shard returned only her reflection and she closed it quickly and shoved it into her purse.

Seconds later, the door opened and Warren stepped in. He studied her red eyes. "Sweetie, what's the matter?"

"Nothing. I'm tired. I was about to go to sleep."

"Nonsense. You can tell me." He sat next to her and put an arm around her.

Lucy started to cry again and spoke between sobs. "I'm trying to build energy up for tomorrow but you're drawing it as fast as I can store it."

"Oh. So it's my fault." His arm became rigid and his voice dangerous.

"I'm not saying that, not at all. It's my fault. I'm not as strong as you need me to be."

"You know I have to keep drawing to keep the glamor in place. People will ask awkward questions about why we did this." He indicated his face, ruined with scars.

We? He'd forced her into it.

She felt herself shaking and looked down. "I'm simply tired, I guess."

"Tell you what. If it helps, I'll lock my door tonight to be sure that no one will see me, and I'll take the glamor down while I sleep. That should help you build your strength up for tomorrow."

"Thank you, Warren." She gave him a meek smile.

He leaned closer and kissed her forehead. "Goodnight, my dearest."

When he stood abruptly, it made her flinch. He chuckled and left.

The mage looked at the rest of her energy-infused stones. She would have to use all of them if she had any intention of going to New York tomorrow, which she didn't.

CHAPTER ELEVEN

Lexi smiled at Louis as he stepped onto the deck holding two cups of coffee. He passed one to her. "It's early for visitors round here. I keep to retired times." He nodded at Dick. "I'm afraid I don't have any of what you drink. Not to spare, at least."

The vampire smiled. "I'm fine, thank you."

She took the cup and nodded her thanks. "I didn't know if we'd get onto the property."

The old man sat beside her. "You're welcome here. The house knows that."

"How did the rest of last night go?" she asked after a small sip.

He frowned. "She was weak but able to spend a little time with her family. Her Grandma passed her over."

Dick leaned against the rail. "It wasn't too awful for her, was it?"

"She told us she'd felt a little dizzy. That was the last thing she remembered."

Lexi leaned forward. "You need to be careful with that information. He's protected by one of the Grandfathers who isn't a good guy either."

Louis looked into his cup. "I wonder how we came to this—giving Kindred so much power."

"If I only had a dollar for every time I've heard that sentiment uttered." The vampire glanced at her. "No offense."

She didn't have an answer for them and merely shrugged.

Their host frowned and inclined his head as though listening to something.

Dick grinned. "It's Scott. He's snoring in the back of the car." They glanced at the mage's leg hanging over the seat in front of him.

Lexi opened her mouth to say something but felt the oxygen being pulled from her lungs. The air felt thick and heavy around them. She looked at her hand holding the cup. It was shaking.

Her teammate sat heavily in a chair with his hand on his stomach. "I feel like my insides need to be scrubbed with bleach and a wire brush." He shuddered.

Louis seemed to be in a trance. The cup tumbled from his hand, landed on the deck, and shattered. She glanced at Dick, whose eyes were closed. In all the time she'd known him, she'd never seen a dropped object hit the floor in his presence before. He was always there first.

The old man blinked to clear his focus, took a few breaths, and stared at her. "Your eyes are shining silver. I've never seen anything like it."

The car door opened and Scott stumbled out. He scrambled to his feet and spun with balls of energy in his hands, looking for something to fight. "Are we under attack?"

"We felt it too—" Lexi began,

The door to the house swung open. and Heidi rushed through. "Grandpa? Did you feel that?"

Simultaneously, the phone in the house, Lexi's, Dick's, and Scott's cell phones all began to ring. They looked at one another. The young witch returned to the house while the others answered their respective devices.

"Hello?" Lexi didn't know whose voice to expect. It certainly wasn't the one she heard.

"My clock must be running slow or that came early." The voice was familiar but she couldn't place it.

"Who is this?"

"It's Anne, dear. Anne Lown from Emmersley."

She remembered the seer. "Is everything okay?"

"I thought I should remind you about what you left behind. It's still here at Emmersley. Oh, good grief. I have to go. The place is in an uproar now." The woman disconnected.

Lexi didn't recall leaving anything at the care home for supernaturals. She shook her head.

It can't have been important or I'd have noticed it had been left.

Somewhat absently, she wondered if she was missing some underwear. They traveled so much that she could never keep track of her socks.

Scott was still talking into his cell and Dick put his onto speaker.

A shuffling sound issued over the device. "Sorry. I'm gathering the papers I dropped all over the floor. Wait, I'm getting a text. That's a shifter friend in Norway asking if I felt that. It must have been everywhere."

"How's Marcel? Did Limpet react?"

"I don't know. I was in the bedroom. I'm looking at them now and they're both sleeping on the couch as usual. I've never seen such a lazy pair. But they seem fine."

"Could it have affected the wards?"

"That's what I wondered too. I guess there's only one way to find out. I have to go to the museum to assess some pieces coming in today. I'm getting ready to leave now. Hopefully, I can be there and back before anyone else gets into the office."

"Okay, we'll be back soon." The vampire took the cell off speakerphone. "Me too." He disconnected.

Heidi stuck her head through the kitchen door. "It seems like only the supes felt it. The chat group went nuts."

Dick waved his phone. "From what Albin says, it could be all the supernaturals on Earth."

Scott appeared at Lexi's side. "And possibly in Fae. That was Dolores. She's coming for us." He looked at Louis. "If that's okay."

The old man nodded.

The young witch stepped out of the kitchen and closed the door. She walked to her grandfather. "Do you know what it was?"

He frowned. "Something evil has awoken. Something very old and very evil."

Lexi sighed. *What now?* She turned to him. "Maybe this is why we have Kindred. Whatever's going on, this is their situation to fix and they're welcome to it."

The kitchen door opened. Heidi jumped and spun to face Dolores as she walked out. "There you all are."

Scott grinned. "Hi, Dolores."

The young woman tilted her head sideways with a puzzled expression. Lexi assumed she saw the inside of a strange apartment where her kitchen should be.

The newcomer glanced at the corner of the porch roof. Lexi's gaze followed. A glowing, insubstantial ball hovered in the corner. The little fae woman turned to Louis. "I see you have a call waiting. We'll hurry along."

"My ancestors aren't going anywhere. They can wait a minute. It's nice to finally meet you."

"And I you, Louis. Hopefully, there will be time to get together for a real gossip when all this is over." She stepped out to the car.

Lexi wondered briefly at Dolores's choice of words. *When all this is over.*

Her boss closed the door and tapped it to shrink it to a tiny size. She picked it up and dropped it into her jacket pocket. "Come along, team. We have work to do." She walked into her apartment without a backward glance. Scott and Dick muttered their goodbyes and followed her through. Lexi patted Louis on the shoulder and hugged Heidi. As she walked to the corner, she glanced up. The little ball had grown larger and began to clear. The figure of a woman was inside and she stared out.

Suppressing her curiosity, she stepped through the fae door and closed it behind her. She turned to face Dolores's apartment and froze. Seated around the dining table was her Kindred unit—her sister Maggie, her brother Isaac, and the only father she had ever known, John Braxton.

For a few seconds, no one spoke. Finally, Maggie waved. "Surprise."

Lexi looked from them to Dolores.

Her boss shrugged. "We have a situation. By which I mean we have another situation."

John Braxton stood and stepped around the table. He opened his arms. "Come here." He didn't wait but walked up to her and enveloped her in a massive hug.

When he stepped back, his eyes brimmed with unshed tears. "I've been beside myself."

Scott shuffled forward and put out his hand. "Hi…sir…"

"This is Scott, my match."

The man frowned, looked at her, and ignored the mage's hand. "From what I heard, the two of you messed that up and you're merely a regular human now. I didn't think that was possible but I don't sense anything from you. You're as human as he is." He pointed at Dick.

The vampire's eyebrows raised almost to his hairline and he turned to Dolores.

She pointed. "It's on the shelf."

Lexi rolled her eyes. "There's nothing wrong with our bond. We've been undercover." She turned to Scott. "Can you let them see I'm exactly as I was before?"

He understood her meaning and amended his cloaking spell to reveal a Kindred legacy.

Dick removed himself from the group and stepped across the room. He retrieved the bourbon bottle and a glass. Isaac and Maggie watched him with puzzled faces. They had met him before when they hired him to find Lexi and knew he was a vampire, even if he didn't look like one right now. A little confused, they shared a look and glanced at her. It seemed they had decided not to say anything.

Braxton checked his watch. Lexi smirked. It was a little past seven am in Illinois and in Texas where her unit lived. Braxton wouldn't like that.

The vampire had noticed the look too. He held his glass up in a mock toast. "It's Happy Hour somewhere in the world."

She recognized John's look of disapproval. It had been directed at her many times and she felt a little homesick.

"We don't have time for this." Dolores looked at Maggie. "Tell them what you told me."

"Lucy contacted us. Warren's match. She says he's been—"

Lexi finished the sentence. "Translocating across the country without her?"

Braxton's gaze returned to her. "How did you know?"

"He's done far more than that." She pulled a chair out, sat at the table, and told them about the murder.

The man shook his head. "You shouldn't mess with Kindred issues. The Council needs to know about it. This young man has to be stopped."

Scott snorted derisively. "I wouldn't rely on much help from the Council. We—"

"Scott tried to warn them about Warren," she interjected. "No one would listen. And that was before he was protected by Eric." She knew he'd been about to start talking about Caleb and she didn't trust Braxton with that information. He might not take it well if he knew that she had been involved in the man's death.

Isaac drummed his fingers on the table. "Lucy could be telling the truth."

The mage put a hand on the back of Lexi's chair. "She could still be lying or is being manipulated by Warren to lead us into a trap. I know him and what he's capable of. He's insane but he can charm the birds out of the trees when he wants to."

She turned to look at him. "There's no doubt that he'll kill her, deliberately or otherwise. We have to get her out of there."

Dick cleared his throat. "Are we simply ignoring the weird, soul-crushing sensation virtually everyone felt only moments ago?"

They all looked at him.

"I merely thought that as Louis described it as—what? The birth of evil or something? I don't know. It sounded quite pressing." He looked at his sleeve and picked at a non-existent thread.

Dolores sighed. "One problem at a time, dear."

"Lexi, why don't you come back?"

Everyone looked at Braxton.

Maggie slumped. "Dad, you promised you wouldn't."

He took Lexi's hand. "Bobby misses you. He asks about you every day."

She felt it like a kick to the stomach. The little brother she barely knew but loved with all her heart thanks to a Kindred counselor's tricks. She turned on him. "Don't pull that crap with me. I know, okay? I know I only met Bobby twice."

"What's this nonsense? He's your brother. I don't know what these"—he gestured to Scott, Dick, and Dolores—"people have done to you."

Her eyes widened. "You're not kidding. You don't know."

The fae woman frowned. "Lexi, one problem at a time, remember?" She turned to Maggie. "We'll take the case and rescue the girl. How can we find her?"

Maggie lifted her purse onto the table. She removed a little bundle of cloth and opened it to reveal a shard of black glass. "She appeared in my dresser mirror."

Lexi leaned closer to look at it. "This is from your mirror? Why is it black?"

The other woman looked at it and tilted it this way and that. "It's connected to Lucy. Wherever she's keeping it, it's hidden somewhere dark. She hasn't taken it out again since we spoke last night. She said Warren and Eric are going to New York to Kindred headquarters today. The plan was to use the connection between the mirrors to teleport to her and get her out."

Across the room, Dick put a hand up. "Why can't she use the mirrors to come to you? For that matter, why can't she wait until they leave and get on a bus?"

"If she uses her magic to translocate," Maggie explained, "she'll leave a trail. Maybe she could run with a cloaking spell to hide her whereabouts like Lexi did, but I don't think she has a clue how to look after herself alone. She's terrified and I don't think she'd last a day on the run."

Scott folded his arms. "I know for a fact that I'd never have been able to get away from Warren if it hadn't been for Lexi. He knows me too well and could probably have quite easily guessed my actions back then."

Lexi nodded. "Maybe that's why he's been trying to find out about me—to get inside my head and learn my actions." She turned to Maggie. "Should I wait until she appears in the mirror and teleport to her?"

Isaac raised an eyebrow. "Only if you've become a sorcerer since we last spoke."

"I mean with Scott, of course." She smiled.

Braxton frowned. "Perhaps this should be a joint mission."

"What?" Isaac almost bolted out of his chair. "That's a terrible idea."

Lexi stared at him, surprised at his sudden anger. "I'd feel better if you weren't involved too. There will be consequences for you if they know you're a part of this."

He leaned back. "They already think we're involved since they found Warren with a bolt hole through his throat—my weapon of choice. I've seen as much of that lunatic as I have of my reflection."

Braxton turned to him. "I didn't mean the two of you. I'm talking about myself. I could go with them."

Lexi looked from Isaac and Maggie to Braxton. "Why wouldn't you go with your unit?"

No one said anything.

Finally, Dick spoke from the other side of the room. "She's pregnant." He waved his glass at Maggie. "Congratulations, by the way."

Braxton turned quickly. "How could you possibly know that?"

The vampire smiled demurely. "I'm a…witch."

The other man narrowed his eyes. "You don't smell like a witch."

Dick sniffed his wrist. "Tom Ford: Fucking Fabulous. Wonderful stuff but quite strong. It could drown the scent of a vampire." He returned to his drink.

Isaac guffawed. "Nothing's that strong."

The vampire's face remained passive.

Lexi rolled her eyes. He would get himself into trouble. It was time to wind things up. "Right. Maggie, give us a call when Lucy contacts you. We'll be with you immediately."

She hugged her Kindred family and Dolores opened the door. It led out into a street the girl recognized as being in Austin.

When it closed, she sighed. "Can we get breakfast?"

CHAPTER TWELVE

Azatoth opened his eyes and breathed in deeply. The air was different—clean and cool. He looked around the room and felt the soft bedding around him. He raised an arm and gazed at the hand, amazed as he flexed and stretched the fingers.

Finally! He sighed.

As he lay there and flexed his toes and the muscles throughout his new body, he wondered how much time had passed since he had slipped his consciousness through the breached veil and inhabited the waiting vessel. He remembered that there had been some kind of disturbance when he left Caleb's mind and joined with the new meat shell. The details were sketchy.

He was aware that time had passed and that he had slept even while he spread himself slowly through neural pathways and along nerve endings, inch-by-inch. Almost certainly, he had crept around inside this body for days, if not weeks. The mind had been as strong as the body that housed it, so he had not been willing to risk making himself known until he was ready to take control. In the end, there had been no battle. The former owner had merely drifted away. He smiled, touched his lips with his new human fingers, and practiced smiling and frowning a few more times before he ran his tongue across his teeth. They didn't feel very sharp and probably wouldn't be very good for rending flesh.

Once he was assured that he had control of everything, he sat and swung his legs until his feet touched the floor. He looked at the limbs. They were muscular but shorter than he would have liked. He stood. After a moment's dizziness, he stepped to a full-length mirror and assessed his new body.

He gazed at the curves and the breasts and was momentarily taken aback. *I am female. Yes, I remember now.*

He recalled seeing the vessel through Caleb's eyes as the revolting sorcerer applied the magic-imbued fat that marked the woman as the target for his consciousness.

I am a she-creature. Azatoth altered his…her self-perception. She tilted her head as she selected memories from the mind. There was some confusion at first. This face looked like the one Caleb had battled several times, but that was a different human with the same face. He found the name in Caleb's memories. That was Alexa.

I am Alicia.

It didn't matter. He was now a she and she had work to do.

She turned and gazed at the man lying with his back to her, still asleep in the bed.

Azatoth looked at her arm. The white magic flowed through the painful magical scar.

He is the source of her magic but I am already the source of greater magic. She stood and stared down at him. Should the human live or die? She decided that he should live for now. He might prove useful and she could always remove him later.

Relying on the vessel's memory, she dressed, left the apartment, and felt the blast of the New Orleans heat immediately. An arm reached out of its own volition and closed the door behind her and she looked at it in surprise. *Muscle memory.*

She walked through the city. This world smelled so different and she didn't like it. The temperature outside was preferable to her—suffocatingly hot. But she would have to get used to the smells. This would be her world. While she had experienced it recently through Caleb, she hadn't experienced it fully. Still, she had all his memories and many others.

As she walked through the French Quarter, she watched the humans. She wanted to devour them and punish them, but this was merely step one. There was so much more to do. She stared at a glass-fronted store. Inside, people were eating and she realized she was hungry.

Azatoth entered the store and watched as two young women sat with trays of something that smelled vaguely like food. The vessel's stomach gurgled and seemed to respond to it as though it was food. She followed the women to a booth and sat with them.

They stared at her with confused expressions that changed quickly to annoyance.

"This table's taken," said one of the females.

She gazed at them for a moment, then looked at the tray. "What is this?"

The woman on the other side of the table answered. "It's a McMuffin. Look, we have no money. You need to go somewhere else."

The demon stared at the patron seated next to her. "I want your McMuffin."

When the woman simply stared at her, Azatoth imagined yanking her guts out. That should have given her pleasure but her body reacted in a curious way. She tasted bile. It wasn't the first time she'd tasted it but it was the first time she'd tasted her own.

She reached out with her mind. "Can I have it?" She smiled.

Wordlessly, her victim passed her tray to her while her friend watched, open-mouthed.

The demon bit into the food. She chewed, swallowed, and repeated the process. With her mouth full, she pointed at the other tray. "I want that one." The tray was passed to her without protest and she continued to eat.

Finally, she looked at the woman across the table. "I want more. Get me another one. No, I want five."

Wordlessly, the customer pulled her purse out and walked to the counter to place the order.

While Azatoth waited, she gazed at the woman beside her, who stared into the middle distance. She leaned close to her, inhaled, and licked the side of her face. *Salty.* The woman didn't even notice.

In moments, the blonde returned with a tray of food, took her seat, and stared vacantly like her friend while the demon dug into the sandwiches. She ate savagely, snorted continuously, and ignored the crumbs that fell down her shirt. When she realized that people were watching, she returned the stares coldly and they looked away.

Finally, she burped loudly and threw the last sandwich onto the plate, unable to take a bite.

"You have pleased me." She smiled at the women and burped again. "I would pleasure myself upon you but as you can see, I have no penis." She put her hand over the woman's hand on the table. "Between you and me, Caleb wasn't much of an improvement. I think he had one but I couldn't see past his stomach." The demon lowered her hands into her lap and sighed. "I miss my penis. It was magnificent."

Crumbs fell from her clothes as she stood and left the restaurant.

CHAPTER THIRTEEN

Eric, Warren, and Lucy arrived at Kindred HQ in New York. The busy office block looked like any other in the financial district—endless glass walls with inspirational quotes.

The older man looked around. "It looks like the old building has been modernized."

The witch wandered closer to read them while he checked them in.

"Don't Count the Days. Make the Days Count." Warren put an arm around her. "How does that inspire anyone? Surely it merely reminds them that their lives are leaking away in this shiny glass prison." He turned to her. "I'm surprised you didn't feel stronger after your good night's rest. I can't believe you would have preferred to miss out on today. Most units don't even know where HQ is, never mind set foot in the place. You look much better now but you need to calm yourself. I can feel how tense you are."

Eric listened as Lucy thanked him. He wondered briefly if this kindness meant that the legacy was settling down. Maybe he'd drop his obsession with Scott.

Warren leaned closer to her. "It's good that Eric had a secret supply of charged crystals and I saw where he keeps them. I'm sure we'll get some good use out of those."

The older man suppressed a snort of irritation and made no outward sign that he'd heard. He'd have to hide them somewhere else.

"Eric, darling. What on earth are you doing here?" The woman's voice echoed around the lobby and drew looks.

Eric glanced up and didn't smile. "Hello, Millicent."

She air-kissed him from about ten feet away. "I've been meaning to get in touch to offer my condolences after Lilith died. How long has that been now? It must be months."

He felt a sharp pain in his jaw from gritting his teeth. "Three years."

"Oh. Well. Condolences." She glanced at Warren and Lucy. "I heard you had adopted a matched pair. How touching. So, what brings you here?"

Although he didn't want Millicent to know his business, he couldn't resist rubbing her nose in it. "I'm meeting Gordon about a position."

"A position?" The woman considered this, her thoughtful expression exaggerated. "Surely not the Council one?"

Eric straightened. "As a matter of fact—"

"Really?" She smiled in a way that made him uncomfortable. "Well, how about I take you up there?" As she led them to the elevators, her pointed heels struck the marble floor and echoed across the lobby.

"Actually, Millicent, I think Gordon was going to—"

"Well, there's no need for him to bother now. Come along." She waved her hand over a panel on the wall and the elevator door appeared.

When it opened, the four of them stepped in.

Millicent waved a hand across the panel and buttons appeared. The only ones available were P—presumably for the underground parking lot—L for lobby, and level number one-thousand.

She gave him a haughty, smug grin. "I have the express spell."

Eric smiled uncertainly.

When they stepped out, he approached the receptionist. "Eric Dale. I have an appointment with Gordon."

The nosey woman hung around.

He inclined his head. "Thank you, Millicent. I think we'll be fine."

"I don't mind keeping you company, Eric. I was coming up anyway." She looked at her watch. "I had another meeting so I've missed the Council meeting."

"You're on the Council now?"

"Yes. I have been for a couple of years now."

Eric didn't like the way she was smiling. He felt there was a joke he had somehow missed.

A pair of large wooden doors opened and a crowd of people stepped out, laughing and slapping one man on the back as they passed.

A tall, overweight man with a large red nose shook the man's hand. "Congratulations, Carson. You'll be a terrific addition to the Council." He glanced up and saw the visitors. "Eric, you're here. I thought we were meeting in the lobby."

Eric glanced at Millicent. Her grin was wide and made him think of a shark.

Warren snorted and he bristled.

"I'll leave you to it, then, Eric. It was lovely to see you again." She turned and walked to the receptionist, her heels silenced by the carpeted floor.

The group dispersed and only Gordon remained with the visitors.

Gordon glanced at the younger two. "Eric, I did need to speak to you alone."

"These two are heading to the Overseer's Office. But I'm not sure what there is left to discuss."

"Great! Let's get your kids to their destination and we can get down to business." He led them to the elevator.

When they entered, Millicent hurried to join them.

Gordon put his hand up. "Sorry, Millicent, this one's full." The doors closed on her offended face.

No one spoke until they stopped on floor 726 and the doors opened. Warren and Lucy stepped out and Gordon pointed. "For the Overseers office, turn left and it's the last door on the right."

The elevator doors closed, leaving Lucy and Warren in the hallway.

Eric turned to the other man. "I thought you intended to offer me a place as your proxy on the Council. Did you merely invite me here to humiliate me and force me to watch you give it to that idiot from Oklahoma? Why did you ask me to come?"

His companion smiled. "Yes, he is an idiot. Did you see them pile out of there? They're all idiots."

He raised an eyebrow. Despite what many people most likely thought, he'd never heard anyone speak so disrespectfully of the Council.

Gordon stopped the elevator. "I have a different proposition for you. Come to my office. We need to have a little chat before I can explain properly."

They entered a corner office with floor to ceiling glass panels. "Drink?"

"No thank you." Eric was still angry and embarrassed.

The other man sat behind his large and mostly empty desk. "Eric, how long has it been since Lilith died?"

"Three years."

"Did you ever consider getting matched again?"

"Lilith and I were a good match. She was a powerful mage. I've never felt inclined to settle for less."

Gordon looked at his watch. "We'll have to hurry this up. I

have an important meeting in a few minutes so I'll be blunt. Would you consider settling for me?"

"You want to bond with me? Why? And why would you need what's-his-name as a proxy if you planned to offer to bond with me?"

"I know you think the Kindred Council is where the power is. That's what everyone thinks, including the Kindred Council, but it's not. What you're looking for is not too far away, but it's not the Council."

"Go on." Eric leaned forward. He noticed his reflection in the glass bookcase behind Gordon, where his scarred white eye was illuminated by the light from the window. Even to him, the effect was dramatic.

"I'm afraid I can't. This is a one-time offer. I can't tell you until you've committed to bond with me. If you say no, I'll have a counselor brought in and you won't remember a thing. But if you say yes, you will have access to power the likes of which you have never experienced."

He was tempted to ask why the man didn't simply tell him everything if he intended to counsel him anyway. But he could see time was short. He recognized this as one of those fleeting moments in life—an opportunity that was solid and there to be grasped but would turn to smoke in seconds as though it had never existed.

Eric was a strategic player. He was calm and ruthless but overall, he was curious. He leaned back in his chair. "I'm in."

Gordon smiled. "How far in would you say you are?"

The legacy knew what he was asking. He stood and removed his jacket, unbuttoned his shirt sleeve, and rolled it up to reveal his unhealing scar, empty of magic and raw. It was a constant and painful reminder of his loss.

Eric gazed at his scar, filled once again with the white light of pure mage magic. He rolled his sleeve down.

Gordon smiled. "How does that feel?"

"I've missed it. I guess you have your meeting now."

"No. We have our meeting. You're on the inside now, Eric." He stood and the legacy followed and shrugged into his jacket as they reached the door.

They left the office and returned to the elevator.

As soon as they stepped in, Eric turned to the other man. "So why have a proxy instead of a blood match in the council?"

"When new members join, they're usually voted in as pairs. I didn't have a blood match so my intended proxy had to be unanimously voted in. I floated you as a possibility but there was one dissenter."

"Let me guess. Millicent."

"I'm afraid so. Do you two have a history?"

"Yes. We also had a future until I met Lilith." He smirked.

The doors closed and he felt the pulse of Gordon's magic as he waved a hand in an odd gesture. The elevator doors disappeared and a new one appeared on the back wall.

Eric detected the increase of ozone in the air. "A fae door?"

"I have it on loan. It's terribly useful. Much faster than teleporting long distances in leaps." The mage twisted the handle and opened the door.

They entered a room with a large table in the center. Thirteen chairs surrounded it and thirteen more lined the walls behind and slightly to the left of each of the others.

As Eric glanced around, he made eye contact with a few people he recognized—people he respected, some he even feared a little, and one he had believed was in prison.

Gordon walked to the largest chair at the head of the table and indicated that he should sit behind him. He hadn't told him that he was the head of whatever this was and he worked to keep the surprise from his face.

They sat and the mage turned in his seat to view him. "Eric. Welcome to the Cabal."

It wasn't the first time he had heard the word. There had been rumors for years but he'd always ignored it. Like people whispering Illuminati, he thought it was nonsense.

The others in the room smiled or nodded. The men seated on either side of him leaned forward to address each other. "You owe me a hundred dollars. I told you Carson would never see the inside of this room."

"Right. To order." The men and women turned to face their leader. He raised his hand, the palm facing forward. The mages did the same, then the blood matches and proxies seated around the outside held their hands up. Eric was uncertain if he should do the same. He half-raised his hand and caught the eye of a woman across the room who nodded discreetly.

Light issued from the mages' hands to join each one to the next, then spread to the outer ring to create a lattice of light around the room. The space hummed with magic. They lowered their hands but the lattice remained above them.

"The first order of business is to welcome Eric to the Cabal," Gordon began. "Raise your hand again, Eric."

He complied and bright lights moved around the lattice and gathered in his palm. He felt powerful magic trickle down his spine and pool at the base to spread a warmth throughout his body.

The woman across the room nodded again and he returned his hand to his lap.

"Appropriately," the leader continued, "the second order of business is to nominate a Second. I know this has taken a while and I haven't been dicking around intentionally. I merely felt I owed it to Caleb to give it as much careful thought as he did when he chose me."

So Caleb was the head of the Cabal too. It's interesting but hardly surprising. He was always where the power was.

Gordon continued when no one spoke. "I hereby confirm Dominic."

One man, presumably Dominic, raised his hand and the lights traveled again.

"Right. We have to discuss the project Caleb and his…friend were heading. As he is no longer with us, we've no way to communicate with the contact."

Dominic leaned forward. "We know his name so we could initiate contact again. That's a great deal of power to lose."

Gordon leaned back in his chair. "Are you offering to host our strategic partner?"

The man's eyebrows raised in alarm. "No, no. I merely— If you want to end the project, that's fine."

The woman at the other end of the table spoke. "I think the project ended when Caleb was killed."

A few soft chuckles came from those around the table.

"Thank you, Gina. How are things going in Las Vegas?"

"Chad has a meeting planned with the casino representatives and their respective unions. We should get them all under the city wards by the end of next week."

Gordon nodded. "Can you report on the investigation into what caused the wards to malfunction?"

Eric had heard about the wards. It seemed the Cabal was investigating it too.

"The investigation is going in circles as requested," Gina responded. "Chad will report to you and the Council that we have no leads."

The leader chuckled. "I'll remember to look appropriately disappointed."

The legacy couldn't help raising an eyebrow. The Cabal had been behind the problem with the wards and the Kindred Council didn't have a clue.

"What about the site?" she asked.

Gordon sighed. "Bury it."

Eric wondered what they were talking about but decided he'd ask Gordon later.

The meeting continued and he garnered a few interesting tidbits but on the whole, he didn't have much of a clue as to what was going on.

Their leader finally looked around the room. "Right, then. Any other business?"

The lattice flickered and everyone looked up. Eric noticed the narrowed eyes and frowning faces.

Gina asked the question on everyone's lips. "What was that?"

A young man Eric vaguely recognized chuckled. "Did someone forget to pay the utility bill?"

Dominic leaned forward. "We still don't know what Caleb was doing at Emmersley."

"We may never know. I suggest—" Gordon stopped speaking when the lattice flickered again. It became brighter until it was blindingly bright, then shattered. While it sounded like glass, the shards of light simply fizzled away as they fell. In the next moment, a portal burst open.

CHAPTER FOURTEEN

The room filled with magic as balls of energy were hurled by the mages and legacies toward the portal. They struck the figure in the doorway but simply dissipated.

Eric gaped when the light faded to reveal Lexi. The last he'd heard, she had lost her legacy abilities, but this woman was the essence of power. Her eyes were yellow with black vertical slits—like a cat's but much more intelligent and dangerous.

"You started without me. I'm disappointed." She walked straight to Gordon. "I think you're in my chair."

The man looked outraged. "I don't know what you think you're doing—"

She flicked a finger and he catapulted out of the chair and collided with a woman seated on the outer edge of the room with such force that it knocked her out and she slid to the floor.

Eric started to stand but a signal from Gordon made him resume his seat. He looked at Lexi.

"Good choice." She smiled at him.

The new arrival sat in Gordon's chair, put her booted feet on the table, and crossed her ankles.

An elderly man who sat to the left of the chair lashed out with a spell that had no effect on her.

Eric knew it hadn't been a weak spell and could feel the electricity in the air. Lexi should have been a smoking pile of charcoal.

She looked at the old man. While her elbow rested on the arm of the chair, she extended a finger and drew it down. A line of red appeared on the man's face. He slid from the chair and onto his knees.

"How dare you—" he croaked.

Lexi opened her hand palm down and continued to move it in a downward gesture. The man fell completely to the floor but didn't stop there. He folded as though a great weight had descended upon him, and his bones crunched and flesh burst. When she had finished, he was little more than a flat puddle.

Her smile was smug as she looked around the room. "I am Azatoth. You work for me now. Would anyone else like to discuss it?"

Eric opened his mouth to call the woman a liar but looked at the others in the room. They all looked utterly terrified and he forced himself to remain silent. The name seemed familiar but he wasn't sure.

Gordon made no effort to stand. "My lord. We didn't recognize you. We thought you were lost to us when Caleb died."

"Oh. He's dead? I wondered why he hadn't greeted me. He provided this vessel for my transition but it took longer than anticipated. I finally took full possession of it this morning."

A chill ran through Eric when he realized with horror that this wasn't merely an ordinary demon. It was high-level, well beyond anything he'd encountered before.

What the hell was Caleb thinking?

He glanced at Gordon on the floor, whose chin trembled with fear. It occurred to him that the problem with seizing unexpected opportunities was that very often, they were too good to be true.

He had chosen a very bad day to join the club and he now wondered if he'd get out of the room alive. Having recognized Lexi when she entered, he couldn't quite understand how she had come to be possessed by this monster. If Caleb had captured her, what had become of Scott?

Azatoth smiled. "Gordon. What are you doing down there? Take a seat. It looks like there's one free."

The man scrambled to his feet and walked to the empty chair. He slipped in the remains of the old man and held onto the back of it to regain his balance before he sat carefully.

"Excuse me?" Eric couldn't believe he'd spoken. All eyes turned to him.

Azatoth fixed him with her gaze and the yellow eyes bored into his for long moments. The whole room seemed to hold its breath. Her face brightened. In fact, she looked delighted. "Eric, isn't it?"

"Er… Yes."

"Sorry, I was with Caleb for a very long time. I have many memories to search through. How can I help you?"

She sounded like a customer services representative and the incongruity made him extremely nervous. "Your vessel was Alexa Braxton?"

The demon frowned and the face went blank again. "No. She was Alicia Rand." She paused. "Now that's interesting. This meat shell has no memory of her sibling but Caleb remembers them. And I remember Alexa. She and her mage stopped me from coming through the veil in my form. Caleb and I had worked on that for a long time."

Whispers began around the room. It was clear that no one had known Caleb was attempting to release a demon.

Eric frowned in confusion. "I didn't know there were two of them." He recalled the redacted sections in Lexi's file. "But maybe it makes sense."

"I know you want the mage. Good heavens, you didn't let

Caleb hear the end of it, did you? You're quite the whiner. The problem is, I planned to pull both their entrails out an inch a day when I found them. Perhaps we could come to an arrangement. I'd be willing to merely take his eyes or his toes and you can have the rest. Let's put a pin in it for now and talk later."

Azatoth spun her chair to face the table. "Now. How are things going with our little project in Las Vegas?"

The meeting finished and the attendees dispersed as one to leave Gordon and Eric with Azatoth.

The mage turned to her. "How should I contact you, my lord?"

"I'll come with you. We still need to talk about the young mage."

They walked through the door and out into the elevator.

Eric felt Gordon's nerves through their new link. He was a wreck. When they left the elevator, his secretary stood and walked to him with a folder. The legacy noticed she didn't seem to give their companion a second glance. When he looked more closely, he saw her demon's eyes were normal brown human eyes.

She seemed to sense that he was staring, returned his gaze, and fluttered her lashes like a little girl. Eric looked away.

Azatoth strode into the office, went immediately to the window, and rubbed her hands together. "This world—there's so much to do." She looked at Eric "Don't get me wrong. The demon realms aren't without their distractions but many of them are like..." She paused in thought. "I want to say termite mounds. A few are okay but they're cliquey, you know?"

He decided that he'd pay good money to be out of that conversation.

"I have questions about this Alexa. Caleb was under the impression the sisters didn't know about each other but something's missing." She looked away over the city but turned quickly to Eric. "I need the mage."

"Scott?"

"No, the one belonging to this vessel. Bryan. What's the fastest way to find him?"

"You should be able to call to him through your link."

Azatoth frowned. "I feel the link." She sighed. "I don't have time for this." She disappeared.

CHAPTER FIFTEEN

Alicia appeared in the kitchen and Bryan jumped. "Where the hell have you been? We're an hour late for the job."

His wife shrugged. "I was walking. I feel disquieted." She sat on the kitchen table and picked a banana up from the fruit bowl. She sniffed it, screwed her face into a grimace, and dropped it again before she turned to him. "It's like something's missing from my mind. I can't quite put my finger on it."

He stared at her in shock. She shouldn't have been able to tell that anything was amiss. "We'll have to fix it later. Dad's going nuts. The manticore was traced to an abandoned school in the Seventh Ward. We need to get there now."

She jumped from her perch. "I'm ready when you are."

Bryan reached out to her and translocated both of them to the entrance of a tired-looking building. It smelled of rat urine and death.

Azatoth rather liked it. "And why are we here again?"

The mage turned and looked at her as he took hold of the door handle. "The manticore who ate a half-dozen tourists yesterday is hiding out here."

"Well? What are you waiting for? Come on." She shooed him with her hands until he opened the door.

They stepped into the abandoned school and he cast a spell to cloak and silence their progress. He glanced sideways and whispered, even though their words were silenced beyond their immediate space. "You should get the poisoned dart ready."

Alicia stopped and turned to the mage. "Listen, this is all very entertaining, but I feel like we have an unresolved issue."

He halted and stared at her in shock. "We have a what?" He glanced down the hallway toward the staircase beside them several times before he focused on her again.

"The memories." She tapped the side of her head to emphasize her point.

"Ali, I think we can talk about this later."

She removed the cloaking spell and spoke loudly. "No, I think we should talk about it now."

A clattering sound came from one of the classrooms farther down the long hallway and shuffling from the floor above.

"You seriously want to do this now?" he whispered.

Azatoth smiled serenely at him to make it clear that she wouldn't budge in her resolve.

He restored the cloaking spell and dragged her into the first classroom on the right.

She strolled around the empty space as though they had all the time in the world.

Bryan remained near the door to keep one ear tuned to the hallway. He gave the classroom a cursory glance to ensure it was indeed empty before he faced her. "What's wrong with you?"

"If there's something wrong with me, I think it's the result of someone messing with my memories."

"Look, I took some memories from you to protect us and…" He sighed. "Stay there."

More noises issued from down the hallway. "This is insane." After a quick look toward the corridor, he put a hand on her head and pushed the memories of Lexi into his wife's mind. He removed his hand and watched as she smiled.

"I do have a sister called Lexi."

He narrowed his eyes at her phrasing and wondered how she had suspected it.

Alicia's gaze flicked around, evidence that the memories filtered into her mind again.

She would soon remember stabbing Scott on the riverbank and the fistfight with her sister and he waited for the inevitable reaction.

Seconds later, she froze and locked gazes with the mage. "She's a dark sorcerer?"

"Don't panic. That's why it was such a bad idea to do this now. There is so much to process. Wait a few moments for all the memories to return."

"But how? I was told there were no shadow mages left."

"Shadow what?"

Growls issued from the hallway.

Bryan spun toward the door and whispered to her. "Take the poison darts out—now." He crept closer to the doorway and realized the growls came from both directions in the corridor outside, which certainly meant more than one manticore. This was bad news. He didn't think they had enough poison for two of them.

A rattle sounded a familiar warning and he lurched back as poisoned spines embedded themselves in the wall an inch from his face. Bryan turned to Alicia to check if she was ready with the poison but she was no longer there. The room was empty. He spun in a circle and couldn't quite believe she'd disappeared without saying anything.

He turned to face the classroom's doorway as the face of a man peered slowly around the corner. The top half of the head was crowned with golden-blond hair and his eyes were a piercing blue, but that was where the similarity with a human ended. He grinned to display row upon row of pointed teeth. Two huge paws padded into view before the body of a winged lion became visible, along with a rattling, poisonous, spiny tail that waved hypnotically above the creature. The monster was halfway into the room when something heavy and fast raced toward it and it was thrust against the door by the other manticore.

As the mage watched in horror, the two creatures began to fight over their next meal—him.

Common sense insisted he should get out of there but he didn't know where Alicia had gone. He hadn't felt a pull on his magic when she left, although his anxiety level was high so he could have missed it. The beasts wrestled viciously and tried to bite each other while they launched occasional spines from their poisonous tails to bolster their attack. The second one swung its tail out of view, ready to fling another spine, but yelped. It was dragged out of sight by something.

A third manticore?

The monster being dragged scraped its claws on the tiles and left gouge marks as it was hauled away. It disappeared around the corner but squealed loudly before a spray of blood washed across the floor. Silence descended in the hallway.

The first creature—which had been losing the fight—staggered to its feet and crept toward Bryan with its mouth gaping and salivating.

He decided it was probably time to get out of there but Alicia reappeared between them, covered in blood and holding the tail of the dead manticore. She thrust its poisonous spines into the creature's mouth and stood back. It howled and released spines from its tail in all directions. The projectiles streaked toward the young couple and bounced off Bryan's magical shield. It shook its head to try to dislodge the mass of spines embedded in its tongue and the roof of its mouth. The creature staggered, then simply sagged and fell.

The mage sighed. He gazed at Alicia, who stared as if mesmerized at the dead beasts. As he stepped to her side and looked into her eyes, he did a double-take. They seemed to be yellow for a moment but when he looked again, they were the same soft brown they had always been. Confused, he rubbed his eyes.

She spun to him and her brown eyes glittered in her red spattered face. "That was wonderful. I love this job. I think I'd rather do this than rule this whole dimension. We should eat their hearts in celebration."

Bryan froze. He couldn't think of a single word to say in response.

Alicia frowned. "Too much?"

"You could say that."

"Then we should copulate amid the ruins of their bodies."

"Alicia, you're kinda freaking me out. How about we get cleaned up and go out for something to eat."

She took hold of the manticore tail and tugged. "I stuck this thing quite far in there." She heaved and pulled it out. "Oh, some of the spines are missing."

Bryan pinched the bridge of his nose. "I suspect they're still jammed in its throat. Why do you want it?"

"Trophy." She stood slowly. "Well, I can't dawdle with you all day. I have a meeting."

"With who—" He stared at empty space and shook his head. She was gone.

CHAPTER SIXTEEN

Eric dropped into a chair, exhaled slowly, and watched through the open door as Gordon continued to sign documents shoved under his nose by his assistant for another ten minutes.

The man finally walked into the office. "Where is she?"

"God knows. Gordon, what the hell have you dragged me into?"

"I'm sorry. I think we're only now beginning to get an inkling of what Caleb was up to. We knew he was in contact with Az—"

He thrust a hand out, his palm up. "Please don't say her name."

"Quite." The man nodded and walked around to his chair. "He told us he had access to new magic. It was so strong it was even capable of bringing the Las Vegas wards down."

The legacy's jaw dropped. "Wait—that's what's been happening in Las Vegas? It was Caleb showing off?"

"The rest of us had no idea he was helping the demon to cross over."

"What did you imagine were the demon's reasons for helping you?" He fixed the man with a steely gaze from his white eye.

Gordon seemed momentarily lost for words. "Well, there was some discussion of quid pro quo, of course, but Caleb was handling it—"

"The fact is," Eric interrupted, "you didn't care what the price was."

His companion's cheeks bloomed red. "Now listen here."

"I'm not judging you. Having seen who is in the Cabal, I know most of them at least by reputation. There isn't one of us who wouldn't murder our grandmother for the kind of power this demon has."

"Well, when you put it like that—"

"Now, Caleb's left you—sorry, us—to deal with his mess. He must have had a plan to get rid of her."

"Get rid of who?" Azatoth asked from the corner of the room.

Gordon froze.

Eric scowled at the man. He turned to the demon, who swung what looked like a manticore tail in circles. "Alexa. It seems she's interfered with all our plans too many times but we don't know where she is."

She smiled and paused long enough for him to get the message that she knew that wasn't who he'd been talking about. After a moment, she spoke calmly. "Yes, Lexi. I've had a short meeting with the mage. It appears this vessel and her mage were hiding secrets. He was holding her memories of her sister. It was a fortuitous meeting for other reasons. You can have the mage. I'm not interested in him. The sister is not to be touched, however. I know where she is but I need another little job done." She looked at the office door. "Which creature should I command to do it?"

Gordon straightened. "You can command me and I'll know the right person to take it to."

Azatoth sat on the edge of his desk, leaned forward, and pinched his cheek. "You are so accommodating."

Eric wasn't sure what it was, but when she smiled and became polite, she was at her most terrifying.

The telephone rang and the mage jumped. He picked the receiver up and listened before he turned to Eric. "Young Warren has passed his interview with flying colors. They're delighted to offer him a position on the team."

He looked uncertainly at Azatoth. "May I leave?"

"Nonsense. Let's get this young superstar up here." Alicia's face smiled brightly but her eyes returned to yellow-and-black.

Gordon turned to the phone. "Send him to my office."

The legacy did his best to not shiver. "There may be a problem. He's familiar with Alexa and he hates her. When he sees you, he might shoot first and ask questions later. It would be a waste for this promising young man to die over a case of mistaken identity."

She grinned. "How thrilling."

Eric stepped toward the door. "Perhaps I should warn him." He found himself unable to take another step.

"Perhaps you shouldn't." The demon twirled a finger and he turned involuntarily.

Having no alternative, he submitted. "As you wish, my lord." He stood aside.

Warren strode into the office with a triumphant smile. When his view into the room widened, his gaze settled on Azatoth. The smile slid from his face and he hurled an energy blast at the demon, who merely stood motionless with a smirk of open amusement. Simultaneously, he hurled a knife and three spiked shurikens at her. He spun without waiting for the results. Eric watched his face when he realized Scott wasn't in the room.

The young legacy seemed to have noticed belatedly that there hadn't been an explosive sound from his energy ball. At the same time, he saw the look of shock on Lucy's face from where she stood at the entrance to the room and stared past him. He turned again.

Azatoth remained standing with the same serene smile on her face. She looked at Eric. "He is fast, isn't he?"

"He's one of the best I've ever had, my lord. I don't doubt he'll serve you well," he said carefully.

Warren's face became neutral and calculating. The older man could imagine what went through his mind. He would sense that the aura of the person in front of him was demonic and probably thought the same as he had when he'd first seen her—that Lexi had been possessed. At the very least, he would realize that things weren't as they seemed.

The demon approached the young legacy and stared critically at him. "What's wrong with his face?"

Gordon looked at Warren. "His face, my lord?"

She waved a finger and pointed at Warren's cheeks. "The scars."

Eric shared a look with his mage. It was clear that Azatoth saw something they couldn't.

Azatoth's eyes lit up. "Ah! I see. I think you and I will get along very well."

He was relieved that Warren wouldn't be murdered in front of him. But while he'd had some concerns about his protégé's mental state, it didn't feel like a positive reinforcement to hear that a high-level demon felt an affinity with him.

The young man smirked when she held his weapons out and dropped them into his waiting hand.

The demon stepped closer to Lucy and flashed her yellow eyes at the girl. Eric could see the waif clamp her jaw to stop it from shaking. "I don't think so much of this one."

"She is Warren's mage," he said hastily, fearful she might be about to strike the girl and kill her. His energy source, my lord."

Azatoth forced out a sigh and a groan. "I know how it works, Eric." She spun and approached him, put her face close to his, and tilted it to stare into his scarred white eye. "You would be amazed at the things I know."

She raised a finger, pointed it at his face, and poked the end of his nose. "Boop." The demon spun away and sat on the desk. "Thank you all for stopping by. Have a great day."

CHAPTER SEVENTEEN

Lexi, Scott, Dick, and Braxton appeared in the street. A man immediately bumped into Lexi and jumped back with shock on his face. She looked at him in disgust. "Watch it, dickwad."

He walked around her and shook his head.

She grinned, having found it was best to brazen it out in these situations. The man would more easily believe that he hadn't noticed her than that she'd appeared out of thin air.

They looked up and down the street but detected no sign of Lucy.

The vampire raised an eyebrow. "Well, this isn't Denver."

"Perhaps this is why she didn't contact us. They must have forced her to go with them to Kindred headquarters."

Scott looked at the building they'd appeared in front of. He turned to Braxton. "Is this it?"

"How would I know? I'm way too far down the pole to know about this kind of thing."

"I'd guess it's the one with all the wards." Lexi pointed across the street.

"I don't see any wards." Braxton squinted at the building. "I sense them but I don't see them."

"Oh. It's merely a spell Scott uses. It lets me see magical wards and that building is covered in them." She gazed at the white designs streaking across and around the skyscraper in front of them.

"Hmm…I've not heard of that one." The man sounded annoyed.

Dick shrugged. "It looks like a regular office building to me."

She studied the door. "How are we going to get in?"

Braxton gaped at Lexi. "What? No. We don't need to get in. Lucy didn't contact us because she's in that building, which means we should stay outside. We'll get her when she contacts us."

"But what if she needs help?"

"This isn't up for discussion. We're lucky she was in there and the wards wouldn't let us inside. Come on. Let's get out of here."

Lexi looked around. "Where's Dick?"

The three of them studied their surroundings until Scott pointed across the street to where a tall man climbed out of a delivery van with *Lunch-2-U* written along the side. As he turned toward them, he put a baseball cap on and they recognized their teammate. She smirked and shook her head when a foot dangled out of the back of the van and he shoved it in again.

Braxton muttered, "Dear God."

She whispered, knowing Dick would hear it. "What the actual fuck are you doing?"

He reached into the van and removed a tray of sandwiches, closed the van doors with his butt, and walked through the wards into the building.

"Well, I'll be damned." She stared through the big glass windows as the vampire walked brazenly to the desk and leaned the huge tray of food across it.

The security man helped the receptionist unload the bags of

food from the wide tray and he left the building, turned, and waved at the guard on the way out.

Dick threw the tray and baseball cap through the back doors of the van and jogged across the street with a sour look on his face. "They wouldn't let me through security."

She chuckled. "No shit."

"Language, Lexi." Braxton reprimanded her. He turned to Dick. "No shit."

"I managed to pick one of these up, though. In case you planned to go in." He slid his hand into his pocket, withdrew a lanyard with a visitor card attached to it, and passed it to Lexi.

Her eyebrow raised, she waved it at Braxton.

"No." He turned to Dick. "I hope you didn't cause that delivery guy any lasting damage."

"Of course not. I…whammied him with a witch…thing."

Scott asked, "A hex?"

"A hex bag, yes." He turned on his heel to face the young mage. "But perhaps you could double-check that I didn't…uh, over-hex him."

"Over-hex." Scott rolled his eyes, glanced at their surroundings, and disappeared. He returned a few seconds later. "He must have fallen on his face when you hexed him. He'll have quite a shiner."

"My bad." The vampire shrugged. "Well, I'm ready when you are. Daylight's burning."

"Is he new?" Braxton murmured to her. He shook his head. "You've taken up with some real weirdos."

She smiled. "I can only agree."

"Oh, hello."

Lexi spun in surprise. "Bryan."

"Where is sh—" He froze when he glanced to his right to see Braxton.

She looked at the older man too but saw no recognition in his eyes.

Bryan turned to her again. "I'm sorry to interrupt." He paused, then finally asked, "Do you have a second?"

They stepped aside. "Where's Alicia?" he asked quietly.

Lexi shrugged. "I haven't seen her."

He blew out an aggravated breath. "She is behaving very strangely."

She rolled her eyes. "I'm sorry Bryan but it makes me feel—"

"No, not that kind of weird. She just suggested having sex in the gory remains of a manticore."

At that, her mouth hung open.

"She's been missing all morning. Then she appeared in the apartment about a half-hour ago and started asking about missing memories. She shouldn't even have known they were missing. It seemed so odd."

Dick stepped beside them. "Maybe you've lost your mojo." He stepped back when he felt the full weight of the young man's unimpressed glare. "If you fought a manticore, maybe she went a little berserk."

The mage considered it. "I'm very sure she ripped one of the monsters in half."

Lexi nodded. "Perhaps she's still trying to deal with her strength."

"I explained that she'd given some of her memories to me for safe-keeping and I gave them back."

"She remembers me again?" She sighed with relief.

"Look. I know you think I'm talking crap but I feel like someone else is looking out of her eyes when she looks at me. Anyway. She seemed particularly excited when she remembered you're a…" He glanced up the street at Braxton. "Uh, what you are. Then she said she had a meeting and simply disappeared." He looked at the man who had been his unit leader until he was fifteen. "How is he?"

"He hasn't changed much."

"I did sneak back a couple of times but it was too difficult to keep doing it." He turned to her again. "Anyway, I followed her when she left. I appeared here but she didn't."

Dick looked across the street. "She must have gone into Kindred HQ, which I guess means she has clearance and you don't."

Bryan's gaze followed his. "That's Kindred HQ? I'm fairly sure that knowing even that much is way above my pay grade. I guess I'd better get back. I merely wish I knew what the hell is going on." He looked once again at the father who didn't remember him and vanished.

CHAPTER EIGHTEEN

Limpet nudged Marcel. He was lazy for a pup but the little demon understood that he had been somehow damaged on the inside from a fire and that made him tire easily. It worked for the little creature, who didn't like to do too much either. He stood, jumped to the floor, and wandered to the kitchen. It took little time or effort to clamber onto the counter and stretch in the sink.

The thinner demon turned the cold faucet on. As cool water splashed onto his belly, he extended his leg and pushed his toe into the faucet to divert the spray to his open mouth. When the sink was half-full, he turned the water off and dozed.

He blinked awake at the sound of the door and sniffed the air. It wasn't Albin or any of his other bipedal pets. Cautiously, he risked a peek over the edge of the sink. Two pretty creatures with pointed ears had wasted no time and had already begun to search the apartment.

Fae. He raised an eyebrow, slid the dishcloth carefully from the side of the sink, and spread it over himself, then watched through the fabric as a shadow passed, peered into the utility room, and passed again. The little creature lay there motionless and tried to decide if this was one of the situations that necessitated him eating the fae. He didn't think he'd eaten one before and he was all about new experiences. As he came to the conclusion that it would be okay to eat these guys, the door clicked closed. He peeked out. Everything was silent—too silent. *Where is Marcel?*

Alarmed, Limpet scanned the room. He bolted from the sink, across the room, and placed his hand on the wall. His ability didn't merely thin the walls between dimensions, it thinned physical walls between rooms. He pushed his head through the wall to the hallway in time to hear men's voices in the elevator.

"I thought it was supposed to look like a cat."

"Did you see a cat?"

"No, only the dog."

"Then they were wrong. It looks like a dog, not a cat. Maybe it can look like both."

"We'd better have it right."

The voices muted as the elevator doors closed.

He thrust through the wall, ran along the hallway, and pushed through the elevator doors. For a moment, he teetered on the edge of the shaft and rocked back against the door to watch the descending carriage with his huge, round amber eyes. He snarled, studied his surroundings, then vaulted into the cables and scampered down them. Carefully, he pushed his face through the roof of the elevator and looked inside. They had Marcel in a sack with magical symbols drawn over it. The bag wasn't moving.

The elevator slowed to a stop and the doors opened on a lower-ground level.

One of the fae turned to his partner who held the sack. "Stay there while I check that it's clear."

The dog-napper stepped out and looked around. Limpet dropped silently onto the remaining elf and bit him hard. He grasped the sack and was about to step out of the elevator when the doors began to close. Intending to stop them, he put his foot in one's path when the other man turned, saw him, and began to run toward him.

The little demon pulled back his foot hastily and allowed the doors to close.

Before the elevator could go anywhere, the fae man jabbed repeatedly at the elevator call button. As the doors slid open, Limpet pushed through the rippling wall with his captive friend.

Without assessing his new location, he turned his attention to the sack. Thankfully, the magical warding on it was designed to keep whatever was in there from getting out. He had no problem getting in. He shredded it with his teeth and claws and made sure he didn't harm Marcel. He was so intent on his efforts that he remained completely unaware of his surroundings. Concerned now, he dragged the unconscious puppy out by his collar, keened sadly, and prodded him.

A voice came from far-off. "Where are you, Daisy?"

Another voice responded from much closer. "I heard something."

Limpet turned to see a little girl push through the bushes.

When she appeared, he had taken the form of a cat.

"It's a cat and a dog." The girl squealed with excitement.

He turned to Marcel. The puppy's eyes fluttered open.

Before he could create another portal, he and his friend were swept into the girl's arms. He turned to see she was a fae child. The significant chunk he'd taken out of the fae sat uneasily in his belly. If they all tasted like that, he'd have to find a different way out of this situation.

Marcel whimpered and began to struggle.

Limpet glanced at him. *Stay.*

The dog did as he was told.

The girl carried them through the bushes. "Look. A cat and a dog."

An elderly fae lady approached her and looked closely at the two of them. "Hmm…I'm not sure about that cat. Be careful, it might be a witch's familiar. Or the witch herself."

"Can I keep them?"

"What did I just say?"

"Can I keep the dog?"

"What's wrong with it?"

"I don't know. It crawled out of a sack covered in runes like the elders make."

"Show me."

"That way." Daisy walked in the opposite direction with Marcel and Limpet tucked under her arms.

They reached a clearing with a little cottage and garden. The girl put the creatures down on a blanket. She had wooden cups and plates stacked up in the middle of it.

"We're going to have tea."

Limpet considered the situation. There was no hurry and he was partial to tea.

Daisy passed the cups around. One for her, one each for Limpet and Marcel, and a cup for a little creature that seemed to be made from straw-filled fabric with string for hair.

The little fae picked a pot up and poured…nothing. She took her cup and held it to her lips.

The demon wondered if they were enchanted. His cat paw darted out and knocked his over. It was empty and he looked at the girl, unimpressed.

"Daisy, Daisy." The elderly fae ran and huffed along the path. "Stay away from the dog. Those runes are designed to subdue a very powerful demon."

The girl scooted away from Marcel and closer to the cat.

Limpet burped. He truly didn't feel well. Unable to stop himself, he sat on his haunches, leaned forward, and vomited the fae head into the middle of the blanket.

That was when the screams started.

He grabbed Marcel and ran.

CHAPTER NINETEEN

Albin climbed out of his car and tapped the remote as he walked through the underground parking lot. The silent space lit up twice in the flash of his headlights as the locks engaged.

He stood at the elevator, pressed the call button, and waited, shuffling the folders he would have to go through for his next meeting.

The doors opened but he didn't enter. Instead, he paused and frowned as he sniffed the air. He smelled blood and worse, a significant amount. While he was sure it wasn't human, he couldn't identify what it was.

A little on edge now, he didn't want to enter the elevator. As he hesitated, the uneasy feeling seemed to increase and he scowled. He wanted to reach his apartment as quickly as possible. After a furtive glance at his surroundings, he stepped in and pressed the button for his level.

The incubus walked along the hallway, looking for signs of anything amiss. He opened the apartment door. "Marcel." No excited puppy came running.

"Limpet." Again, his call met with no response.

A cursory search told him that both were gone.

He sighed and took his cell phone out.

Dick pressed the accept button. "Albin, darling. Are you missing me?"

He got straight to the point. "I just got back from work. Marcel and Limpet are missing. I think something's happened because I smelled blood in the elevator. Not human I might add."

The vampire's voice lost all its joviality. "I'm on my way."

"I'll meet you at the diner."

"Are you sure?" He knew Albin was uncomfortable beyond the wards of Las Vegas and with good reason.

"It'll be the fastest."

Dick was silent for a moment. "Pick my day car up from the condo. I'll sit in the back."

Albin retrieved a baseball cap and sunglasses. He drove to the condo and went inside for the keys. He drew a breath in. The place had been ransacked but the keys were still in their little dish near the door, fortunately. He snatched them up and paused as he stared at the key to the condo next door. He reasoned that it had either been searched or it hadn't. If it had, there wasn't anything he could do about it. If it hadn't, he could get caught up in some magical security system of Scott's. He chose to go to Dick's car and drove to Boulder City.

The vampire stepped out of the diner and climbed into the back of the car the moment he stopped. The dark glass partition remained up until they crossed through the city wards.

When the partition came down, he reached through and squeezed Albin's shoulder. "Lexi and Scott will be along soon. There isn't much more we can do there."

The incubus patted his lover's hand.

"Maybe they went for a walk," Dick suggested.

"There's more. I found your home ransacked."

"Was anything missing?"

"I didn't stop to check. I simply grabbed the keys and I didn't enter Lexi and Scott's condo at all."

"Was your apartment ransacked?"

"No. If they were after Marcel or Limpet and they were able to get them immediately, they wouldn't have needed to." Albin was silent for a few moments. "Dick, I'm so sorry. I've been over and over the day in my mind and I don't remember seeing anything or anyone out of place."

"I wouldn't blame you for a moment. You can't be everywhere at once and neither can I."

The incubus sighed. "But the blood I smelled in the elevator." The idea that they might have been butchered in there made him nauseous.

"That makes no sense. What's the point in taking them from the apartment and killing them seconds later in the elevator?"

"There could have been a struggle."

"I don't fancy anyone's chances with Limpet. Don't torture yourself. We'll assess the situation when we get there."

They arrived in the parking lot and Dick climbed out of the car. "I can smell it already. Let's get closer." He started to walk toward the elevator and Albin kept an eye on their surroundings.

The vampire covered his nose. "Good grief, that's strong. It's not dog, though. I think they've tried to disguise the smell."

Albin exhaled slowly. He hadn't even realized he had been holding his breath.

"It's supernatural," Dick continued. "Not anything I've ever smelled from the demon realms, although the demons I've seen tend to produce something like rancid, foul-smelling jello." He looked at his boyfriend. "Not you, obviously." He was silent for a moment. "You use luminol in your work on artifacts, don't you?"

"Yes, I have some upstairs. I'll go and get it."

The elevator doors opened and the vampire stepped back. "I can't see a speck of blood anywhere. I don't understand why it smells so strong."

Albin raced to the apartment, let himself in, and hurried to his leather case. He stood silently in the bedroom doorway, hoping to hear the sounds of a puppy scratching at a cupboard door or the crunch of Limpet eating lightbulbs. There was no sound and he moved away regretfully and returned to where his friend waited. He stepped out of the elevator but stopped it from closing with a foot in the doorway. "Would you mind vandalizing the lights?"

The vampire raced around the underground parking lot. While his strength and speed were reduced by the wards, he still had the capacity to run quite fast and jump fairly high. He left a trail of destroyed light fittings behind him. When he returned, he punched the elevator light out and all was pitch-black. Albin sprayed and the area lit up in bright pink.

The incubus frowned. "Pink. That's different." He looked at his feet. Some of the luminol had landed on his shoes and was also bright pink.

Dick thought for a moment. "Fae."

Albin sprayed more luminol and this time, his companion's shoes also glowed. "I don't think the scene's been cleaned at all. I think they've simply used magic to hide it. I bet fae blood has been trampled all over the place since this happened." He sprayed more of the chemical around and it revealed a trail of pink through the parking lot. Something big had been dragged and footprints were visible beside it. The trail ended at an empty parking space.

"There were probably two of them," the vampire mused. "The dead one and his pal."

The incubus narrowed his eyes in the darkness. "Not one in the car?"

"I don't think so. If there were more, whoever owns these footprints wouldn't have had to drag his friend's body alone."

"And they may or may not have our little guys."

Dick patted his back. "Let's get upstairs. I need to burn these shoes."

The two stepped into the elevator again. Albin sprayed more of the chemical and blood spatters appeared throughout from the ceiling to the floor. As it settled on the wall to their right, a circle of bright pink appeared but the center of it remained black. Albin smiled.

The other man voiced his thoughts. "Limpet escaped and there's no way he would leave Marcel behind."

As they exited the elevator, the incubus sighed. "I've walked through the apartment in these shoes. Twice."

Dick smiled, clearly relieved by the revelation that the two pets had most likely escaped. "We can scrub it thoroughly. I'm sure it'll be fine. If not—" He stopped speaking abruptly.

His companion frowned. "What?"

He looked away from him and along the hallway as they walked. "I merely thought…well, you could move into the condo with me."

Albin's lips twitched but inside, he grinned like the Cheshire Cat. He still had his original luxury apartment but until that moment, he hadn't realized how empty it might be alone. He didn't feel any inclination to move there. None at all. "That's very kind of you."

After only a moment's hesitation, he opened the door to the apartment and looked at the carpet.

Dick sighed. "I don't know whether it's worse to take my shoes off or leave them on."

The incubus shrugged and walked in. "Leave them on. We can clean it later. What do we know?"

The other man looked sadly around the empty apartment. "We know some kind of fae was after either Limpet or Marcel."

"Do you have any fae enemies?"

"You collect enemies of every race when you've lived as long as I have."

"Fair point. What does your gut tell you?"

"The only reason to take Marcel is to hurt me. I don't think I currently have any enemies who would steal a puppy. There are quite a few who would eat him and leave his bones in my bed, however."

"In your bed?"

"I went through a phase of being attracted to bad boys."

Albin smiled. "Well, thank goodness you're out of that phase. Or at least you've upgraded to friendly demons."

Dick frowned. "It's someone who's after Limpet, isn't it?"

"That would be my guess. Who knows we have him?"

The vampire considered the question and finally shook his head. "Only friends as far as I know. Dolores, Lexi, Scott, Alicia, and Bryan. There are others who have known he's with us but wouldn't know where we are. Many people think he's a cat and at least one thinks he's a cat-monkey hybrid."

Albin stood. "I'm going to change out of my suit." He entered the bedroom and shouted to his companion as he kicked his shoes into the corner and threw his pants after them. "Could someone have forced him to make that portal?"

"It was a very small hole. Few fae would fit through it. Although I've seen a fairy shrink to two inches so we can't discount the possibility."

The incubus pulled his jeans on and went to the door. "Right, your choices are to stay and wait or go out and look."

"I don't think I can simply wait around. I'll go mad."

Albin nodded and threw his shirt and tie into the corner of the room, yanked a t-shirt on, and stepped out.

"Let's find a witch to do a locator spell."

Dick picked Marcel's lead up. "They'd need something belonging to one of them but what about the wards? Would they need to be beyond the city limits?"

"Possibly. I don't know for sure. A spell like that might be possible within the city and if not, it's only a short drive out of town."

The vampire narrowed his eyes. "I have an idea. Scott should be able to do it with a map. And I'm very sure Lexi has some dog toys in that funny little pocket of hers." He reached for his cell phone.

While he spoke to his teammates, Albin retrieved a plastic bag from beneath the sink, returned to the bedroom, and shoved his foul-smelling, blood-soaked shoes and clothes into it. When he entered the living room again, Dick was waiting. "They're getting ready to leave Austin but Scott will do the locator spell with Marcel's ball. They'll call us back. Let's head out, but where to?"

"We can head to the supernatural bar. We might find a witch who can do another locator spell on the dog lead. Two spells are better than one. But I think we should check your condo first. You never know, they might have made their way there. And you should see if anything's missing."

The vampire sighed and sat on the edge of the couch. "I don't care about my possessions. I care about my dog and that stupid little demon."

Albin stepped forward and sat beside him. He put an arm around him, pulled his head closer, and kissed his temple. "If it'll cheer you up, we could talk about all the ways we can kill the remaining fae fucker who Limpet didn't eat."

When they stepped out of the apartment, he started to walk the other way but turned when Dick didn't follow.

The vampire looked puzzled. "Where are we going?"

"We can take the other elevator. I don't want to stand in stinky, invisible gore again."

"Good call."

They headed to the parking lot, walked past workmen on ladders fixing the lights, and drove out.

The condo wasn't as bad as Albin had first thought. Seat cushions had been pulled out and cupboards opened and emptied.

Dick checked his room. Clothes had been pulled out of the closets but his little jewelry box hadn't been touched. He opened it, found his lion's head pin where he had stored it, and sighed with relief. His companion was relieved too as he knew how much the pin meant to him.

The incubus looked around. "Do you think they could have been here and left?"

He shook his head. "No, they haven't been here since yesterday. I'd have smelled it." His cell phone rang and Lexi's name appeared on the display. Dick sat on the bed. "Hello?" He put the call onto speaker.

"Scott can't pick anything up from the ball. I'm sorry."

After a long moment, he sighed. "So, he's either in a demon dimension or—"

"Don't even go there. We're wrapping up here," Lexi added. "There's not much else we can do. We'll be with you soon." She disconnected before he could reply.

Albin stood in the doorway and looked at Dick as he stared into space. "Right. I could help in two ways. We could go to the Strip and search up and down it all night, or I could try to take your mind off things with a catalog of moves I can guarantee you've never even heard of in your hundred or so years."

He smiled at the man. "Can we go to the Strip and search up and down it all night?"

"Of course." The incubus opened his hand to reveal that he was already holding the car keys. "I'm ready when you are."

Dick jumped up. "I'll change out of these clothes."

While the other man was changing, Albin set about clearing the mess left by the home invasion. He was returning the cleaning products to the cupboard under the sink when Dick stopped in the doorway.

The vampire folded the lead and dropped it into his jacket pocket. "What if I'd chosen option two?"

He straightened. "You would never have chosen option two. Let's go look for your puppy and that crazy face-eating demon."

They entered the loud bar and the vampire had to shout into Albin's ear to be heard. "This doesn't feel like a supe bar to me."

"The action's in the back room."

"Do you know many witches in town?"

"I know a few. I work with one at the museum. She told me about this place. It's not my scene, to be honest."

"You are certainly more of an upscale dining guy than a throwing it down on the dance floor guy."

The incubus grinned. "I can bust the moves when I have to."

"And now I have new goals."

As they approached the back of the room, he shouted in Dick's ear. "Watch yourself. There is usually a horde of wannabes in here."

"They're everywhere." He rolled his eyes and altered his voice to a simpering whine. "Make me sparkle."

They wove through the crowd to the door to the private club at the back of the bar. The doorman put a hand up. "Sorry, members only."

"He's with me." The man nodded and allowed them to pass. Albin led them down the hallway.

The vampire stopped walking. "I forgot. Scott spelled my watch to hide my nature." He removed his Rolex watch and slid it into his pocket before he pulled his cell phone out and tapped it. "I'm letting Lexi know where we are. I need a drink."

The other man hated places like this and as they approached, he felt the thumping bass in his chest. As expected, the room was heaving.

He turned to see Dick raise his face and turn his head in all directions. His companion was most likely responding to the smell of human blood in the room. He knew that with his vamp vision, he'd be able to see into the dark corners where vamps were feeding on donors.

Albin touched his arm to get his attention. "Let's head to the bar. It should give us a good view of the room."

The incubus stood with his back to the bar and studied the dance floor. It was a little quieter where they stood and he could hear his companion ordering the drinks. "A Chardonnay and a Jack and O-neg, please."

"We have some fae red if you'd prefer," the barman answered. "It's just in and still warm."

He thought immediately about the foul-smelling fae blood in the elevator and glanced at Dick, who screwed his face up in disgust, clearly thinking the same. "No thanks. I'm right off fae."

A young woman in a short, revealing dress spun on her barstool to face the vampire. "Hello, handsome."

He nodded politely. "Good evening." He started to turn away from her.

She continued to speak. "You don't need to get the bagged stuff. You can have it straight from the source."

"No thank you."

"I like your eyes," she persisted.

Albin turned to search the crowded dance floor, but he grinned.

"I'm with someone." Dick began to sound annoyed and he knew how he felt. He'd received unwanted attention his whole life. It was worse now that he simply wanted to get on with finding Marcel.

The woman spoke again. "He's with someone."

The incubus turned to find another stunning young woman on the other side of Dick. The vampire flashed an eye-roll to him.

The first woman asked, "Do you offer an exchange?"

Albin sighed. *Wannabes.* He knew she was referring to the exchange of blood.

Dick frowned. "Not to complete strangers, no."

As he leaned an arm on the bar, the other girl tried to lower her head to make him put his arm around her.

With a scowl, he spun away from the bar to avoid it. "Ladies, I'm honestly not interested. Not only are you barking up the wrong tree, you're in entirely the wrong forest."

One of the girls giggled. "Oh. Well, it was worth a try."

Albin turned his gaze to the dance floor and located his colleague. He signaled as much to Dick, who gave him a discreet nod to continue. The vampire picked his drink up from the bar and knocked it back.

He made his way to his colleague. "Cassie."

"Albie? Holy shit, I never thought I'd see you in here."

"Can we chat for a minute?"

They moved to a table away from the dance floor. "Sorry to disturb you but my friend has lost his dog. He's distraught over it. Would you mind doing a locator spell on the lead?"

She stared at him. "You are so freaking hot right now." She blinked and shook her head. "Sorry, it's the wine. Sure. I'll help." She held her hand out for the lead.

"Shit, Dick has it. I'll be right back."

He started to walk to the bar but when he looked for his friend, the vampire was nowhere to be seen.

CHAPTER TWENTY

Lexi pushed through the crowd. "Can you see them?"

Scott shook his head. "No."

"This is ridiculous, Dick's six foot three. And what's Albin? He must be six foot eight. How can we not see them?"

"Maybe they're behind the bachelorette party of giants on the dance floor."

She looked at the women who were at least twelve feet tall. One wore a sash with *Same Penis Forever* written on it. "Let's head to the bar. It'll give us a better view."

They continued to push through the crowd, taking care to not offend anyone.

"Lexi, Scott."

She turned as Albin hurried toward them and she realized that she'd never seen him look so frantic. Her stomach sank when she came to the conclusion that they'd found Marcel and it was bad news.

The incubus shouted over the music. "Someone grabbed my Dick."

Scott helicoptered his finger and the club noise reduced.

Lexi raised an eyebrow. "Surely that kind of thing happens to you all the time."

"No. Not my dick. My Dick. My vampire. The love of my life."

His statement took a little time to process. "What happened?"

"He was being solicited by a couple of donors at the end of the bar. I went to talk to a friend who was going to help us. But when I looked back, he was gone and so were the girls. It was about ten minutes ago. I've looked everywhere. I have a very bad feeling about this."

She looked around. "Have you asked the bartender?

"He didn't see anything. He said they were there and then they weren't."

"Bartenders never see nothing." She marched to the bar. "We're looking for a friend of ours, a vamp. He was chatting to a couple of girls."

The bartender frowned. "I already told your friend. I didn't see them leave. Are you sure he didn't take them into a corner to snack on?"

Lexi glanced at Albin with an eyebrow raised.

He shook his head vehemently. "No chance."

"Sorry to bother you. I've had a dare to kiss someone and you're it."

She turned to where the giant bride-to-be towered over Albin and grinned at him.

The incubus gestured impatiently. "I'm sorry. We're dealing with something here."

Large patches of red appeared on her cheeks. "Dude, all my friends are watching."

Lexi glanced at the dance floor and sure enough, they were staring and giggling.

She continued. "And I thought since your drunken friend ditched you, you wouldn't mind."

He gave her his full attention. "My what?"

The giant stooped a little to make sure she was heard. "I've never seen a vamp in that condition before. I didn't even know they could get drunk. I thought the bartender would throw him out when he flopped over the bar."

Albin grabbed her face and delivered a full-on kiss, tongues and all.

The giant girl's arms flapped and almost felled everyone in the vicinity.

Across the room, a cheer went up from her friends.

After the kiss, she hovered, still bent over. "I think I love you."

He smiled. "Don't worry. It'll wear off."

Lexi returned to the bar. The bartender glanced at her face and as if on cue, little spots of sweat appeared at his hairline and began to trickle down his face.

It shows there's nothing wrong with his instincts, except maybe his fight or flight. Lexi decided he should be running because she planned to wipe the floor with his smug face. Scott stepped closer and put a hand over hers on the bar. "I see at least fifty infringements of Kindred laws here."

The man turned his attention to him and clearly preferred the idea that he might be able to talk his way out of it. "They went out the back." He pointed to a door.

The group started toward it but she didn't move. She continued to glare at the man while her fingers grasped the edge of the bar-top. The mage leaned close to her ear. "Let's find Dick." She exhaled slowly, then marched out of the club through the door the douche had indicated. Beyond a short hallway stood another door that led to the alley behind the building.

Scott turned to the others. "Has anyone got something of Dick's we can use to find him?"

"Shhh!" Albin was listening.

Lexi heard a groaning sound coming from a dumpster.

The young mage opened it and the three of them looked in. Dick lay barely conscious inside. She looked with horror at the collar of his shirt, which was soaked with blood.

The cut had healed but it was clear from the amount of blood that it had been a bad one.

Albin climbed up and dropped into the dumpster in one fluid movement.

She marveled at how strong and capable he was as he lifted his lover out.

"Lexi, you're drooling," Scott remarked as he took the vampire so the other man could climb out.

"It's not my fault," she told him with a shrug.

He held their teammate in his arms until Albin stood beside him. They placed Dick on the ground and examined him carefully.

Scott put a hand on his head and muttered a few words. He turned to the incubus. "It was a hex." He continued to mumble with a hand on their friend's forehead.

Dick's eyes snapped open fully. His fangs appeared and he was on his feet in a second.

Albin stood but kept his distance and Lexi prepared to jump between Dick and Scott. After a few tense seconds, his teeth retracted and he looked at his shirt. "Urgh! I've been violated."

"What happened in there?" The mage indicated the club's back door.

"I rejected some wannabes and in the next moment, I was sprawled on the ground with you three around me. Was I simply lying there? In the gutter?"

"No. We found you in that dumpster."

"Thrown into a dumpster again? Why does this keep happening to me?" He sighed. "Well, however they do it, I hope it hurts."

Scott frowned. "Do what?"

"They took my blood, which probably means they want to turn. But they have to die first and they'd better hope I never see them again or their second lives will be a damn sight shorter than their first." He straightened his jacket. "Any luck with the locator spell on Marcel's ball?"

Scott took the ball out and bounced it a few times. It showed no inclination to roll in any direction. He looked at Dick with a shrug. "Maybe they're in a demon dimension."

"Our little Marcel in a demon dimension." The vampire shook his head. "Let's head to the condos and decide what next."

CHAPTER TWENTY-ONE

At the condo, Albin made a pot of coffee, popped a straw into a bag of blood, and handed it to Dick.

The vampire sighed. "Could I have a bourbon?"

"After that." The incubus pointed at the bag.

"Yes, Mom." He stared at the others as they sipped their coffee. "I envy people who can drink coffee. You drink it and you're set for the day."

The sun was beginning to rise and they had found no sign of Marcel and Limpet. Albin yawned, then smiled, but it didn't reach his eyes. "I think you're exaggerating the magical properties of coffee."

Lexi drained her cup. "I plan to get a couple of hours of sleep, then start looking for them again. You two should get some sleep too."

Dick shook his head. "I don't think I could."

His cell phone rang and he picked it up quickly. "Yes."

Dolores's voice issued through the tinny little speakerphone. "Any news?"

He rubbed his face wearily. "Nothing."

The fae woman sighed audibly. "I'll be along this afternoon. We can try the locator spell in Fae."

"Okay, message us when you think you'll be there we'll meet you. Thank you, Dolores."

Lexi stood. "I'm dead on my feet. Scott?"

"Yep. I'm ready for some shut-eye."

They headed out the door.

At the entrance to their condo, Scott touched the lock and frowned.

"What is it?"

"Someone's been in here."

She put her hand into her pocket and grasped the katana. He stood aside and allowed her to enter first. Bonded again, they had slipped easily into their old routine. This was what they did.

Lexi moved silently through the hallway and rounded the door to the living room. She couldn't quite believe her eyes. She retrieved her cell phone, called Dick, and heard his ring through the wall. "Can you two come in here, please?"

"Was yours trashed too?" he asked

"No. But there's about to be some damage around here." She disconnected.

Running footsteps indicated that the two men had rushed out of the other condo and they arrived a few seconds later.

Scott leaned his head into the hallway and signaled for them to come to the living room.

They joined the two young people and stared at a male fae frozen in a block of ice up to the neck.

The mage nodded at the little man. "This is Dralog."

Albin raised an eyebrow. "That looks uncomfortable."

The fairy turned to him. "No shit." He tried to struggle but the ice held him securely and all he could do was move his head. His hat fell off and lay on the ice beside him.

He stopped moving and sobbed. "I'll freeze to death."

The vampire's expression had fallen into flat, unreadable

lines. His voice was quiet and terrifying and his fangs grew. "Where are they?"

"I don't know. I'll say it again. I don't know where your pets are. I also don't know where my friends are. They were supposed to come back and get me out but they left me here." His voice trembled. "And for the fifth time, I don't know who hired us."

Dick ran his tongue over his teeth. The look on the fae's face told Lexi he was getting the message. "You're not looking very useful right now, my friend," she told him.

Dralog seemed unable to drag his gaze from the dangerous-looking vampire. "We were told to find a thinner demon and that it would be in here or next door. We were tearing the other place apart when Burdok got a call saying the creature might be in an apartment at one of the big hotels down on the Strip. I didn't hear which one. We planned to go straight there but Burdok said we should check here in case before we left the area and he sent me in. They didn't tell us a mage lived here."

"How many of you ransacked my condo?"

The fae's face was quite easy to read. Lexi studied his expressions and saw that he thought about lying but relinquished the temptation with a sigh. "There were three of us."

She believed him. It also fit the theory that there were only two at the hotel.

"It took three of you to go through my home, but they sent you in here alone. Are you sure no one knew there was a mage here?"

The fairy's face fell in the instant when he realized he'd been sent in alone to set off any traps. His face turned a deep red. "Like I said. I don't know for sure who hired us, but Bardok does work for Kindred sometimes. Quite often, actually. He might even be on the payroll."

Dick spoke through gritted teeth. "Why did they take my dog?"

That drew a startled look from the captive. "We weren't after a dog. Maybe they took him by mistake. Does your dog look like a cat?"

"No! How dare you." The vampire was offended on Marcel's behalf.

"Bardok was given a sack with runes all over it. He told us it was supposed to make the demon sleep and be no trouble."

Albin frowned. "Where were you supposed to take him?"

"I don't know about that. It was Bardok's job."

Scott turned to Lexi. "I don't understand the Kindred connection. Could Caleb have been working with someone else?"

She turned to the fairy. "Did they talk about someone called Caleb?"

"No. The only name I heard was Azatoth."

"What did you say?" She froze.

Dralog gulped. "Azatoth, maybe—something like that. Bardok said, 'If we don't get that thinner, Azatoth said he'd pull our guts out.'" The terrified fae tried to shrink away. "Are you going to kill me?"

"Of course we are." Scott waved a finger and the fae's head slapped forcefully against the ice block and stayed there.

Albin blinked. "Did you kill him?"

"No. I merely knocked him out. We didn't need him for anything else, did we?"

They all looked at each other and shook their heads.

Scott took hold of the corner of the ice block, disappeared, and returned a minute later.

Lexi grinned. "What did you do to him?"

"I left him in the middle of the desert."

Dick's eyes narrowed. "In that ice block, I hope."

"Yes. It'll take a couple of days for him to get out."

"Unless he shrinks himself." Dick picked a piece of fabric up. "Oh, here's his little hat."

"The ice block will prevent him from using magic."

Albin raised his eyebrows as the vampire waved the hat

around. "His head will burn and his body will freeze. I don't fancy his chances much."

Lexi frowned. "I don't understand. I ripped his heart out."

The incubus turned to face her. "Whose heart?"

"Azatoth's heart."

He frowned at her in confusion. "I thought you said he didn't get through."

"He didn't. I ripped it out of his chest and crushed it with my bare hand while he was still in his dimension."

When the man continued, his voice sounded slightly shaky. "You…reached through the veil?"

"I punched through it and—" She froze. "I… I…" She looked at Albin in horror. "What have I done?" Her thoughts flew to the conversation they'd had the previous day with Bryan. "Bryan kept saying she was different."

Scott's phone was already in his hand. "Dolores, how fast can you get here?"

Lexi turned to the mage when he finished the call. "It's starting to make sense."

"But we only saw her a couple of days ago. She seemed fine."

Albin rubbed his chin in thought. "If he's on this side, he's either in the body that was prepared for him or he's looking for it."

"I'll call Bryan." Scott raised the cell phone but she covered it with her hand. "The other way."

He nodded. His gaze went distant for about thirty seconds before he focused again. "I sent a message asking him to contact us ASAP. I don't want to freak him out by putting this in a message."

Dick leaned against the wall with his arms folded. "Maybe we are jumping to conclusions. If Azatoth did get through, why would he still need Limpet? The icicle fae could have embellished the truth. Or maybe his information is out of date."

Lexi looked away. "Maybe." She wasn't convinced and when

she looked at her companions, it was clear that no one else was either.

Albin took his cell phone out. "I have to leave a message at the office." He walked out into the hallway. "Hi, it's Albie. I need to take a personal day or week—probably the week. It's a family thing."

Dick's lip twitched. He was listening too. The world was going to hell or hell had come to the world, but Lexi was fairly sure the vampire was in love.

She walked out onto the deck, sat in the first chair she found, and went over the scene in her mind. The details remained vivid in her memory. Alicia lying unconscious and covered in foul-smelling grease. Overpowering Caleb. Punching through the veil where the outline of the beast stood.

"Are you okay?" Scott sat beside her.

"No. I let him through. It was me." She felt sick.

"Not necessarily. How did you get the strength to overcome Caleb's paralysis spell?"

With a frown, she thought back to the moments before she'd overpowered Caleb. She was reminded of the feeling of her magic reserves being filled when Limpet thinned the veil and allowed the energy through from the demon realm. Startled, she looked at Scott. "You think it was Limpet?" She considered the events again. "So…when I ripped his heart out and crushed it, his essence had already left that body behind."

"It's a possibility. Or he could have somehow come through after we had all left the room." The mage leaned forward. "But try this. Think of another scenario where we wouldn't have all died right there and then. I don't think there is one. We're still here and we can fight him. If he's possessed Alicia, we need to get her back."

Lexi could see he was trying to make her feel better and she knew he was right. The only reason they had walked away from that tower was because Limpet had made it possible for her to beat Caleb's paralysis spell. "Okay, but how do we unpossess someone?"

Dick stepped out to join them. "This isn't something you won't hear me say very often, but I think we need a priest."

CHAPTER TWENTY-TWO

Limpet dived through a portal with Marcel in his arms. It was the fourth and the puppy was shaking.

The sudden heat was shocking but strangely comforting. For a moment, he thought he was in his dimension but realized moments later that the air was not as acrid as his home. He felt uneasy about taking his furry friend through these demon realms but there hadn't been much choice. He assessed the ground before he placed the dog beside him. They were at the mouth of a cave.

The puppy trotted forward two steps before Limpet looked at him. *Stay!*

Ever obedient, the French Bulldog froze.

After listening for a minute, the demon edged forward and the puppy walked close beside him.

They crept into the light of a strange, orange sky. Marcel scratched at his nose and sneezed and didn't seem to like the air.

The little demon sniffed while he turned his head in all directions. He knew how to find the best places to cross. His companion followed him as he picked a careful path through the dirt and rocks into a hot basin. The thinner paused for a few seconds and took a few tentative steps before he realized Marcel wasn't with him.

The puppy was about twenty feet away, seated on his haunches with his head tilted as he stared at a yellow worm-like creature that had risen from the ground and now hypnotized its new, curious prey. Limpet managed to cover most of the short distance to his friend before it struck. The rest was covered by the demon's arms, which stretched to three times their normal length. He managed to divert the spray of poison from the dog but took a fair amount of it in his face. Without hesitation, he bit the creature, separated the head from the body, and spat the rancid creature's foulness from his mouth. He took hold of Marcel, who had begun to bark in fear.

He sent a hasty thought to the puppy. *Shut up.*

The bulldog whimpered.

Be a good boy. Be quiet. The little demon had never been responsible for another creature before. He couldn't even begin to explain to himself why he felt responsible for this one. A creature such as this was food where he came from.

Limpet glanced at the worm. Its body seemed to thrash around with more energy than he expected from death throes, and it was still somehow anchored in the dirt. As he watched, the body rolled itself closer to the head and began to reattach itself.

Marcel watched too. He sat on his haunches, tilted his head, and stared at it with suspicion.

I hate this dimension. The thinner snatched Marcel off the ground and ran.

As he raced across the basin, the ground shuddered. Dust and stones fell away and yellow worm-like creatures appeared everywhere, writhing as they emerged from below the surface. He leapt onto a rock and climbed quickly.

When he reached the top, he put Marcel next to him. It wasn't a solution but it gave him a moment to think. They were in the middle of the basin. He could see that a run of a few minutes would take them to the edge and out of there. Of course, he could make a portal in the air but they were so unreliable. He studied the rock they stood on. Downward portals always worked out badly for him.

Yellow worms' heads popped to the surface and squealed. They rose above the ground as far as the eye could see and thrashed and undulated in what looked like an orchestrated joint activity. It moved as one, he realized a moment later, because it was one. This creature was also not happy and sounded as though it was in agony. He turned to Marcel, who had cocked his leg and now peed off the rock onto the worm, which hissed and blistered. Limpet caught him under his front legs and held the puppy penis-outward. The worm shrank away. He continued his race across the basin and this time, he wasn't pursued.

A short climb brought them into a pass. He sprinted along it and did his best to ignore the skittering sounds behind him. *What now?*

He didn't release Marcel until his nose led him to a sheer rock face. The sound behind grew louder but he didn't turn. Instead, he hoisted the puppy under one arm, slapped the rock to create a portal, and jumped through to land heavily on the other side.

A shadow fell over them. The little demon pushed his furry companion behind him and snarled as he spun to face a huge horned creature that held a large, ugly wide-bladed weapon.

His would-be assailant raised the weapon in his hand and the blade descended.

CHAPTER TWENTY-THREE

An hour later, Lexi stepped into a bar. It was a real dive and in a bad part of town—the kind of place people went to drink until they could no longer think. A few patrons sat in front of poker machines at the bar, their faces mesmerized. They didn't even look up when their drinks arrived.

She located Albin and a woman seated opposite a man whose face was flat on the table. The sight of the incubus in a dump like that seemed incongruous. Dick and Scott entered behind her and they walked to the table together.

The mage tapped her arm. "Do you want a drink?"

Dick looked at him in horror. "Are you insane?"

He looked around and grimaced. "You might be right."

Albin gestured to his friend. "This is Cassie. She's one of my colleagues at the museum."

The girl nodded a greeting.

"And this is Father Anthony," he continued. "He's agreed to help us."

The man's head jerked off the wood surface. "But it's thirsty work, all this talk."

Dick headed to the bar.

The priest straightened fully. Lexi had expected him to be in priest's attire and the surprise must have shown on her face.

Father Anthony brushed his hand down the front of his t-shirt. "Forgive my appearance. I'm undercover."

She looked at Albin. The unimpressed look in his eyes said everything she needed to know.

The vampire placed a fresh glass and a bottle in front of the bleary-eyed priest, who poured himself a drink. As drunk as he was, he didn't spill a drop. He downed it and poured a second before he spoke. "You want an exorcism?"

Lexi waited until he'd emptied the glass again. "Do you know how to do one?"

"What do you think put me in this condition, girlie? I've seen things you wouldn't believe were possible."

"Right back at ya," Scott mumbled.

She leaned forward. "My sister is possessed by a high-level demon. Can you get it out of her?"

"How strong is it? The stronger they are, the tighter they hold on." The priest clenched his fist in front of his face and focused on her. "Sometimes, they'll pull the vessel's guts out as they leave."

All expression fell from her face. He laughed until it dissolved into a coughing fit.

Once he'd recovered, he looked blearily at her. "You know what you need, child? You need faith."

Lexi rolled her eyes and glanced at Albin as if to ask if he couldn't have found someone better.

Father Anthony finished another drink. "Oh, I don't mean faith in God. Don't get me wrong, he exists all right, but we ain't gonna get much help from him. No, you need faith in me." He looked at each of them in turn. "Let me take you to church." He stood, snatched the bottle off the table, and staggered toward the exit.

She rounded on the incubus. "Are you insane? I won't put Alicia's life in the hands of a drunk."

Several people around the bar raised their heads.

"No offense. We were just leaving." Dick guided her out with a firm hand under her elbow.

Cassie stepped beside her when they stood outside. "Give him a chance. He honestly is the genuine article."

Lexi walked along about twenty feet behind the drunken priest, who now talked to himself or maybe to God, she wasn't sure. A large church with stained glass windows and a spire loomed ahead of them but before they were even close to it, he stopped outside a large abandoned building with boards over the windows and graffiti covering the entire front façade.

As she approached, he bent over, held himself steady by leaning his head against the iron gates across the door, and unlocked a padlock. He opened the door and pulled a light cord in the corner of the space. It had clearly been a hall of worship at some point but the only thing that remained was the font off to the side.

Plastic chairs were piled along one wall and hundreds of crosses were spray-painted onto all the walls all among other symbols. All the pews were gone and a pentacle was drawn in the middle of the floor. Lexi looked up. The same was drawn on the ceiling. A metal loop was buried in the center of the circle on the floor and chains hung on the wall. She recognized some of the symbols between the crosses on the walls, ceiling, and floor.

Cassie nudged the priest. "Show her."

He pulled his t-shirt up to reveal a large ugly scar that stretched the length of his chest and stomach. "When I said they can yank the guts out, I wasn't kidding."

Dick stared at the scar. "You performed an exorcism on yourself?"

"Weren't no one else to do it. It took three days. It was a messy one, for sure, but that was in the early days. I've tightened my processes since then." Father Anthony gave him a lopsided grin.

Lexi chewed her cheek in thought. "Are you still good with the church?"

"Do I look like I'm still good with the church? They moved to new premises up the street and left me here. But if you're asking if I've been excommunicated, the answer is no. But I'm no longer on the payroll." Father Anthony took a long swig from the bottle he still held.

She stepped in and walked around the space. Curious, she felt the weight of the chains and kicked some bags of salt which were piled at the back. They created a low wall between the main area and a bed of dirty blankets and pillows on the floor. A bible lay beside the bed. She knew the others were waiting for her to say something so she turned and regarded them with her silver eyes. "This will do nicely."

The priest crossed himself and Albin's witch friend put her hand into her pocket and held whatever was in there that gave her comfort. Lexi surmised it was an athame but it could have been a gun as far as she knew.

Until the moment she stepped into the church, she had thought the priest was a fake. But there had been demons in that room and many of them. She felt the memory of their passing like echoes in a cave.

She jerked her head to indicate she needed to speak to Scott. He walked closer and secured their privacy.

"Can you sober him up?" She glanced at the priest.

"Not a chance."

It wasn't the answer she expected. "But I've seen you sober yourself up. And you did the same for me with the vamp blood."

Scott shook his head. "This is completely different. God knows how long he's been drinking this hard. If I sober him up, he'll go into extreme withdrawal and his organs will likely go into failure."

"I guess we'll have to sober him up the old-fashioned way." She walked to the priest. "Come on, I'll buy you lunch."

Cassie pulled her purse over her shoulder. "I need to get back to work. One question though. How will you get her here?"

***

"More coffee?" The server looked suspiciously at the scruffy, smelly, drunken priest.

He shook his head. "No thank you."

Lexi glanced at her and nodded. "Fill it up again, please."

The woman refilled all the cups and left.

Father Anthony frowned. "If you get me too sober, I won't be able to do it. I have to be at least half-drunk to do the job. No one in a sober condition would do this."

"That's fine. If we can start to sober you up tonight, you might be half-sober by tomorrow. This won't be easy, Father Anthony. Do you want more food?"

"I don't eat much anymore. Can't keep it down." The priest shrugged.

She leaned forward and held his gaze. "Bryan has already told us she's enthusiastic about the job. The killing part anyway. I think I should simply invite her along to work."

Dick retrieved his flask and took a sip of bourbon before he dribbled some into the priest's coffee and winked at him. He turned to Lexi, who gave him her I-will-cut-you face. Unperturbed, he shrugged. "When should we do it?"

She rolled her eyes and turned to Father Anthony. "What do you need?"

"I've got almost everything I need. Incense, the Good Book, the candles, and the chains. All I need is the holy water. I can get that in the morning."

They finished their meal and walked along the street to the abandoned church. As they approached it, Scott touched Lexi's shoulder. "I'm getting a nine-one-one message from Bryan. He says to look at his live feed." He shrugged but pulled her into his dimensional pocket where he turned a computer screen on and looked at the email. There was a link at the bottom of the one-line message.

The mage clicked on the link and a window opened to reveal what looked like an office. "This must be what he sees right now."

Bryan was in an office. The door flew open and Lucy stumbled in, followed by Warren. The young mage had a split lip.

"Warren, what in the name of—" Bryan's gaze flicked to Eric, who had spoken.

"She was planning to leave." He held a shard of glass out.

"Oh no." Lexi slumped.

Eric approached the girl. "Is this true?"

She started to talk quickly. "I wanted to trick them into coming for me so Warren could get Scott back." The lie now carried weight.

The older man struck her with the back of his hand and blood trickled from her nose.

Warren grasped her arm and she winced. "Are they coming?"

She started to bleed from her eyes before she coughed up blood.

"They'll come, I promise. Please make it stop."

The young legacy looked at her with disgust on his face. "How could you plan to leave me?"

Scott looked horrified. "What the hell is he doing to her? Why doesn't she cut off his access to the magic and get the hell out of there?"

Lexi was at a loss. "And why is Bryan mixed up in all this?"

Lucy tried to speak but coughed up more blood. "I'll contact them again. They said they'd come."

Eric frowned and looked at someone she couldn't see. "Would someone be able to translocate into this building?"

Bryan looked at a man in a suit but Lexi didn't know who he was.

The man slapped his forehead. "Of course not. The building has protective wards. If anyone tried to translocate inside, the wards would drop them on the other side of the street. Nora," he shouted loudly.

A nervous-looking middle-aged woman entered the room. "Yes, Gordon?"

He spoke quickly. "Take security outside to see if there's a legacy and a mage across the street trying to get in."

She paused at the door. "How will I know who you're looking for? What do they look like?"

"She looks like me, Nora."

Lexi froze as Bryan looked at Alicia—*no, Azatoth*. The demon blinked and her eyes turned black-and-yellow. "But her eyes aren't as pretty as mine."

With a hissed intake of breath, she retrieved her cell phone and called Maggie. "Has Lucy called you again?"

"Yes. I told her we'd contact you but Dad said it wasn't worth it. She said she was at home alone and we came to get her but we're standing on the street outside what Dad says is Kindred HQ."

"It's a trap. She's in there with Warren and something much worse. They're sending guys out so get out of there."

She waited for a response while she watched the young mage try to stem the blood with her sleeve.

"Please, My Lord Azatoth." Eric said, "Warren needs his mage."

Warren sneered. "I don't care what you do to her."

Bryan looked at the white-eyed Kindred Grandfather who faced Azatoth.

Once outside the dimensional pocket, Lexi turned to Dick. "Get the holy water. We have to do this now." She watched as he raced—faster than a human but not as fast as a vampire would—

to the church doors. He held his flask out as though to pour the contents onto the ground but guzzled what remained hastily.

She sighed, rolled her eyes, and returned her focus to the office.

Bryan stared at Alicia, who gazed around the room. "I'm beginning to tire of all of you." She looked at Lucy. "Why am I still waiting?"

Azatoth picked at her nails, then stared at a man in a suit Lexi didn't recognize. "Has there been any news of the thinner?"

"No, my lord…lady. I…"

"Gordon, your people are incompetent. That makes you incompetent." She pulled a spine from the manticore tail and threw it at his neck.

He yanked the spine out and looked from it to the demon. A gurgle emerged from his mouth and he clutched his throat and fell, his face still a mask of confusion. As they watched, he thrashed wildly before he lay paralyzed with his eyes wide and staring.

Azatoth stepped closer and prodded him with her foot. "Damn, that stuff's effective." She leaned closer to him. "Don't worry, Gordon. It'll wear off in a few hours."

Maggie came back on the phone. "Okay, we're twenty miles away."

"You need to cover your backs and send a message through official channels about Lucy contacting you. It looks like it's too late to save her now. I have to go."

She disconnected the call and quick-dialed Alicia's number.

A phone rang in the office. Azatoth paused and looked around before she pulled the cell phone from her pocket. She looked delighted. "Ha!" She brandished the device at those with her in the room. "Seriously? No one thought to tell me I could simply call her?" She answered in a sing-song voice. "Hi."

Lexi turned away from the screen. "Hi, sis. How's it going?"

"Oh, you know. Work, work, work."

She couldn't help it and simply had to look at the room again. Through Bryan's eyes, she watched as Alicia turned to face the room with her hand over the phone. "Sorry, everyone, I have to take this." She dropped into a swivel chair and crossed her legs over the sides. "Hey, where are you?"

"We've been in Peoria in Illinois." Lexi looked at Scott as she spoke. "An old friend of mine, Louis, had a problem he needed our help with. Scott's still there tying up loose ends, although there wasn't much we could do."

The mage immediately retrieved his cell phone and began texting.

"Oh. Scott's in Peoria. You've never mentioned a Louis before." Azatoth looked at Warren, who smirked and disappeared. Lucy gasped and fell against the filing cabinet as the legacy used what little magical energy she had left.

The demon covered the cell phone and shushed the girl. "Can't you see I'm on a call?" She waved an arm dramatically before she returned to the call. "So, where are you? Do you want to meet tonight?"

"I'd love to but I've had a job come in. Half a dozen wild vamps are holed up in an abandoned church in Las Vegas. I'm on my way there."

Azatoth straightened and her face lit up. "Half a dozen? Do you want help? I'd be happy to help out. Sisters taking the bad guys down together."

"I'm not sure. I don't want to get you involved in non-Kindred jobs. It might compromise you."

Lexi watched through Bryan's eyes as the demon leaned forward and dropped the manticore tail onto the desk. She looked like an excited child. "Please say yes. It'll be fun."

She looked at Scott. "Okay. Yes. We can go for drinks after." She frowned and focused on the faces of the people in the room. They were motionless and had begun to turn red. She moved closer to the screen. Bryan's vision was beginning to blur and she realized they weren't breathing.

"Right," she said quickly. "Well, I need to shoot. I'm waiting for the address to come through. I'll message it to you when I get it."

Azatoth turned away from the frozen, dying people in the room. "Oh, no time to chat?"

"Sorry. I have another call coming in. I need to run. See you later." Lexi disconnected and stared at the screen.

The demon remained in the chair and spun it to face the room again. She still held the cell phone against her ear. "Okay. Look, something needs my attention. I'll meet you later." She looked at Bryan and unknowingly, directly into Lexi's eyes. "Bryan's dying to see you." She put the device onto the desk.

Scott shook his head. "Was she pretending you hadn't disconnected the call?"

She put a hand on his arm. "Tell Bryan to get the hell out of there."

He started to type.

The demon stood and gestured laconically. Eric, Gordon, and Lucy sucked in desperate breaths and leaned on the furniture.

Azatoth looked at Lucy. "Well, I don't need you after all." She picked up the manticore tail and waved it. About twenty spines launched from the end of it and struck Lucy in the face. She fell and the screen went black.

Lexi's jaw dropped. "What happened to the feed? Did something happen to Bryan?"

Scott started clicking keys. "I don't know."

A message popped up on the screen. *I'm hiding out.*

Let us know where you are, Scott typed in return.

Back on the street, Lexi turned to Dick "Did you get it?"

The vampire shook the flask. "Yes, the baby's father tried to hit me, though. In a church, can you believe it?"

"You interrupted a christening?" Scott's eyes bulged. "Why didn't you simply use one of the little stoups at the door?"

He raised an eyebrow. "Oh, is that what they are? Well, I'll know for next time."

Lexi walked into the center of the pentagram. "Right. This will happen in less than an hour. I want everyone out of sight until she's bound."

Father Anthony removed his grubby t-shirt and replaced it with a shirt and collar. He opened a grate in the wall and withdrew several candles and silver religious items. Finally, he placed a large silver cross around his neck. He glanced up and caught her surprised expression. "You're surprised a drunk like me hasn't pawned this?"

She responded with an exaggerated shrug. He couldn't blame a girl for thinking that.

The priest snorted. "Lady, this has been hocked so many times it has its own shelf in the back of the store."

"How do people usually find you when they have a possession problem?"

"Mostly, I come home and find them here. Occult groups break in and summon something, then they can't get rid of it. I have to exorcise the damn thing before I can get to my bed."

Lexi frowned. That wasn't great news. The demons she had sensed might have been from someone else's summoning. "Scott will help you to make sure the demon can't leave the circle. He has some…skills."

He looked at her. "I can guess what he is—a witch or a mage, I suppose. I'm quite familiar with your world." He sat back on his haunches. "I'm not sure what you are, though."

"If you ever find out, let me know." She smiled.

Dick looked around. "Can I do anything to help?"

She thought for a moment. "Yes, run around and make a smell."

The vampire gaped at her. "I beg your pardon?"

"This is supposed to be a nest of feral vampires." She shooed him away.

With a resigned expression, he removed the watch Scott had imbued with a cloaking spell and wandered around the room, flapped his arms, and stared at her like he wanted to rip her arms off.

Albin chuckled and Dick stopped and pinched the bridge of his nose. "The humiliation of it."

Within a few minutes, they were ready. Lexi ordered Albin, Dick, and Scott into an anteroom.

She stepped outside and messaged Azatoth with the address.

CHAPTER TWENTY-FOUR

Seconds later, her sister appeared beside her. "So, let me get this right. Since you're not with Kindred and I'm off the clock, we don't have to worry about those pesky accords."

"We're here to kill." Lexi emphasized her point by drawing her katana from her dimensional pocket.

Azatoth looked around and picked a fallen branch up. She snapped it in half and hefted it to test the weight. "I'm ready."

So she can't access the dimensional pocket. That's good to know.

She thought back to how Azatoth had hidden the fact that Lexi had hung up on her. *The demon has ego issues.* She decided to test her theory and looked at the branch. "Interesting choice. I'll go first to keep you safe." She stepped forward to open the gate.

The demon put a hand on her shoulder and gave her a wide grin when she turned. "You'll what?"

"I don't want you to break your little stick and then have no weapon. So, I'll—"

Azatoth frowned. "Do I need to remind you who won our little fight? Don't forget, I have all the Legacy strength."

Lexi circled her blade so it pointed away and held both palms out as she stepped back. "If you insist. I'll back you up."

"Yes, you will." The demon stepped through the gate and opened the big wooden door. "There is a strong vampire smell in here. What a stink." She scowled. "And something else—cheap cologne."

A soft, high-pitched squeak issued from inside.

She chuckled softly as she waved a hand in front of her nose. "Is your friend Dick in here?"

Shit!

Lexi recovered quickly. "He'd better not be in there. He did recce the place first but that was hours ago. His cologne does have the habit of hanging around long after he's gone." She whispered, "Go slowly."

Azatoth charged in ahead of her as she knew she would. She moved directly into the center of the pentacle. Scott's shield went up around the circle and Father Anthony stepped out. He opened his book and sprinkled holy water onto the demon.

Azatoth spun in fury. "What is this?"

"This is an exorcism, vile devil." The priest read aloud but it wasn't in English. Lexi couldn't fathom what language it was.

The demon looked at Lexi with a crestfallen expression. "How did you know?"

She rolled her eyes. "You weren't psychotic enough."

"It was Bryan, wasn't it?" She swung her stick at the woman's face and it bounced off the shield. "He'll wish he hadn't done that."

Unperturbed, she held the demon's stare. "You should settle down. This might be a little uncomfortable."

"Fuck!" Her eyes glowed yellow with a slash of black down the middle of each. She spun and hurled the stick at the priest with the same result.

Father Anthony continued his ramblings. "*Sukric et to eybdug dais na, nurt re dekap, tenafeley et eillen.*" He waved the incense in the shape of the cross.

Lexi muttered, "Bind with chains of iron." The chain which

they'd hung from the ceiling snaked down, wound around their captive, and secured itself to the floor.

Azatoth turned slowly and followed the priest with her gaze like a caged animal as he walked around the pentacle. "Will you shut up? I can't hear myself think." She turned to Lexi. "We could work together. You and me, the sisters plus one. We could rule this dimension together. Or battle beasts. I find that very satisfying."

"I'd rather have my sister back."

"I won't give this vessel up," she howled. "I'll tear it to shreds before I release it."

Although she kept her expression deliberately neutral, Lexi prayed it wouldn't come to that.

The demon groaned. "It doesn't matter. She's gone. I tore her out root and stem. This vessel will be empty without me."

She refused to believe that Alicia was gone.

The priest continued to read from the book as he sprinkled his holy water. "*Skold mosjo skadis.*" He switched to English. "Take hold of the dragon, the old serpent, which is the devil and Satan, bind him and cast him into the bottomless pit..."

Lexi was impressed that he was able to translate the book into what was presumably Latin.

Azatoth looked from Father Anthony to Lexi and licked her lips. "If you let me live, I'll tell you about Liz. That's your mother's name. You didn't know that, did you? Caleb knew about her. I can tell you."

She didn't respond. If Caleb knew, someone else in Kindred must surely know.

"I'll make a deal with you. Let me go back to my body on the other side. If you cast me out like this, I may never find my way back."

The priest raised his voice. "*Skarig stomma, Lamplig Ostron.*"

The demon screamed and crumpled. Lexi wanted to look

away as her sister's body writhed on the floor but she stared at the beast as it thrashed wildly.

A door opened behind her and she sensed Scott enter. He walked to her side while Dick and Albin hung back.

Azatoth screamed again, rolled to face Lexi, and caught a glimpse of Scott. She froze and flopped onto her back. "Well, young Warren will be quite vexed when he doesn't find you at the witch's house." She stood and stepped away from the chains which remained secured to the ceiling and floor but not to her. Calmly, she dusted herself off.

Lexi stared at the priest, who now stood open-mouthed and gaped at the creature on the other side of the circle.

Ignoring him, the demon took hold of the chain and pivoted on one foot as she swayed nonchalantly. "All I want is for you to work with me, and you will."

She planted her feet and yanked on the chain. The ceiling of the old building shuddered and collapsed. Lexi was so shocked that she couldn't move. A beam slid half out of the ceiling and Azatoth swiped a finger casually in mid-air. The beam plummeted and drove through the priest's chest to pin him diagonally to the floor. His head flopped back and his arms hung as the rest of the ceiling collapsed. Dick caught hold of Albin and rushed him through the exit and Scott teleported himself and Lexi corporeally into his dimensional pocket.

The ceiling had barely stopped collapsing when Dick hurried into the building. "Lexi? Scott?"

They reappeared. "We're okay."

As the dust settled, they found the body of Father Anthony but as expected, but there was no sign of Azatoth.

They sat in Dolores's apartment, the four of them covered in dust and debris from the damaged ceiling, dejected and horrified by what they had seen.

"That poor man." The fae shook her head in dismay.

Dick closed his eyes and sighed as though something had just occurred to him. "He was a charlatan."

Lexi glanced at the vampire. "How can you be so sure? There had been demons in that church and what about that scar on his chest? Isn't it more likely that nothing as powerful as Azatoth has walked this earth since...well, probably forever, and Father Anthony simply wasn't equipped to deal with it?"

He glanced at Albin. "I think you have shards of silver in your hair."

The incubus stood. "Have I? Sorry, I'll sort that out now." He went to the back door and stepped out to run his hands through his hair.

Dick leaned forward with a troubled look on his face. He opened his mouth to speak but closed it again.

She rolled her eyes. "Spit it out."

The vampire nodded. "I obviously couldn't say this in front of Albin but I recognized some of the words the priest said in his ritual. I have only now realized where they came from." He paused and still seemed reluctant to say it. He glanced at the door, ensuring that Albin was still outside. "I can't explain how I know this, but skold, skarig, ostron..." His voice sank to barely whisper. "They're all Ikea products."

Lexi's jaw dropped. "You are fucking kidding me. I can't believe it."

Scott's eyebrows raised almost to his hairline. He shook his head. "Yeah, right. You knowing the name of Ikea products."

Dick shushed him as Albin appeared in the doorway.

Lexi rubbed her face. "He was a fake and I got an idiot killed."

The vampire fixed her with a frustrated look. "How could we have possibly known?"

Albin rubbed the back of his lover's neck as he returned to the table. "It's possible that even if he was a fake, his rituals could have scared some lower-level demons away. They'd rather have left under their own steam than be cast out to who knows where."

"I can't accept that Alicia's gone." Lexi turned to Scott. "Have you heard from Bryan?"

He shook his head.

She picked up the piece of Azatoth's branch that she'd taken from the rubble, turned it in her hand, and dropped it onto the pile of maps. "We need to know where she is. How can something so powerful be completely hidden?"

Dolores stood. "We've been at this for an hour. I think it would be better if you got cleaned up and had some sleep."

Dick moved to the window and looked out onto the lake. He sighed. "I wonder where Marcel is now."

A further sadness settled on all of them. It was strange how the little puppy was the absolute heart of their little group. The thought that something awful had happened to him was as worrying as what the demon would do to a world that didn't seem equipped to defend itself.

CHAPTER TWENTY-FIVE

"Can you stop that?" Scott stood in the doorway of the kitchen in his shorts.

Lexi bounced the ball off the wall and caught it again before she looked at his bloodshot eyes. "You look like shit."

He shuffled in. "That's because I've only had three hours' sleep. You probably look worse than I do. How much sleep did you get?"

She shrugged. "A couple of hours."

He looked doubtfully at her.

"Maybe less," she admitted.

The mage opened a cupboard on the wall and took out the coffee and a filter. "Go have a shower. I'll put the coffee on."

Lexi complied and avoided looking at herself in the mirror. She didn't want to see the identical face to her sister's.

She rubbed her eyes as the water poured over her. The truth was that she hadn't slept at all. When she tried, all she could see were Azatoth's yellow gaze.

When she went downstairs, Scott had thrown a t-shirt on and Dick and Albin were at the kitchen table.

The incubus looked almost as rough as everyone else did. He

yawned, scowled, and gulped his coffee. "Have you heard anything from Bryan?"

Lexi shook her head.

He frowned and his gaze settled on her. "Do you think he might try to go up against Azatoth alone?" When she shrugged, he continued. "You guys need to find him and warn him how strong that demon is."

"You're right," Dick agreed. "What will you do?"

Albin shrugged. "I can't leave town so I'll do what I can from here."

Scott slathered cream cheese on a toasted bagel. "I made another discovery last night. I looked through the rest of Father Anthony's exorcism…uh, the parts that weren't Ikea products…" He paused.

"And?"

"It was Nellie the Elephant backward."

Lexi put her head into her hands. After a moment, a hysterical giggle burst free and she couldn't stop it. She laughed until tears ran down her face, then Scott joined in, and finally, Dick and Albin.

When the hysteria passed, she sighed. "We're lucky we're not all as dead as Father Anthony."

They sat in silence for a few seconds.

"Do you think Bryan will be in New Orleans?" the mage asked.

She frowned. "Hopefully, he has the sense to be somewhere Alicia doesn't know about. She didn't know anything about his life with me. He could be in Austin. I don't even know if a location spell will work. If he's laying low, he might be completely shielded. I only hope we're not too late."

Scott went blank for a few moments, which indicated that he was doing something in his dimensional pocket. "Have you got anything that belongs to Bryan? I can't find anything."

Lexi thought about it. She went to the windowsill and dug in an earthenware pot that contained wooden spoons. After a few muttered exclamations, she retrieved a pink plastic stick with a flamingo on the top. "Will this do?"

He took it from her. "He gave this to you the other night in the bar."

She nodded. "It should be fine. Do you want me to do it?"

Dick raised an eyebrow. "I'm no expert, but the last time you tried to locate someone you flew off alone and appeared in a jail cell."

Scott nodded enthusiastically. "Good point. That's probably something we should practice. In this case, I'll do it. We'll travel with Dolores. She's meeting us at the diner."

The incubus stood. "I'll continue to look for Marcel and Limpet. I have demon contacts and I know a high magician. He might be able to summon Limpet."

The vampire's face brightened. "Do you think it could be that easy?"

Albin shrugged. "It depends. If he's taken the name Lexi gave him, he could be summoned using it. If not, he won't respond."

Half an hour later, they were in the car and on their way to Boulder City.

Scott's face appeared between the front seats. "I hope we'll have time for breakfast at the diner."

Lexi twisted around in her seat to face him. "You just had four cream cheese bagels."

"Hey, I only had three."

"Four," his companions said together.

Dolores was seated outside with an iced tea when they arrived. "Any updates?"

"No, you?" she asked as she closed the car door.

The fae woman shook her head.

Scott eyed her suspiciously. "I'll go in first and get us a table."

"You do that, dear." She smiled sweetly.

The mage walked quickly to get to the diner door before she

did. He placed a hand on it and turned to her. "I don't have time for your sneaky door tricks. I want bacon and eggs." He turned and stepped into Dolores's apartment. "No! I thought you had to open the door to make it work."

"Yes, Scott. I know you thought that, but you were wrong."

Lexi hid a smile as they filed in. They stood around the table which was already covered with maps.

Scott took the pink stirrer out of his bag and Dolores took a map down from a shelf. One side showed New Orleans and the other the state of Louisiana.

He opened the map to the New Orleans side. "Let's be optimistic and assume he's in the city where he's supposed to be." He muttered his words and placed the stick on its end before he released it. It remained standing before it spun in circles a few times as it moved around the map. The circles began to diminish as it spun faster. It finally zeroed in on one location and remained there.

The mage narrowed his eyes to read the address. "Chestnut Street. That's the chief's house, isn't it?"

The last time they'd seen the house, it had been ablaze. The fire department had reached it within a few minutes and most of the damage had been superficial, but they hadn't seen it since.

Dolores checked the time. "Okay, I'll drop you off across the street. Give me a call if you need me. Any sign of Azatoth—and I mean any sign—get the hell out of there."

They stepped out and she closed the door behind them.

Dick stiffened and his fangs extended. "Blood."

His companions both looked at him.

"Seriously. And a considerable amount too."

They looked in both directions, then walked to the house across the street.

After they eased through the open gate, Dick turned to the others. "I'll take the back entrance."

He vanished before they could respond. Lexi and Scott walked up the steps and pushed the front door open.

The smell of blood was overpowering. Mage and legacy gave each other a curt nod and stepped in. They found Bryan seated on the floor in the entrance hall.

Lexi leaned closer to him. "Bryan. What happened here?"

He didn't respond.

She gestured to Scott to stay in the hallway and see to Bryan and headed into the living room. Barely an inch of the room was not covered in blood and gore. Intestines and body parts were strewn over the floor and furniture. A head rested on a turntable in the corner. It wasn't Alicia, but it was her Kindred mother.

Dick arrived at the door to the kitchen. "The chief's in the kitchen. It's the same as it is here."

They stared at the wall as one. *Psychotic enough for you?* had been scrawled in blood.

"Bryan's in the entrance hall. He's in shock." She jerked her head for him to follow her.

Lexi stood at the bottom of the stairs and looked up, dreading what might be there.

"I'll go." The vampire vanished in a blur and returned as quickly. "Nothing."

She released a breath she didn't know she'd been holding and looked at Bryan, then Scott. "Put him in your pocket. We need to get him out of here."

Dick was already on his cell phone. "We're ready for pick-up." They left the house and went directly across the street into Dolores's apartment.

She paused and turned at the door to look at the house that had only recently survived fire damage.

This time, it won't survive.

This was far too important to mess up with her sporadic magic. She deliberately placed a hand over her unhealing scar, called to Scott's magic, and whispered, "Burn hot. Bone to ash."

The mage appeared with Bryan and seated him on the couch while Dolores made him a cup of strange-smelling tea. Lexi didn't want to look at him. He seemed utterly broken.

Still, he was obedient if uncommunicative. He sipped the beverage and after his third sip, he turned and smiled at the fae. "Thank you. That's lovely. I don't recognize the herb."

She smiled in return. "It's not local."

He laughed. "I expect not."

Dick raised an eyebrow at his swift change in demeanor and wandered to the herb jar. He shook the clear glass receptacle and made to open the lid.

Without taking shifting her gaze from Bryan, Dolores said, "I wouldn't."

Without argument, he put the jar back where he found it.

Their boss sat beside the traumatized mage. "So. Would you like to tell us what happened, dear?"

"Of course. I woke up yesterday and Alicia had already left the house. That's quite unusual. I normally have to coax her out of bed with a gallon of coffee and a promise of beignets." He turned to Lexi. "She loves them."

Dolores prompted him to the story again. "But she'd already left."

"Yes. We'd had a disagreement on Wednesday evening. She was tense and angry and that was before we went out on the pixie-clearing job. While we were working, she was bitten by a pixie—maybe that's what caused it. Are pixie bites poisonous? I've heard that—"

"It wasn't that," the woman interjected. "Carry on."

"Well, she trampled all the pixies—around thirty of them. It was a real mess. Pieces hung from her clothes and blood had sprayed across her face. She didn't seem to notice or care, though. It was so bad, I had to glamor her. She was still moody at home—"

"Let's move forward a little, shall we?" Dolores coaxed gently.

"We had another job where she acted weird. I told Lexi about it. Then yesterday, she said she had a meeting at Kindred HQ and she wanted me to go along. I was relieved because we already knew she'd been there, didn't we, Lexi? But when we arrived, people didn't call her Alicia. They were calling her Azatoth." He turned to the fae. "That's the name of the demon who—"

She patted his hand. "I know."

"Well, she started to hurt people and her eyes…" He remained silent for a few moments. "I contacted Lexi and Scott when I realized they were in danger and it was some kind of trap. But Alicia—" He stopped speaking again and shook his head.

Dolores put the cup into his hand. "Have another sip of tea."

He drank, then smiled. "Thanks. It helps. I left and shielded myself. I hid out but had a text from Mom. It said, *Can you come over? Alicia has been here. It didn't go well and your father and I are in pieces.* I thought she was upset. I guess Azatoth sent it."

Lexi glanced at the little jar Dick had returned to the counter. She didn't know what Dolores had given to Bryan, but he was surprisingly talkative.

"I went there this morning and…and…" He looked at Lexi. "Did you see the words on the wall? I didn't understand it."

Lexi tried to tell him to not worry about it but the words stuck in her throat.

He sat in silence again for a few moments before he finally sighed heavily. "She's gone, isn't she? If she was still there, she wouldn't have done that or let him do it. My Ali's gone."

She sat beside him. "Bryan, I'd like you to let me and Scott into your dimensional pocket. Remember? Like last time. Would that be okay with you?"

"Sure Lexi-Loo. I made it so you can get in there anytime."

Gently, she put her hand onto Scott's arm and pulled him into the walk-in closet. She stepped to the end of the little room and pushed the mirror door open. It hadn't changed much since the last time they'd been there.

He pointed across the hall. "The room with bad memories has gone."

She looked across the hall and realized that he was right. The room she'd found his wolf side in was no longer there. "I don't plan to leave those memories anywhere he can find them."

They raced down the steps. She ran to the booth where the latest memories were and pulled everything after the phone call from Alicia. All the pictures and DVDs came out and scattered on the floor.

Scott looked down and glimpsed one of the pictures. "Holy mother!" He twisted his face away. "Thank you for not letting me see that."

Lexi took a blank sheet of paper from the printer and wrote on it. *Found Mom and Dad dead. It was bad. Azatoth has possessed Alicia.* She pinned it to a board.

She shook her head as her consciousness arrived in the apartment again. Scott was still dazed. "Are you okay?"

"I only need a moment." After a few seconds, he turned to her. "There was more on the printer."

She wondered, from the color of him, if he would throw up. "Are you okay?"

"Yes. It was mostly us finding him and coming here."

Lexi knew he'd seen more than that but she didn't challenge him.

The young mage stood and put his hands on Bryan's head.

As he counseled the other mage, she imagined the security procedures being set off. The shutters would come down and the memories would be preserved—all except the hours since he received Alicia's call.

She turned away because she hated to watch him counseling someone. Instead, she retrieved the bottle of bourbon and filled a glass for Dick and one for herself. She took a gulp.

The vampire glanced at Scott before he turned to her. "I know you don't like it but I'm sure this will help him."

"And I'm sure this will help me." She emptied the glass, then refilled it and placed it in front of Bryan and gazed at the mage for a moment. "They overuse it—the counseling. They use it to manipulate and lie. He does this out of compassion."

Dolores squeezed her arm. "I don't want to imagine what you saw in there. He could take that away for you too."

Lexi felt momentarily overwhelmed but kept it together. "I need to keep it. I need to remember what I'm up against. There'll be a moment when the things I saw in that house will carry me through a much worse time."

Dick shrugged. "Maybe it won't—" He cut off abruptly as if he didn't know how to finish.

They all knew it. Alicia was gone and Azatoth was all that was left. This could only end one way.

Bryan spoke sadly behind her. "When did he get her? She was fine after Emmersley."

She turned to find him standing and looking at her. The strange tea had worn off and he had returned to his senses.

The vampire spoke quickly. "I think the possession had probably already begun before we got there."

Lexi knew he was trying to stop her from taking responsibility for punching through the veil. "I don't think—"

Dick spoke again. "We can argue it until the cows come home. The only relevant question now is how do we get that monster out of her? And what do we do if we can't?"

Bryan picked the glass of bourbon up. "What about an exorcism?"

She hung her head. "We tried that yesterday. It went badly and the priest didn't survive it."

He finished the drink and placed the glass on the table. "I need to prepare the communities and make sure we have back up if we need it." He shook Scott's hand. "Thank you."

"I'll give you a call when I hear something."

Dolores opened the apartment door and he stepped out onto Bourbon Street.

Bryan turned to say something but his brows drew down in puzzlement. "I think—" He vanished.

Lexi's mouth hung open. "What happened?"

The fae yanked Lexi out of the doorway and closed the door. "Nothing good."

She looked at Dolores. "We have to get him back."

Her boss shook her head firmly. "We can't simply stumble into something we're not equipped to deal with."

Her expression like stone, she nodded. "Then let's get equipped."

CHAPTER TWENTY-SIX

The group stepped out of the revolving door one at a time and into the foyer of a restaurant.

Lexi turned to speak to Dolores and froze as the small fae woman elevated without warning. Her glamor fell away and she was a beautiful sylph. The girl looked at her other friends. Dick's teeth descended and the tan he'd been working on disappeared. His skin turned as white as death.

It was looking at Scott that gave her the greatest shock. His blond hair glowed, as did his green eyes. A light of pure goodness shone around him.

Her jaw dropped. *He's beautiful.*

Woah! Lexi's eyes are pure silver. Wait, I'm what?

She froze when she realized she'd heard his thoughts and was fairly certain he'd heard hers.

Albin immediately yanked a hat and sunglasses from his pocket and put them on before he drew the cap low over his face and turned his collar up. Even though his face was hidden, the draw of his magnetism couldn't be masked. Two women stood at a desk wearing staff t-shirts. One garment stated *Ethically-sourced Pixie Brains* and the other stated that *Pixies Eat Free.* Lexi was puzzling over that when one of the women looked directly at the incubus and fainted.

Dolores turned to him. "I'm sorry, dear. I forgot about this. It should wear off in a few moments."

He sighed. "No worries. I should have thought about it. I've been here before."

Lexi heard a growl from behind her. She spun and leapt onto Dick, who was about to go full vamp on his boyfriend. They fell together and she managed to hold onto him until the compulsion had passed.

His muffled voice came from between her legs. "You can release my neck from your thighs now."

She smirked. "Are you sure? We can stay here for a few minutes to be sure."

The vampire groaned. "Urgh!"

"If you're certain." She rolled off him.

He was on his feet in a fraction of a second and pulled her up. "Thank you." He pinched the bridge of his nose. "And we are never to speak of this again." He shuddered.

Albin mussed his lover's hair. "It's going in my autobiography."

Lexi looked at Scott. The strange glow had gone and she could no longer hear his thoughts. She hoped to God he couldn't hear hers anymore.

As Dolores approached the desk, Lexi gazed at a huge chandelier hanging from the ceiling several levels up. The walls and floor were tiled with highly polished white sparkling tiles. The woman who wore a maître d' tag assisted her colleague to her feet and supported her while she wobbled to a chair and dropped into it.

The maître d' tucked her hair back behind her pointed ears and looked unflustered as she focused on her tablet screen.

The young woman's eyes were still on the device as they approached the desk. "What name is the booking under?"

"Dolores."

The girl's gaze flicked to the fae's face. Her eyes went from brown to gold to topaz and finally settled on amethyst. Her face broke into a wide, genuine smile.

She squealed. "Aunty Dolly," she shrieked as she ran around the desk to hug the fae.

"Hello, Cassidy. Is he in?"

The young fae looked confused. "He's always in."

"I was joking."

"Oh." She laughed, then frowned. "I didn't see your name down for tonight."

"It's not. I need to see Phil."

The young girl narrowed her eyes. "There isn't room to swing a sprite in there. I could try to get you a cancellation sometime next week."

"I'm sorry, Cassidy, it has to be tonight. It's quite urgent."

"I'll see what I can do."

They stood in a group and waited. Lexi gazed at the sign on the wall. Glossy white letters stood out from the glossy white wall—*Phil's Cornerdown Kitchen*— and the letters were backlit with a purple glow. A huge glass knife and fork-shaped tanks filled with water stood on either side of the sign. Water nymphs in thin, flowing shifts drifted lazily in and out of a constant stream of bubbles. She found the effect quite relaxing and turned to Dolores. "You've mentioned this place before."

"Yes. It's quite famous among supernaturals."

Scott asked, "What happened earlier?"

"There's no hiding in here. Anyone who tries to hide their true nature will be revealed."

"I think it simply boosted my abilities—like, seriously." She was about to tell her boss that she'd heard Scott's thoughts but stopped, embarrassed. Instead, she added. "I could sense Albin behind me without even looking at him." She risked a glance at the mage, whose shoulders had slumped. Good. He didn't need to get the idea that she thought he was beautiful.

He shifted his gaze from his feet but didn't look at her. "How long will this take? I'm worried about Bryan. Do you think he'll try something while we're gone?"

Albin raised an eyebrow. "If he does, he'll get himself killed. There's not much that can kill a high-level demon like Azatoth."

Dolores patted the young mage's shoulder. "That's why we're here."

Cassidy returned with five white cards. "I'm not supposed to do this. I can't get you into the restaurant but there's a party due in the VIP lounge in a couple of hours. Phil walks past all day so you should be able to get a few minutes with him."

"That's all I need. Thank you, dear." The fae took the cards and Cassidy handed them off to the other young fae woman who had returned to her senses. She led them to a curved seating area, unclipped a plush red rope, and pulled it aside for them to enter.

They sat on the curved couch. Lexi leaned forward and looked into a little bowl on the table. It contained what looked like walnuts. She reached out a hand to take one but was distracted by a little cough from Dolores. When she glanced up, the fae woman stared at her and gave her head an almost imperceptible shake. She withdrew her hand and continued to look around the room beyond their alcove.

The light was subdued and small tables were set out around which supernaturals gathered to chat and drink quietly.

Dick raised an eyebrow at the bowl in the center of the table and snatched the champagne bottle from a bucket beside it. He brandished it at Dolores. "Is there likely to be anything wrong with this?"

"Other than the price? No."

He had the cork out before she finished speaking, turned the glasses over, and poured one for each of them before he held his glass to his nose and sighed.

Scott frowned. "Not drinking it?"

"No. The alcohol content isn't high enough. I simply like to feel the bubbles on my nose." He smiled, then sighed and frowned.

Lexi guessed that he was thinking about Marcel again. As she looked at the vampire, a shadow plunged his face into almost complete darkness. It spread across the faces of her friends like an eclipse. She turned slowly and her field of vision was filled with white fabric. She looked up...and up...and finally, she met the gaze of a huge man who stood beside the alcove. He was so large that the top of his head wasn't visible. While every supernatural sense in her body told her this being was no threat, her Kindred-trained brain went through several scenarios of attack. She shook her head.

I think I'd have to shoot him in the face with a missile.

Scott also had thoughts about the giant in front of them but as usual, his dribbled from his mouth. "Who even makes workwear in that size?"

Lexi glanced at the chef's whites worn by the large man, then dragged her gaze to the mage and found the others looking at him in surprise.

A deep voice brought her attention back to the man. "It's age eight-to-nine from the giant store."

"Phil, dear. Do you have a moment?"

"For you, Dolores, anything."

As he stooped to unfasten the rope, Lexi caught a glimpse of two horns growing out of the sides of his head and curving upward. They were brown at the base and changed to bright ivory at the top. The points looked sharp enough to make her uncomfortable.

It explains the high ceilings.

Phil extended a huge hand to Dolores and she placed hers on it. They shared a look. "I see. Let me open the chef's table in the back. We can talk privately. Follow me."

He walked away and Lexi scrambled to her feet and stepped from the seating area. As she made to follow Phil, a choking sound from behind drew her attention.

Scott was retching. He held a walnut in his palm. "What the hell is this?" He began to scrape his tongue with his fingernails.

"It's pixie brains. They're considered quite a delicacy by elves."

The mage made the kind of noise you expect to hear directly before someone throws up. Dick shoved a champagne glass into his hand. He gulped the drink, then moved along the table and finished everyone else's as he followed the group.

When they reached the end of the long room, they stepped into a small private dining room with a large table in the middle.

Phil introduced himself individually to each person and shook their hands.

"You might as well eat while you're here." He looked at the vampire, narrowed his eyes, and shook his head.

They sat at the table and the giant excused himself.

Dick raised an eyebrow. "What's his problem?"

No one had an answer.

Lexi glanced at the table. "Where's the menu?"

Dolores smiled. "You don't need one. Phil knows your heart's desire and will have it brought to the table."

She raised an eyebrow. "How does he know what I want? Even I don't know what I want."

Her boss shrugged. "He's never been wrong as far as I'm aware."

Phil returned and sat at the head of the table. He was an imposing sight and he immediately looked at Lexi. "I understand you're the reason I lost one of my richest customers."

"I am?" She smiled uncertainly.

"The former head of the Kindred Council was a frequent visitor."

The smile slid from her face. "You miss Caleb? I hope you're not waiting for me to apologize."

He shrugged. "No. He never tipped the staff. We won't miss him."

The waiter entered with drinks and placed them around the table—a sealed thermos mug for Dick with a red napkin, a glass of ice and a bottle of water for Albin, coffee for Lexi, and a strawberry milkshake with a cherry on top for Scott.

The mage looked up in mid-slurp to find Lexi looking at him. "What?"

Her lip twitched and she sipped her latte. It was delicious and already sugared to perfection.

Dick sniffed the top of his flask and raised both eyebrows. "Hello." He took a sip. "Wow!"

Dolores narrowed her eyes at the vampire.

He smiled widely. "It's best to not talk about it."

Lexi guessed it was fae blood.

When the waiter left the room, Phil leaned forward and focused on Albin. "It's been a long time. You can remove the disguise. This place is enchanted to the roof."

Dick smirked. "And a very high roof it is too."

The incubus didn't look confident. "Are you sure? Last time I was here—"

"I remember." Phil interrupted him but seemed amused. "I've had a few more wards added since then." He turned to Dolores. "How can I help?"

Albin removed the cap and glasses.

The fae straightened. "Did you feel the disturbance a couple of days ago?"

The giant's eyebrows raised. "Ah! Not here. It was only in the Earth realm, I believe. Everyone was talking about it but no one seems to know anything."

She narrowed her eyes. "Have you ever felt a magical planet-wide disturbance?"

The huge man shrugged his mountainous shoulders. "Not since the old days. And I mean the *old* days."

Dick patted his mouth with the cloth. "I've never felt it before and I've been a supernatural creature since the fifties. You don't look that old although I can't quite pinpoint exactly what you are."

Phil grinned. "I'm older than that but I have a strict beauty regime."

Lexi wondered how old those old days were.

Dolores dropped the bomb without further preamble. "Have you heard of Azatoth?"

Their host's face darkened and he straightened as though preparing himself for news he knew he wouldn't like.

"He walks the human realm," she continued,

Phil sighed. "Well, it was only a matter of time. He's been trying since the dawn of shadows."

Lexi looked up. That was the second time the word shadow had been raised. "What—"

Dolores spoke across her. "We need to know what, if anything, can defeat him. And we need to know quickly."

"Tell me the rest."

When the fae had finished telling him about Alicia, he placed his giant hand gently onto Lexi's. "I'm sure you wanted to hear that your sister is still alive but I know of nothing that could remove the complete possession of a higher-level demon. If you confront him, you have to be prepared to kill him, and if you're lucky enough to get even one chance, you must take it."

She wondered why he assumed that she would be the one to do it.

Dolores put her hand on his arm. "Which brings us to the reason we're here."

"You need something that can kill a high-level demon. There are things—weapons. Most of which I couldn't tell you where to find."

Dick raised an eyebrow. "Most?"

"I know of one and it's location." As the giant leaned forward, he seemed to grow in stature and intensity. "The sword known as Harpe."

Lexi had the impression he had said something magnificent but it had gone right over her head."

The three teammates looked at each other.

Albin rolled his eyes. "The sword Perseus used to slay the Gorgon, Medusa."

Phil gestured to the incubus. "Thank you, Albin, for restoring my faith in human-shaped creatures."

Dick's jaw dropped. "That happened? I was offered the role of Perseus but the movie never got the green light."

His lover patted his shoulder. "You'd have been amazing."

He sighed. "I know."

Lexi placed the glass she'd been going to drink from onto the table. "So where is this Harpe?"

Phil frowned. "I have it. Kind of."

Now, she frowned, both perplexed and a little irritated. "Kind of? I feel like I'm waiting for the other shoe to drop."

He remained silent.

She sighed. "May we borrow your sword please?"

The giant grimaced. "It's not exactly here and I can't leave to get it."

Scott shrugged. "So when do you get off work?"

Phil spread his arms in an apologetic gesture. "I can't leave here."

The mage's jaw dropped. "Dude, you have to stay at work forever?"

The horned man chuckled. "I have a residence here."

"Well, can you give us directions?"

"It's a little more complicated than that. Give me a moment." He stood and left the room.

Scott's face screwed up in confusion. "What is he?"

Dolores smiled at the mage. He'd been dying to ask. "Minotaur."

"A minotaur? I didn't know they existed."

Albin smiled. "Not *a* minotaur, *the* minotaur."

Lexi raised an eyebrow. "The actual one? From Greek or Roman mythology?"

Albin stared at her and smirked. "Greek."

She frowned. "His English is good. Anyway, he was killed in the movie."

The incubus leaned forward. History was his jam. "The legend says that he was killed. The truth is, he came to an arrangement with a witch who gave him a human head and allowed him this place beyond the maze and no further."

Scott frowned. "What did he give her in return?"

"I don't know. I'm not sure it's polite to ask." Albin shrugged.

The young man shook his head and seemed bemused. "The minotaur changed his name to Phil and opened a restaurant? Weird."

The door opened. "My name was always Phil. Philomenes to be precise. But according to history, a cursed bull-headed creature has no need of a name."

The giant gestured and led them through a side door he had to crouch to get through. Halfway down the hallway, he opened a door that led into an office. They filed in and he closed it behind them. The space was spartan with white walls, a black glass desk and leather chair, and a couch along one wall. The only adornment was behind the desk. While the walls were mostly plain, a gold mural was styled to look like an ornate door with golden scrolls. Phil strode closer to the wall.

Lexi opened her mouth to comment but when he placed his hand on the wall, the drawn hinges began to fill out and glisten like metal. The handle did the same and it became a real door.

He turned to her. "I hope the sword finds you worthy."

She paused and thought of Scott glowing with a pure light in comparison to her eyes, which were black without the benefit of his magic. "Maybe Scott should get it. He's more like the worthy kind."

"If you'll be the one to wield the weapon, you need to go." He opened the door and her mouth hung open. They stood at the top of a flight of stairs that led into a giant maze. She poked her head beyond the door to look left and right. It continued as far as she could see in any direction.

Scott looked at their host. "Is there a map?"

Phil merely laughed.

"Surely you must know your way around."

"Indeed I do. But when I go in there, I change. The longer I stay in there, the more I change and the longer it takes me to change back. None of you would be safe. I'd be as likely to murder you as to bring the sword back."

Someone knocked on the door. "Boss, there's a fight breaking out."

"Throw them out." He rolled his eyes, took hold of the doorknob from the maze side, and twisted it. It came away in his hand, a golden glowing orb with a square protrusion where it fit into the door. "Don't lose this. Put it in when you get back." He handed it to Lexi.

Dick raised an eyebrow. "Why can't we leave the door open?"

"There are other entrances to the maze from other realms. I go in and clear it out every few months or so but it's been a while." Phil stepped close to the door and leaned out. When his head passed the threshold, it grew larger and began to form into the shape of a bull's head. He snorted, then bellowed. It was shockingly loud and echoed through the ancient space.

Lexi and Scott shared a look that said, "Woah!"

The minotaur pulled himself into the office and his eyes stared wildly for a few moments before his head returned to normal. "That should send them scurrying back to wherever they came from."

She stepped into the doorway and looked out. "Let me guess, the sword's in the center of the maze."

He grinned. "See, you're getting it."

The door thumped again. "They won't go."

The massive, horned man groaned. "I need to sort this out." He took one more look at Dick and shook his head, frowned, and headed out of the room.

"What did I do to offend him?"

Scott shrugged. "Maybe he doesn't like vampires."

Lexi looked at the others. "Well, I'll get going then."

Dolores shoved her hand into her purse. "Here, take these."

She knew from the yellow glow before the fae's hand brought it out that it was sulfur and took the little glass vials containing the yellow substance. "Thanks." She stepped out and watched as they closed the door.

CHAPTER TWENTY-SEVEN

Lexi turned away from the door and faced the maze. She stared at it for a long moment, then took a couple of steps down. Her footsteps echoed and it sounded like a parade marching through the impossible space.

She paused when something scratched somewhere and she strained into the odd silence. A sound that might have been a stifled giggle made her jump.

With a heavy sigh, she readied herself to continue.

At least I can use the staircase as a point of reference.

To reassure herself, she glanced over her shoulder and her frown turned to a scowl. The wall and door behind her and the top two steps had vanished. All she could see was more maze beyond. Her heart skipped a beat at the thought of being trapped in this eerie puzzle. She stepped up two steps and the orb, still in her hand, glowed brighter. The wall and door began to appear.

"Well, that's a relief." Her voice reverberated unpleasantly.

Extremely wary now, she took the katana from her dimensional pocket and proceeded down the stone steps. The roof was cave-like and she couldn't quite ascertain where the low-level light came from, but she could see clearly enough. She turned and as expected, the stairs had completely disappeared. When she retraced her steps, the first few reappeared. After a moment's thought, she ascended the stairs quickly, removed a sulfur vial from her pocket, and rested it on top of the wall nearby before she descended again and entered the maze.

It smelled damp. The stone walls were covered with a strange moss but the path below her feet was clear.

"Okay. What do they say? Always keep left." She followed the path ahead and perversely, it turned right. A short while later, she had the option to either turn right again or left. She chose the latter.

Over the next hour, she made all left turns and wondered how long this would take. Not that she was in a hurry to kill her sister. The thought made her heart hurt.

The smell of the moss became even more dank and cloying. It was strong and sweet and earthy. She swept her hand across the green wall. "Ahh! Son of a—" She looked at her finger as a small blossom of blood appeared. With a small grimace of distaste, she sucked it. "Fuck you, wall." She pushed on and continued to choose each left turn.

After about another ten minutes, Lexi heard a noise and froze. It sounded like someone else had been walking and stopped when she stopped. She looked around warily, unable to see more than a few feet ahead or behind. Unwilling to simply walk blindly into what might be an ambush, she slid her hand into her pocket and retrieved a little black seeing ball, then sent it into the air and closed her eyes.

Around the corner from where she'd just been, a few demons had gathered and more were spread throughout the maze. From what she could tell, they were the black multi-eyed beasts she had fought in Palm Springs. She realized her katana was too long to use between the twenty-foot-high walls of the maze so she stowed it and pulled its shorter partner out. As she hefted the weapon and settled it in her grasp, she opened her eyes and readied to move quickly to kill the closest creature. She lunged around the corner but her targets had vanished. They must have retreated around the next corner.

She heard a giggle and spun hastily. When she turned again, she glimpsed the flutter of white fabric as it disappeared around the corner.

"Wait. Be careful, this place is full of—" She remembered what Phil had said about the other entrances. What if this child didn't realize the danger of the place she'd somehow stumbled into? Lexi ran after her, expected to meet a demon around every corner, and tried to be careful at the same time.

Through turn after turn, she pursued the girl in the white dress through the maze. Finally, she stopped and wiped the sweat from her face.

This is ridiculous. I need to know where those demons are.

She released the ball again but as she was about to close her eyes, her cell phone rang. Startled, she took it out and stared at it. Scott's name flashed on the screen

"How is there a signal here?" She pressed the call accept and put the device to her ear. "Scott? Is everything okay?"

He sounded annoyed. "Not really. You forgot about me. I'm stuck in your dojo."

While holding the device, she closed her eyes and opened them in the dojo. Scott was seated on the couch with a bucket of popcorn and a huge coke.

Perplexed, she stared at him. "What are you doing? How did you even get in here?"

The mage slurped the coke. "I'm watching the movie."

Lexi looked up at the large screen that displayed the maze she was in. She was certain she'd been standing with a sword in her hand but according to the display, she was seated on the ground and the moss that grew on the walls had covered her almost completely.

Scott offered her the bucket of popcorn. "This show is the

worst. It started okay and was even fairly exciting. The stairs disappearing and you making all left turns—good call by the way. That's what I'd do. But then you cut your finger and a few minutes later, you slid to the ground. You've been sitting there for hours."

She knocked the popcorn bucket away and it fell with a realistic clatter. He grimaced. "Aww!"

"I've been hallucinating?" She was furious, left her dojo, and scrunched her eyes shut with a muttered curse. When she opened them again, they were silver. The light they gave off bounced off the surrounding walls. When she was taking her time, trying to learn her craft, she would try to emulate Scott in her spell-crafting. It worked sometimes but not always. Still, it mostly worked better in her own words.

Focused now, she brought her will forth. As she unleashed it, she opened her eyes and stared at the moss that shrouded her body. "Get the fuck away from me."

It shrank immediately as though in fear.

Lexi closed her eyes to sense where her seeing ball was but found only blackness. She narrowed her eyes to search the darkness, then sighed.

It's not up there because I never took it out.

She returned to her pocket. "I can't believe—" Her statement ended abruptly when she realized there was no Scott and no popcorn on the floor, and the screen wasn't on. "That was a hallucination too?" Irritated, she returned her consciousness fully to the maze.

With the ball held in her palm, she whispered the spell to make it rise and it elevated to a position a little above the level of the walls. "You have to be kidding me."

Not only were there no demons and no little girls in the vicinity, but she was mere feet from where she had started. She walked around a few corners and stopped beside the vial of sulfur which still glowed on top of the wall.

Her patience finally snapped. "I could be in here for years. Fuck this." She sent the ball out and it rocketed across the maze while she followed it with her mind. On impulse, she spoke loudly to the maze. "I'm sorry if you think I'm not worthy by doing this, but as far as I'm concerned, you cheated first."

She watched through her mind's eye as the ball reached the center of the maze and immediately translocated to it. With a scowl, she realized that she was surrounded by and stood on piles of junk. Helmets, spears, armor, gold, jewels, and thousands of swords were piled haphazardly in giant heaps. Frustrated, she walked around the stacked swords. None of them were rusted but she hated seeing weapons discarded like this. It irked her because each had value. "How am I supposed to…"

A moment later, she sighed. "Right. It was used to kill a demon." She sorted carefully through the weapons and noticed a glow emanating from one deep inside the pile.

Immediately, a familiar smell of sulfur reached her nose.

Lexi stepped back and swept her hand to the side. Hundreds of swords slid across onto the pile of helmets. She stepped closer, moved a few others aside, and found one with a long glowing blade. It was styled with a sharp hook that protruded near the end of the blade and looked extremely vicious. She couldn't imagine using it against her sister.

With her prize in hand, she translocated to the door, climbed the stairs, and slid the knob into place. She turned it and stepped through.

Phil was in the office alone, seated at his desk and working on a computer.

She looked around. "Where is everyone?"

He turned and glanced at the sword in her hand. "You've been in there for half a day. They got hungry."

With a shrug, she handed the sword to him. "Did I choose the right one?"

The big man gaped. "That's the only one you brought back?"

Her jaw dropped. "I thought I had to…you know, choose the right one."

"This isn't Indiana Jones. You could have brought them all back if you wanted to."

Lexi stared at him.

"And why did you go alone? That's not a safe place to be alone. Did you know the walls are poisoned with a hallucinogenic moss?"

"No shit. Yes, Phil, I know that. You mean I could have taken someone?"

"Of course. It's not Indiana—"

"Jones, I got that. Dude, write a list of instructions or something."

"This kind of thing doesn't happen very often." The minotaur looked uncomfortable under her sharp gaze. "Come on, then. I ordered for you. They went only a few minutes ago."

Phil closed the door to the maze and waited until it became a mural on the wall again. They reached the office door and he turned to her. "Listen, I'm not usually squeamish and I've provided what your vampire friend wanted because I happen to have it in stock. But I'd prefer it if you don't bring him back here." He led her back to the private dining room.

She wondered what kind of blood Dick could possibly want that would upset the big man. Her eyes widened after a moment. *Could it be bull's blood?*

Before they reached the dining room door, she thought of something she had to know. "Phil, when I was hallucinating in there, I went into my dimensional pocket and Scott was there. He showed me what was happening to me. How did that happen?"

"I don't know. The maze must have found you worthy. Perhaps it chose to help you."

"It would have been more helpful if it hadn't poisoned me in the first place."

"Maybe."

Lexi entered the dining room and Dick gave her a finger wave. "There you are. Take a seat. Dinner should be along in a moment."

The welcome left her feeling somewhat underwhelmed. "Yes, I'm alive. Thanks for being thrilled."

Dolores patted the chair next to her. "Scott felt you were okay the moment you returned through the door."

"You were triumphant. I felt it." He smiled but it wasn't a grin and she knew why. Having the sword meant killing her sister's body. There would be no hope of saving her.

She sat as the door opened and a waiter brought in a Caesar salad for Dolores and three McRib burgers for Scott.

"Oh, yes!" He tucked in without delay.

The waiter left as another server entered with two plates that held steak for Lexi and Hungarian Goulash for Albin. Phil returned with a large stainless-steel bell jar over a platter. He placed it in front of Dick, shook his head, and sighed.

The vampire's eyes bulged at the grand dome in front of him. He raised both eyebrows. "Gosh. I'm quite excited."

Scott kicked her under the table and she frowned at him. "What was that for?"

He returned her puzzled look. "Huh?"

Despite his apparent confusion, he kicked her again.

"Would you stop kicking my leg?"

"What?" The mage looked under the table. "It's my bag." He leaned down, pulled it onto his knees, and opened it. A tennis ball lurched out of it and bounced onto the surface. They all watched as it rolled slowly and deliberately along the length of the surface and bounced repeatedly against the serving platter.

Dick became a blur. In one moment, he sat in his chair and in the next, stood with his back to the wall and a look of horror on his face.

Everyone looked at one another in shared confusion. The ball was relentless. *Bump, bump, bump.*

When it was clear that the vampire had no intention of moving, Albin reached across and grasped the handle of the cover. Dick raised his hand to his mouth.

Phil stood at the door and looked completely perplexed.

The incubus lifted the dome. A pile of fur lay motionless on the platter.

It moved, yawned, opened its eyes, and saw Dick.

Marcel yapped excitedly, bolted to his feet, and scrambled off the table.

The vampire's eyes widened. He hadn't moved an inch, but as the puppy launched himself off the chair, he crouched and flung his arms out. "Marcel!"

The puppy leapt into his arms and he slid down the wall while Marcel climbed onto his chest.

"Who's a good boy? Who's the best boy?" He didn't need to wipe tears from his face as the dog's tongue took care of it.

Lexi saw that Marcel was alone. While she felt sad, she didn't want to spoil her teammate's reunion.

The others left the table and joined Dick and Marcel on the floor. The tennis ball rolled off the table and continued to follow the puppy as he bounced excitedly around the room.

Dick looked at Phil. "How is this possible?"

"They came through a portal into my kitchen being chased by a giant Slougspider. It almost got the little fella but I hacked the creature's leg off."

She spun to face him. "They?"

"It was with a demon. Vicious little bugger. A thinner. Not seen one those for—"

Lexi grinned. "Limpet? Is he still here?"

"Sure. He wouldn't stop eating so I put him to work pulling the guts out of chickens. This way." She followed him. "He was supposed to save the heads for stock but he keeps eating them too. He'll probably be sick."

They walked through the kitchen and to a cold storage area. A box of headless, gutless chickens rested on a large steel counter but there was no sign of Limpet.

"Now where in the hell—"

He raised his head when high-pitched screams emanated from another room down the hall. "Oh no."

She darted out of the way as the huge man barreled down the hall. He flung the door open. "Damn it!"

Phil filled the doorway and she struggled to see what was screaming. Finally, she pushed past his bulk. It took her a moment to understand the scene. The room was divided into sections. The one to her right contained about a hundred pixies that hid between the wall and the edge of a little swimming pool. They crouched and trembled, some beneath tiny towels. The section next to it was filled with little massage tables. On her right were beds with ultraviolet lamps over them. The pixies there seemed to be sleeping and completely unconcerned about the madness taking place around them. Here and there, others wandered aimlessly, perilously close to the monster at the end of the room.

The monster was Limpet. He stood propped against the back wall of the room with a headless pixie in each hand. Several more of the creatures were scattered around his feet. Some were dead, some sat with vacant expressions on their faces, and others stared at him in horror and uttered seemingly endless shrill, high-pitched screams.

Blood had spattered everywhere.

Limpet burped and waved at Lexi. She didn't seem to receive the enthusiastic reunion Dick had enjoyed with Marcel but she was relieved that the weird little demon was alive. She looked around the room and frowned at the bedding and ultraviolet lighting. "What is this?"

Phil sighed. "It's the pixie spa."

She swung her head to look at the giant man. "S'cuse me?"

"Our pixie brains are ethically sourced. They come here,

donate their brains, and spend time in the spa while their brains grow back."

Lexi was stunned. "They grow back?"

The minotaur looked morosely at the dead pixies scattered across the room. "Well…not those with their heads bitten off, obviously."

She crooked a finger at the little demon. "Come on, you."

Limpet dropped his victims, scampered to her, and climbed onto her shoulder.

The giant leaned his face close to his. "I should have let that slougspider eat you, you little shit."

The demon burped again and snuggled into her neck.

When she walked into the dining room again, Dolores frowned. "Oh, the thinner's back too. Maybe Phil should keep him."

"If he's not out of my restaurant tonight, I'll spatchcock him."

Lexi and Scott looked at each other as they recalled Jamal in New Orleans.

The creature jumped onto the floor and ran to Albin.

The incubus scratched his head. "Hey there, little guy. You did a great job of looking after Marcel. Well done."

Confused, she looked at her plate. "Where's my steak?"

Dick—who was still on the floor with the puppy—put a protective arm around the furball. "Don't be mad at Marcel. He was hungry."

Lexi raised an eyebrow. "And did Marcel get onto the table and eat my steak all on his own?"

The vampire hesitated. "Well—"

"Hey!"

They all turned to Albin, who stared at his empty plate and the thinner demon beside it.

She smirked. "Don't forget, Albin, he did a great job of looking after Marcel."

He pouted. It wasn't a good look.

Dolores stood. "Let's go to my place. We have work to do. Phil dear, can we have the check?"

Phil smiled at the little fae woman. "Don't worry about it, Dolores. Stay safe."

Albin approached Dick. "Are you going to hog that dog all to yourself?"

"Well, that was the plan." He scratched Marcel's belly before he passed him to the other man.

The incubus rubbed noses with the puppy. "I bet you've been on some great adventures."

They headed to the revolving door. Dolores stood beside it and gestured them through to her apartment. Unfortunately, that wasn't where they went.

CHAPTER TWENTY-EIGHT

Lexi entered an office that seemed vaguely familiar and froze in surprise. She looked around hastily and realized it was the same room she'd seen through Bryan's eyes.

Azatoth lounged in a chair with her feet on the desk. "Sorry to interrupt your travels. I had to hijack that nifty fae device you were using."

Dick stepped through after her, followed by Scott who spun, slammed the fae door, and severed the connection to it with a spell to leave Dolores, Albin, and Marcel on the other side.

She stared at the demon, who had fresh blood on her face. Briefly, she wondered whose it was.

A groan drew her attention to a small round meeting table at the other end of the room. Bryan was slumped over it. She recognized him by the clothes but his face was almost unrecognizable. He'd been beaten almost to a pulp.

A fae lounged against the wall next to him. It was Dralog, the fae they'd caught in the condo.

Lexi smirked. "Hey, Dralog." She tapped her forehead with a finger. "You're looking a little sunburned there."

He stared directly at her and twisted one of Bryan's fingers until it snapped. The mage was so out of it that he barely cried out.

She seethed with anger but refused to let it show on her face. Although it took effort, she managed to remain impassive.

I should have killed the little beast.

"Sis, you brought me a gift and I didn't bring anything for you." Azatoth's gaze had settled on Limpet who clung to Lexi's shoulder.

The thinner crept around to the back of her neck to hide from the scrutiny.

The demon picked up the phone on her desk and pressed a couple of buttons. "They're here. Come on up." She replaced the phone and stepped closer to Lexi. "Walk with me." She flicked her wrists at the door.

Scott and Dick collapsed and lay motionless.

Lexi stepped toward the mage but Azatoth put her hand up and in an instant, she stood frozen in place.

"They're fine." The demon swept past her through the door into the hallway.

She found herself free to move and followed.

"Lexi, I feel I've been unclear. When I said I wanted us to work together, it wasn't optional. By which I mean it was—"

"Compulsory?" She tried to think ahead. They approached a set of double doors. If the demon opened one and went through first, she could draw the sword. Could she do it? Could she stab her sister in the back? Maybe that would be easier than watching the light fade from her face. "Why do you want me to work with you?" She truly couldn't understand why her adversary hadn't simply killed her.

"I think we're a great match." She smiled with Alicia's face and it broke her heart.

"A match? You want to bond with me? Like...a Kindred bond?" She was horrified.

Instantly, she realized that the only way Azatoth could bond with her was by getting rid of Scott. She had just been led away from the mage who was unconscious and defenseless against a psychopathic little fae.

"I don't find Bryan to be a great fit." The demon waved the double doors open and strode through. Lexi halted in the doorway of a large conference room. Dismembered bodies lay everywhere.

There must be over twenty of them.

Azatoth turned. "Oh, I don't suppose you've met the Kindred Council before. Let me introduce you to Gordon. Here he is, and here, and here, and I think that's…no wait. That belongs to someone else."

Stunned, she stared at the carnage.

Here's what I'm thinking, Limpet. You communicate with Marcel telepathically, don't you?

There was no response from the little demon.

I could truly use your help right now.

He rested his head against her neck.

I need you to get back to the room where Dick and Scott are and get rid of that fae guy. He was one of those who tried to take Marcel.

She felt him scramble down the back of her clothes.

Satisfied that he understood, she returned her gaze to Azatoth. "What are you offering me?"

"You already know how powerful I am. This room contained twenty-six of the most powerful people Kindred had to offer and I crushed them without breaking a sweat."

Lexi walked through the sickening carnage and stood at the window, looking out. "Well, that's all about you. What about me?"

She sent her consciousness to Scott but felt no answering touch. While she could sense that he was still alive, his mind was completely inactive. She focused on Bryan's dimensional pocket. In a moment, she stood at the top of the stairs and shouted, "Bryan. Wake up, Bryan, and open your eyes."

The screens fluttered to life. He faced the room and from the angle of view, he was still lying on the table. Her gaze went immediately to Scott. There was blood on his face. The nasty little fae had clearly given him a few kicks, but Dick was in a much worse condition and bled heavily from a wound on his neck. It wasn't healing as normal. Dralog had already been distracted, however. He chased Limpet around the room before he snatched up a wastepaper bin and dropped it on top of the little demon.

The elf stood and yanked the pad from the flip chart stand. He started to push the pad under the metal bin like he'd caught a spider. "I've got you now, you little shit."

That idiot deserves what's coming to him.

The moment he realized his target wasn't under the bin was the same moment he discovered exactly where he was. He spun but it was too late. The little thinner's extended jaw clamped down and ripped his face off. Lexi turned away and grimaced.

"Bryan. You have to get up now. I know it's hard but you need to help Limpet get Scott and Dick out of there and get yourself out too."

Lexi hadn't realized it, but she had turned and grimaced in the conference room too.

"If the sight of this bothers you, we can go somewhere else and chat. Come on. I have another surprise for you."

She didn't want the demon to return to the other office before her friends were out and searched her mind for a way to stall. "Exactly what are you planning?"

Azatoth waved a finger playfully. "No spoilers. Come on."

They left the conference room and turned in the opposite direction to the one they'd come from. She almost sighed audibly with relief.

With no way to tell how much time she had, she flicked her consciousness quickly to Bryan. He hung onto the wall as he staggered closer to Scott and Dick.

"Question." Her enemy had spun to face her.

Lexi blinked to return her focus to her physical surroundings. "What?"

"Is there anything I could offer you that would make you join me voluntarily?"

She sensed that Azatoth already knew the answer. Still, she put on her best thinking face.

The ploy gave her a moment to return to Bryan's view. Limpet had stretched his limbs out and created a portal on the floor. It looked like Dick had already left and Bryan now pushed Scott through. He looked into what appeared to be a cave, dropped, and she lost the connection.

Relieved, she pushed a thought to Limpet. *Go with them and keep them safe, wherever you end up.*

Lexi turned to Azatoth and shrugged. "At the moment, I honestly don't feel it."

"Well, prepare to be surprised, because—" She stopped speaking at the sound of footsteps.

Eric ran up the hallway. "Your prisoners have gone and so has the thinner. I just missed the little monster." He held a sack up that had no doubt been intended for Limpet, then threw it onto the floor.

The demon's eyes glowed yellow as she stared at the Kindred Grandfather. "You interrupted my big reveal."

He lowered his head instantly when he realized the shaky ground he was on. "I apologize most humbly, my lord."

"They keep calling me a lord. Do I look like a lord to you?" She arched her back and pushed her breasts out.

The man's eyes were still on the ground. "May I ask my…lady. Have you asked her?"

"Oh! My bad. Lexi, where's Warren?"

"I have no idea."

"There. I asked. Off you go."

Eric took a fraction of a second to stare pure hatred into Lexi before he walked away.

Azatoth sighed. "Where were we? That's right. You told me you didn't feel the inclination to join me. Thank you for your honesty. I truly appreciate it. But I think you'll feel it at any second now." She grasped the door handle. "Lexi Braxton, you thought you'd never see your birth mother again but..."

Lexi's eyes widened.

"I'm kidding. She's been dead for years." The demon opened the door. "But I do have them."

Seated inside the small meeting room was her whole unit—Braxton, Maggie, Isaac, and Bobby. They sat silently, bruised, bleeding, and powerless with K-cuffs sapping their energy and restricting their magical abilities.

Her eyes blazed silver.

"Well, I've never seen that before. Are you some kind of half-breed shadow mage?" Her sister's face screwed up with the demon's disgust. "Well, beggars can't be choosers, I suppose."

Lexi wondered what that meant. Did Azatoth need her because she was a dark sorcerer?

Her adversary stared at her. "Well? I don't need to go through the whole thing, do I?" She counted off on her fingers. "Torture them, kill them one by one, leave the kid for last, or maybe the one with child. I haven't decided yet."

Braxton raised his head and muttered something softly.

Azatoth put her hand over her ear and walked closer to him. "I'm sorry. You'll have to speak up a little. No one can hear your last words otherwise."

Her back was to Lexi. It was time. She put her hand into her dimensional pocket.

"So, it's decision time." The demon turned quickly to face her and walked closer.

Lexi thought about what Phil the Minotaur had said. *Don't miss your opportunity.* Had she missed it? Maybe not.

She stared at her sister's face, then looked intently into her eyes.

Azatoth was still staring into what she would have believed was Lexi's eyes when the dark sorcerer appeared behind the demon with the vicious-looking Harpe in her hand. She swung it at the demon's back but her target was no longer there. She stood facing her with her hand around her throat. Her enemy had done the same thing that she'd done to her.

The demon's eyes were angry and yellow as they stared into hers. "Don't try to kid a kidder. We are so much more alike than you could possibly believe. I told you what would happen. Which one will it be to start? The father? The brother?"

She maintained her crushing hold on her neck. Lexi slid her gaze to her family and they held it sadly as if to confirm that she had let them down.

The hand loosened slightly around her throat and the hard gaze shifted into the soft brown eyes of her sister.

When the hold had almost completely released, Alicia cried urgently, "Whatever you have planned, do it now. I can't hold him. He's too strong."

"Alicia?" Lexi felt Harpe still in her hand. It was time. But the young woman was still alive.

She dropped the sword.

Her sister blinked and the eyes that opened were no longer her own. The hand tightened again. Azatoth didn't seem to have noticed that anything was amiss.

Lexi choked the words out, as much from the hold around her throat as from her reluctance to concede to the monster's demand. "All right. Spare them. I'll work with you." The demon's hand slackened around her throat. "But I won't bond with you. You can simply kill me now or I'll kill myself."

The crushing grasp released immediately. "I'm so happy you reconsidered." She threw her arms around Lexi. "It's fine about the bonding, which was only a nice-to-have anyway. Welcome to the team. Let's go chat about it over coffee." Azatoth was already walking toward the door. "I'll rebuild the organization. I have huge plans."

She looked at her unit.

"Oh, right. Of course." Azatoth looked back "You can go now. I know where to find you if I need you again." The threat was clear. She flicked her wrist and the K-cuffs fell to the floor.

They huddled together and each gave her reproachful and disappointed looks before they disappeared. They knew she'd had her chance and hadn't taken it. She followed the demon to the door but remembered the sword. When she looked down, it was gone. She turned to Azatoth again, who smiled at her.

No need to guess where Harpe went.

There would be no more opportunities with the magical demon-killing sword.

Her new and very unwelcome teammate led the way to her office. She glanced in at the faceless fae corpse. "Is this a problem for you? It's only one, right?" She walked in and sat at the desk.

Lexi stared at the corpse with a raised eyebrow.

Her sister's face rolled her eyes, the gesture impatient and cold. "Fine. Nora!" she shouted.

Shuffling drew her attention outside and she peered into the hallway as a thin, middle-aged woman crawled out from under a desk. She looked a wreck. Her clothes, hair, and face were disheveled.

She looked at Lexi in fear.

Azatoth called. "In here."

The woman frowned and stepped into the office. She looked from one woman to the other and back again.

"I'm the one with the pretty eyes, remember?"

Nora simply nodded.

"I hate to ask again. Would you be an absolute sweetheart and get that out of here?"

The woman tottered in on her heels, grasped Dralog's feet, and dragged him out of the door.

The half-headed corpse disappeared around the doorframe and the demon shouted. "Oh, and two coffees when you're ready." As the dragging sound receded, Azatoth looked thoughtful. "I wonder where she puts them all."

Lexi sat opposite her. "How long has she been here?"

"I don't know her life story." She shrugged.

"I mean how long since she last went home? She looks a mess. Don't you think she should go home and get some sleep?"

The demon shrugged. "I could simply get rid of her."

"Azatoth, how many people have you killed in this building?"

"Some. But only to make a point."

"Keep in mind that she probably knows all the important stuff. Like where the coffee is." She looked at the floor. "And the phone number for the people who clean the rugs."

"You're such a nag. Honestly, you're lucky I like you." The demon spun around in her chair and began to toss balled-up papers into the wastepaper bin in the corner.

You don't like me. You want something. I only wish I knew what it was.

The door opened and a man entered with an armful of documents. Lexi's eyes widened. It was the man she'd seen watching her and Scott on the Las Vegas Strip. She opened her mouth to say something, but he looked at her and shook his head so slightly it was barely noticeable. She frowned but remained silent.

"Lady Azatoth, here are your daily reports." He dropped the pile onto her desk and waited.

The demon spun the chair to face him. "Lady Azatoth. I like how that sounds." She laid a hand on the documents. "Ah! I've been waiting for these."

She took the top sheet and looked up when she realized he hadn't left. Her gaze returned to the document. "You're dismissed."

He bolted.

Azatoth screwed the document up and threw it into the bin.

Lexi frowned. "Not important then?"

"I don't know. I didn't read it." The demon leaned closer. "Nora sneaks in when I'm not here, flattens them out, and gets them dealt with. She doesn't know I know. Shh…she's coming." She winked.

Nora entered the office with two cups jangling on a tray.

She put them on the desk.

Azatoth smiled. "Thank you, Nora. You can go home now. I'll see you bright and early on Monday morning."

Her assistant turned to leave.

"Oh, Nora."

The woman turned to face her again.

"Remember, not a word."

"Of course." Her walk out of the office was closer to a run.

Lexi put two spoons of sugar into her coffee and watched her hands as she worked. They were steady, thankfully, and didn't betray the extreme level of consternation inside her mind. She tried periodically to reach out to Scott and Bryan or even Limpet but with no success. Calmly, she poured the cream into the cup and stirred.

As she looked up, Azatoth took her cup. No milk, no cream, no sugar, exactly the way Alicia took hers. Was that a sign? Was her sister strong enough to grow and take the body back? Was anyone that strong? Lexi had to believe that Alicia was. It was all that kept her going. She smiled.

CHAPTER TWENTY-NINE

An hour later, Lexi stepped out of the elevator on the first floor of Kindred HQ. To her amazement, people bustled around her. They had no idea what was happening on the executive floor.

She walked out of the building and drew several breaths. Her cell phone beeped and she read the screen. The message was from an unknown number.

Turn right. There's a coffeehouse two blocks down on the same side of the street.

Warily, she looked into the venue through the glass facade. She half-thought she'd see the man she'd recognized in Azatoth's office, but she couldn't identify anyone in there she recognized. With a shrug, she stepped through the door and into Dolores's apartment. The little woman hugged her. She looked around the small home. Albin sat at the dining table with Marcel in his lap. The dog scrambled down and ran to her.

Immediately, her heart dropped. "They're not here? Have you heard from them?"

Dolores shook her head. "We've been in the dark since Scott broke the link. If Albin hadn't seen a glimpse of the New York skyline out of the window, we wouldn't have had a clue where you were."

Lexi crouched to stroke the dog. "They escaped. Limpet and Bryan got them out."

Albin sighed. He leaned his elbows on the table and rubbed the back of his neck. "Did you kill Azatoth?"

"No—"

"Don't worry. I'm sure you'll have another chance."

"I had the chance. I merely couldn't do it. Alicia's still in there. I get the feeling she's hanging on by a thread, but I'm sure Azatoth doesn't realize she's there."

Her companions both stared at her.

She frowned. "I won't kill my sister if there's a chance I can get her back."

Dolores sighed. "Do you still have Harpe?"

"No. I think Azatoth has it."

Neither of them would look her in the eyes. She knew they were disappointed but didn't want to burden her with it while they were still missing their friends.

"At least you're not looking at me like my unit did. I don't think I'll get any Christmas cards from them again."

The fae woman straightened. "Your unit was there? Leverage, I suppose."

Lexi nodded.

"Where do you think they went?" Albin asked and she knew he meant their missing friends.

"All I saw was a cave as Bryan dropped into it."

Dolores grimaced. "He opened a downward portal? They can be problematic."

She rubbed her forehead. "In what way?"

"You never know how high they'll be."

"They're fine." She sighed heavily. They have to be." She stood and went to the shelf to retrieve the bourbon and waved the bottle at the others.

Her boss nodded. "Do you know what Azatoth's planning?"

"He's butchered the Council and taken over Kindred, although from the look of things on the first floor, I don't think the rest of the organization is even aware of it." She returned with three glasses and poured each of them a drink.

Dolores's face grew thoughtful. "But to what end?"

Albin threw his back and crooked a finger for another one. "How did you get out?"

Before she answered, Lexi took a lanyard out of her pocket. "I work for Azatoth now."

He stared at it but his attempt at a smirk was more a grimace. "Congratulations on your new job. Do you have your own office?"

She exhaled in sharp disgust. "I suppose if I could find one that's not full of body parts I could lay claim to it."

"What is she up to?" Dolores spoke more to herself than to Lexi.

"She wanted to bond with me." She waited while Albin choked on his drink. "But I said I'd rather kill myself. I think she wants me because I'm a dark sorcerer. I don't know why."

Her boss frowned. "Interesting."

"I thought if a high-level demon ever got through to our realm, they'd rampage through the streets and slaughter the masses. She's focusing entirely on Kindred at the moment." Lexi thought about it, a scowl on her face. "Unfortunately, she seems to have decided to keep Eric around. I suppose I could dismember him and add him to the pile. She might not even notice. Although he's not happy that I'm there. He can't find Warren and he's fairly sure I'm behind it, which I think I probably am."

The fae woman shook her head. "Not yet. I've had a call from Louis. Scott told him to prepare for Warren's probable arrival after you told Azatoth that Scott was still in Peoria. The coven's been on high alert and set up all kinds of nasty surprises, but there's been no sign of him."

The young woman sat alone in the kitchen with the flowerpot in front of her again. She leaned forward to smell the flower. It wasn't yet ready to release its perfume.

The herbs had been added to the oil and this time, the empty vial sat front and center with the stopper already loose.

She moved to dip her fingers into the oil but paused at what wasn't so much a sound but a feeling that someone had moved into her space. Despite the sensation, she knew that if she turned, she would see no one. Instead, she continued her work, dipped her fingers into the oil, and rubbed her hands together. The next thing to do would be to put her fingers into the earth and speak the spell to release the flower's perfume. But that would never happen.

A knife appeared at her throat.

The athame was a few inches from her hand. Instinctively, she flexed her fingers toward it.

"No." Warren emphasized his word with a tiny jab. "Get up. Slowly and quietly. We don't want to wake your grandfather, do we?"

She stood slowly.

"Move. Let's go outside." He guided her to the door. Before they left the kitchen, he dipped his hands into her pockets and disposed of the hex bag from one pocket and a bag of salt and sand from the other.

Once outside, he pushed her through the trees that led to the coven's sacred space. Twice, he jabbed her in the neck with the knife. She felt the sharp sting and the warm blood trickle down her flesh.

"I've looked forward to seeing you again. I even took the bus.

That's how much I wanted to see you. And Scott. I know he's around here." He pushed her out into the circle, past the torches, and up to the altar.

She swallowed. "He was here but he left."

The crazed legacy spun her around. "Where? Where did he go?"

"I swear I don't know." She answered truthfully and looked into his face. It was full of ugly scars.

"When I was here with your friend Carolyn, we played a game. You'll play it with me tonight." He caught her hands and put them on his forehead. "Say the words. Give me the magic." His hands remained there to force hers against his flesh, holding her to his clammy skin.

She muttered words and magic began to flow into him. He closed his eyes and laughed as the power entered him. "More. Give me all of it."

"All of it? Well, if that's what you want, Warren. All of it you shall have."

His eyes snapped open and he stared into the bright, silver eyes of Lexi Braxton. He tried to pull his hands away but they were stuck. "No. Get off."

"But I'm giving you my magic, Warren. Can you feel it? Flooding into you?" She pushed the magic in.

He looked beyond her and jumped when his gaze darted around the clearing. It took a moment to register that they were not alone. The coven was assembled in a circle around them. The torches burst into life to illuminate the faces of those who had gathered.

The legacy howled as the energy began to burn the very core of him. His unhealing scars filled with silver energy but it wasn't his, nor was it power she allowed him to use.

Warren screamed and finally, she released him and stepped away. He stared at his hand with a look of horror on his face before he burst into flames and stood stock still for several seconds. Without a word, he sagged and crumpled into an ungainly heap at her feet.

Lexi watched as her burned hands healed. She looked into the eyes of Carolyn's mother. They held each other's gaze for a moment. There was no jubilance or sense that anything had been made right, merely a promise kept. She walked away from the circle.

Albin stood in the cover of the trees. He carried a ward created by Scott, one by Dolores, one by Louis, and one by Lexi. As she approached, she still had to forcefully push away the image of ripping his clothes off. When she reached him, she kept walking. He turned and fell into step beside her. He glanced over his shoulder. "How long will he burn for?"

She didn't bother to look back. "Until there's nothing left."

EPILOGUE

Lexi wandered from one room to another in the condo. She sat on Scott's bed and unrolled and rolled his laundered socks. It had been two weeks and she still hadn't heard from her teammates.

Things had been quiet for her at Kindred HQ. Azatoth was most certainly up to something big. She was constantly in meetings with her new Council.

She suspected they were Caleb's shadowy Cabal that had run Kindred in the background all along. Most of them seemed to be missing the end of a finger or two, a sure sign to mages of a certain level that forbidden magic was being practiced. She wondered how council members didn't notice all those bandaged fingers. Surely they'd put two and two together and come up with thirteen.

Perhaps they hide them behind a glamor.

The Kindred units out in the communities remained the same, blissfully unaware of the changes at the top. Her old unit wouldn't take her calls, which wasn't surprising. Because of her, they lived on a knife-edge. If she put a foot wrong with Azatoth, their lives were forfeit.

Despite her heavy reluctance, she had been in the office every workday. She arrived at 8:50 with three coffees from the coffee shop for herself, Azatoth, and Nora. Occasionally, she had lunch in the break room with Nora. The woman looked like she was falling apart at the seams from the stress of it all. She had mentioned during one of their lunch breaks that as Caleb's and then Gordon's secretary, she had been a part of the secret Cabal but very much on the periphery.

Lexi didn't press for information. She didn't want to scare her off or send her running to Azatoth. There would come a time when she might need her, so she outwardly adopted the same approach—one of self-preservation.

When the demon called one of them into the office, the two women would share a look that suggested *what now?* or *good luck*. It seemed to be Office-Survival 101. Always make friends with the secretary.

Every day, she brought Azatoth's coffee five minutes before the first meeting with the Cabal. She didn't want to spend any longer with her and only wanted to see the demon and look for a sign that Alicia was still there, fighting to live. There had been no more signs since the day she failed to kill her.

Despondently, she wondered how many people Azatoth had murdered in that time. All that blood was on her hands. She wasn't sure she deserved to get her sister back.

After work, Lexi would meet Dolores and Albin to search for their friends. They were reaching the point where every possible lead had been followed and led nowhere.

She put Scott's socks on the bed, stood, and straightened the covers where she had been seated. In search of a distraction, she descended the stairs and wondered if anything that resembled food remained in the fridge.

When she reached the bottom step, someone knocked on the door. She prayed it wasn't Azatoth. The demon had arrived twice, wanting what she kept referring to as a sisters' night out.

Both had been exhausting for her. She had labeled them, *The nights I spend all my time convincing Azatoth not to murder people for sport.*

With a sigh, she opened the door.

Albin stood in an evening jacket. He also wore Dick's silver lion's head pin. He looked smoking hot but he frowned at her. "You're wearing that?"

"Huh?" She looked at her leather vest and pants in confusion. They were her regular clothes.

He rolled his eyes. "You haven't seen the message."

"Sorry, I've been upstairs."

Albin stepped in. "Dolores wants to take us to dinner at Phil's."

"Thanks, but I was about to make myself dinner. There's coffee if you want one." She headed to the kitchen and he followed.

The incubus stepped to the refrigerator and opened it, picked up a white box and looked inside, and grimaced. "Is the coffee to go with the week-old chow mein?"

She shrugged. "I've worked out a spell to kill the mold."

"That's what you're doing with your magic, is it?" He shook his head.

"What else should I do with it? I'm thirty and I'm only now coming into my birthright, but I've never felt so powerless. Anyway, I should stay here in case."

"In case someone sends you an important message and you miss it because you left it in the kitchen? Come on. Dolores is right. We've moped around enough."

Lexi stared around the kitchen and sighed. "Sure, okay." She snatched her cell phone from the table and they left the condo. Both glanced at Dick's door but walked away quickly.

As they hurried through the pool area toward the gate leading to the street, a girl strolled past the pool in a sleeveless silver pantsuit. Lexi looked at her drab clothes and decided she'd like to wear something like that.

Ooh! That's what I need.

She brought her will forth to create the outfit and looked down. It was perfect for dinner at Phil's Cornerdown Kitchen.

A blood-curdling scream made her and Albin both jerk their heads around. The girl in the pantsuit now stood in her underwear. She spun and tried to cover herself with her purse, then stumbled and fell into the water.

The incubus stared open-mouthed at the commotion. "What on earth is—" He looked at Lexi in her new outfit, complete with a look of embarrassment. "Oh."

"I didn't do it intentionally." She watched in horror as the woman spluttered and swam to the side, then walked quickly around the corner and out of sight.

Albin shook his head and followed. "We need to find Scott. You're a walking disaster as a mage."

Lexi and Dolores stepped through the revolving doors into Phil's Cornerdown Kitchen and Albin followed. He crouched behind them with Marcel in his arms and tried to remain hidden until the entrance spell had completed its truth search. Lexi gazed at Dolores, who was young and ethereally beautiful with diaphanous wings. After a few seconds, she became a little, middle-aged, power-suit-wearing, no-nonsense woman.

The incubus straightened and removed his hat and glasses.

Cassidy greeted them as enthusiastically as before. "Hi, Aunty Dolly. Your table's ready."

The young fae led them through the restaurant. "We're running a half-price promotion on our ethically-sourced pixie brains."

Lexi frowned. "Why do you need to run promotions if Phil already knows what the customer wants?"

The girl indicated their table. "You might want pixie brains—"

"Which I don't, by the way," Lexi assured her.

Cassidy continued as if she hadn't spoken. "But not be able to afford them. Knowing they're more affordable might change your mind."

Which it won't. She shuddered. The idea of eating the brains of anything was a hard no.

Their hostess laughed. "I don't need to be Phil to know I won't be bringing PBJ to the table." She smiled and left them.

Lexi screwed her face up in disgust. "I'll take a massive leap and guess she's not talking about peanut butter jelly."

Dolores patted her arm. "You have the jelly part right."

She shuddered again.

"Dolores! It's lovely to see you again so soon. I'm happy to see you don't have that little beast with you this time." Phil gave Lexi a sad smile. "I'm afraid I can only grant food-related wishes."

The fae woman nodded. "Good evening, Phil."

The minotaur walked around to Albin. "I hope to see your vampire friend again. I have to apologize for assuming he wanted to drink the puppy's blood. In all my years, I've never had one here who wanted anything more than blood. It was most curious."

"He's one of a kind."

Phil sighed. "Your food will be along shortly." After a brisk nod, he walked to another table.

Lexi opened her mouth to comment on what he had said about Dick but noticed that the incubus was staring across the room.

"Can you excuse me for a moment? I see someone I need to speak to." He picked Marcel up and headed toward a large table with a party of at least twenty people who were being seated. As he approached, a man noticed him and waved.

"Albie, mate." The speaker appeared to be British. He swept his blond hair back and threw a camel trench coat over the back of a chair to claim it before he went to meet him part-way. "You didn't call me back."

They met and shook hands. Albin responded but Lexi couldn't hear what he said. He pointed toward the bar and the man nodded enthusiastically.

Lexi's gaze followed them as they walked to the bar. "I wonder who that guy is."

"I'm sure Albin has many friends we don't know about." She stared at Lexi. "I'm certain it's not a new boyfriend."

She was embarrassed that the thought had occurred to her, and more so that Dolores had guessed what she was thinking. Still curious, however, she glanced again at the two men chatting.

Her gaze slid along the bar to two shifters who seemed to be having a disagreement. They began to get loud and gesticulated wildly at each other. She glanced at a mural on the wall next to the bar which she hadn't previously noticed.

No fighting! By order of the management, fighting will result in expulsion to a dumpster realm. How you get home from there is not our problem.

Curious, she leaned closer to Dolores. "What's a dumpster realm?"

Her boss raised an eyebrow. "You should pray you won't ever have to find out." She shuddered.

Lexi had never seen her friend look so uncomfortable and completely serious. She looked at the bar again. The men had seen the mural too and it seemed to defuse their altercation.

Albin handed something to the man but they were too far away for her to see it was. A minute later, he returned to the table.

"Sorry about that." He noticed her staring at him, waiting for more. "That's Craig, an old friend of mine. I'm sure I've mentioned him."

She opened her mouth to inform him that he had not, in fact, mentioned him. At the same time, the food arrived.

He looked at his bowl of Hungarian Goulash. "Maybe I'll get to eat it this time." Then, he sighed. Limpet had eaten it the last time.

Lexi missed the crazy little demon. She checked on Marcel who was seated under the table. He whined and she knew he missed his little friend too.

It reminded her of something and she looked at Albin and pointed to his chest. "Dick's pin. It's fallen off your jacket."

"It's fine. It's safe, don't worry." He started to eat.

Understanding that he would offer no more information, she looked at her plate and the three McRib burgers on it. She missed Scott so much, she should have guessed this would be her meal. With a sigh, she opened the burger, took the pickle out, and put it on the side of the plate.

Dolores looked up from what looked like coffee and walnut cake and stared at the pickle. "You must have wanted it or it wouldn't be there."

Lexi was about to explain about Scott's strange eating habits when an explosion rocked the restaurant and a door at the end of the dining room blew off its hinges. It careened toward the diners but was zapped by so many mages, witches, fae, and other magical creatures that it disintegrated into nothing.

Smoke billowed out of the room.

One of the diners stood and shouted, "Fire!"

Phil marched through the restaurant, his features pulled into a scowl, and bellowed, "It's not a fire. Stay in your seats. There will be no stampeding in this establishment."

The nervous patrons began to return to their seats except for one man who remained standing when the giant strode past. The huge minotaur stopped and stared at the man, who squeaked plaintively, "I was going to the toilet."

Phil looked lower. "Well, you've been now. So sit."

The man snatched a napkin up and held it across the front of his pants. He noticed all the people staring at him. "It's beer. I was drinking beer when— Oh, for God's sake." He sat and lowered his head into his hands.

Lexi noticed Albin's friend wasn't in his seat at the big table. She looked at the bar to see if he was still there and glanced again at the mural.

There will be no stampeding in this establishment. Stampeding will result in expulsion to a dumpster realm. How you get home from there is not our problem.

"He's nothing if not consistent." She turned to face the smoke that continued to billow out of the room.

The minotaur stopped at the edge of the dining area and stared intently across the space. "When I find out who's been casting spells in my establishment..." He turned and joined a couple of staff members outside the room and stood there for a few minutes, waiting for the smoke to dissipate.

Her gaze automatically shifted to the mural painted on the wall.

By order of the management, there will be no rituals practiced in this establishment. Practicing rituals will result in expulsion to a dumpster realm. How you get home from there is not our problem.

Her arm itched. She rubbed it absently and decided that she would never attempt magic there.

"I wonder what was in that room," she commented to Dolores.

"It's a storage room but there are no chemicals or anything," Cassie answered from where she stood nearby, watched the drama, and chewed the tip of a lock of hair absently.

Movement came from deep within the room. The smoke swirled and people started to file out. Lexi could see they were staff members by the *Phil's Cornerdown Kitchen t-shirts* they wore.

Realizing it was a restaurant internal staff issue, patrons began to turn to their meals again.

She ducked her head under the table to check on Marcel. The commotion didn't seem to have bothered him. She offered the puppy a piece of her burger and waved the food at him before she noticed he had a bowl filled with chunks of steak. "Well, you're an expensive date."

With a small smile, she threw the burger in with the steak and stroked the dog. "Hey, Dolores, I bet someone will go to the dumpster realm for that one."

"I certainly hope not," Dick replied.

Lexi jerked her head up and smacked it on the underside of the table. As she sat and rubbed it vigorously, she gaped at Scott, Dick, and Bryan. The three of them were filthy. They stood in bare feet and wore brightly colored chefs' pants and restaurant merchandise t-shirts. Bryan and Scott were thin and had beards —extremely long beards. In fact, she wouldn't have recognized the young mage if not for his green gaze that held hers. But his eyes were red-rimmed and she looked again at the length of his beard.

That's way more than two weeks' growth.

Her jaw dropped and she wondered if she might be hallucinating.

After watching Albin bolt to his feet, take Dick's head in his hands, and almost kiss the face off him, she finally stood and hugged her green-eyed mage.

Scott's response to the hug was not encouraging. "Ouch."

She released him and decided to scold him instead. "Where the hell have you been? I've been worried sick."

He chuckled although he sounded exhausted. "Funny you should say that."

"Say what?" She drew her brows down in confusion.

"Hell."

"Oh." She grabbed a burger. "Would this help?"

He finished it in three bites. "Urgh! Pickle."

Cassie brought them three more chairs, two jugs of water, and a thermos that Dick snatched and gulped before she'd left the table. As he drank, he signaled to her and waved his finger in circles.

Albin interpreted. "Keep them coming, please."

A soft voice beside Lexi asked, "Did you do it?"

She turned. Bryan slid into the seat placed between her and Dolores.

"Did you kill her?"

She took his hand. "No. I almost did but she's still in there, Bryan. Alicia revealed herself for only a few seconds and we have to get her back."

"Are you sure? How?" The hope in his eyes was all the confirmation she needed that she'd done the right thing. It had been a question she'd asked herself relentlessly over the previous weeks. She leaned forward. "I have a theory about that and you are the perfect person I need to help me."

"Urgh!"

Lexi spun to look at Scott as he spat food from his mouth and scraped his tongue with his fingers. He had Dolores' plate in his hand.

In between heaves and gulps of water, he asked, "What is this?"

The fae pulled her plate back indignantly. "Hey, that's my coffee and pixie brain cake."

Before the mage could say anything, Albin's friend stopped beside the table. He placed the lion's head pin on the surface.

The incubus shook his friend's hand and thumped his back. "Craig, I can't thank you enough."

"No problem, mate. It was easy. Your little demon must like his new name. He came straight away."

Lexi frowned. She looked under the table. Marcel was seated on Dick's dirty feet but there was no sign of Limpet.

She looked at Craig. "Didn't he come back with them?"

He nodded. "He hurtled out of that room first under the cover of all the smoke and confusion, followed immediately by me."

Her face fell. "Then where is he?"

They looked around the room.

Then, they heard a tiny scream, followed immediately by others.

"The pixies!" Lexi, Albin, and Dolores all said at once.

Phil ran ponderously through the restaurant. "Leave my pixies alone, you little savage."

The fae woman stood. "Excuse me a moment. Damage control." She hurried after him.

Craig looked uncomfortable. "I'd better make myself scarce before I end up in a dumpster realm. I'm honestly not dressed for it. He pulled his coat on. "Hey, Albin, do me a favor, will you? If you ever find out why they came back stark bollock naked, I'm dying to know." With that, the mage walked away.

Lexi stared at the three of them. The workwear made sense now. "Why were you naked?"

Scott opened his mouth to explain.

Dick silenced him with a look. "Not. One. Word."

Thanks for reading **Dawn of the Shadow!**

Book 5 in the series, **Order of the Shadow,** is coming soon to Amazon and Kindle Unlimited.

So… The world's a bit of shit show at the moment, isn't it? I hope the book took you away from everything for a while. Most of it was written in lockdown with all kinds of other hellish stuff going on, which I won't bore you with. Lexi and her friends have been my happy place this year and gave me respite from the craziness out there.

Here's hoping next year is kinder to us.

I've had a fun time writing about Phil's Cornerdown Kitchen. The inspiration for Phil is my husband who unsurprisingly, is called Phil. If you follow the Phil's Cornerdown Kitchen Facebook page, you'll see he's been keeping me fed while I work on the books. It was all going really well until I threw him a curve ball a few months ago; something along the lines of "Hey, this cheesecake is great but I'm starting a low carb diet next week."

I had to do something, the guy was fattening me up. He's been cooking me some excellent low carb dishes since then. If you're on my mailing list, you'll know that in a moment of pure madness, I promised to share some embarrassing before and after photos. I'm waiting until the difference is more noticeable.

It'll be worth it, my worst photo is of me standing next to William Shatner, and he's the skinny one!

Hubby says that since he is now the boss of PCK, I have to call him "Chef" while he's cooking (which is actually quite cute.) Also, he now wants an apron with the name of *HIS* restaurant on it. I'm going to make that happen!

I'm looking into setting up a PCK store online, hopefully in time for Christmas because he's notoriously difficult to buy for, but this year everything's going to have the PCK logo on it. Bwahahahaha! He asked for it.

I've started book 5 and hope to have it with you by the end of the year. I'm speeding up though right? I'm no Sarah Noffke but she's my inspiration.

Anyway, as evidence that Phil (husband, not minotaur) is getting too big for his boots, he insisted I put one of his recipes into the back of the book.

PIXIES are curious little creatures, they are kind and terribly polite in their own communities, but let them near a sprite and they turn into absolute monsters. I think it's because of the ozone emitted by sprites. The little guys seem to react to it in an extremely negative way; setting upon the sprites and eating them, to be precise.

Two more interesting facts about pixies. Their brains are considered a culinary delicacy by many fae, and those brains grow back. It takes a couple of weeks but if you harvest a pixie's brain correctly, you leave behind the nucleus, the part with all the memories and motor functions. They don't seem to use the rest of it.

Phil's Cornerdown Kitchen uses only ethically-sourced pixie brains. In fact, we run a pixie spa where those little dudes can come in for elective brain removal and spend the next two weeks using the hot tubs, having daily massages and mani-pedis (and boy do those sharp little claws need it) while they wait for their brains to grow back.

They have their own entrance to the spa so sprite diners don't need to worry about having their meal interrupted by marauding pixies. Now that I've wetted your appetite for pixie brains, here's a recipe.

COFFEE AND PIXIE BRAIN CAKE

Ingredients

For the sponge:

- 50g butter
- 80ml full-fat minotaura milk (regular cows' milk will do)
- 1 serving of espresso, cooled
- 2 eggs
- 225g caster sugar
- 100ml oil (sunflower or vegetable)
- 100g pixie brains*, chopped (remember to thank the pixies)
- 250g self-raising flour

For the frosting:

- 250g butter
- 500g icing (confectioners) sugar

- 3 tablespoons instant coffee granules
- 1.5 to 2 tablespoons boiling water
- 9 pixie brains* halved (or walnuts)
- This should be enough frosting for both layers

*If you are unable to access the magical realms to purchase fresh pixie brains, WALNUTS are an acceptable substitute.

Instructions

Preheat the oven to 180 degrees C/ 350 F/gas 4 and grease two 20cm (8 inch) tins.

In a pan, melt the butter and stir in the milk and espresso. In a bowl, whisk the eggs and sugar until foamed, then add the butter, milk, espresso and oil. Add the chopped pixie brains then fold in the flour.

Divide the mix between cake tins and bake for 25 minutes. Cool on a wire tray.

Frosting: Mix together the confectioners' sugar, butter and coffee. Use half to fill the cake and half on top. Decorate with pixie brains.

ACKNOWLEDGMENTS

This book could not have been written without the support of so many people. My sincere thanks to the wonderful people who make LMBPN the great organisation it is. Michael, Judith, Kelly, Steve, Judah, Lynne, Jen, Grace, and Moonchild for the beautiful covers. Huge thanks also to the beta readers who took the time to read and feedback my errors and inconsistencies, and to the JIT team who repeatedly save our skin in the neck of time.

To Micky and ladies (and honorary ladies). What an absolutely cool group of people you are. I can't wait to hang out with you again.

Thank you to my husband who stops the world around me from grinding to a halt, and for keeping me fed with awesome food and who doesn't judge me when I work until 6am then sleep for half of the day.

Thank you to the friends who help me to consistently move forward and stop me from losing my shit on a daily basis. Anne, Erika, Fatima, Kate, Craig, Sam, Jon, Nat, Sarah, the Hellcats, and the Coronitas.

https://www.bookbub.com/authors/michael-anderle